A

LIBRARY-NEWARK, OHIO 43055

P9-CSH-915

WITHDRAWN

UNCOMMON
CLAY

*Also by Margaret Maron
in Large Print:*

Storm Track
Home Fires
Killer Market
Up Jumps the Devil
Southern Discomfort
Bootlegger's Daughter
Fugitive Colors

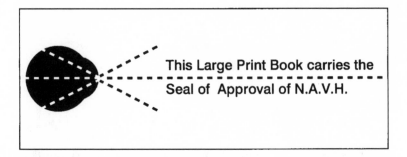

UNCOMMON CLAY

Margaret Maron

Thorndike Press • Waterville, Maine

Grateful acknowledgment is given for permission to reprint
from the following:
Raised in Clay: The Southern Pottery Tradition, by Nancy
Sweezy. University of North Carolina Press, 1994. © 1984 by
Smithsonian Institution. Used by permission of the author.
Turners and Burners: The Folk Potters of North Carolina, by
Charles G. Zug III. The University of North Carolina Press.
© 1986. Used by permission of the author.

Published in 2001 by arrangement with Warner Books, Inc.

Thorndike Press Large Print Mystery Series.

The tree indicium is a trademark of Thorndike Press.

The text of this Large Print edition is unabridged.
Other aspects of the book may vary from the original edition.

Set in 16 pt. Plantin by Christina S. Huff.

Printed in the United States on permanent paper.

Library of Congress Cataloging-in-Publication Data

Maron, Margaret.
    Uncommon clay / Margaret Maron.
      p. cm.
    ISBN 0-7862-3370-2 (lg. print : hc : alk. paper)
    1. Knott, Deborah (Fictitious character) — Fiction.
    2. North Carolina — Fiction.   3. Women judges — Fiction.
    4. Potters — Fiction.   5. Large type books.   I. Title.
    PS3563.A679 U53 2001b
    813'.54—dc21   2001027459

In memory of
Edith Elizabeth Stephenson Johnson,
who loved blue flowers, writing poetry,
and staying up late

ACKNOWLEDGMENTS

Seagrove, North Carolina, is a real town and the surrounding Randolph/Moore/Montgomery County area is populated with real craftsmen, but as usual, I have taken enormous liberties with geography, creating roads and potteries where none exist. A few real people appear in cameo and by their permission. All the others are figments of my imagination and any resemblance to anyone living is purely coincidental.

As always, I am indebted to many for their help and technical advice, in particular, District Court Judge Lillian O'Briant Jordan and Chief District Court Judge William Neely of District 19B (Randolph, Moore, and Montgomery Counties, North Carolina).

My thanks to the many potters who talked to me of their craft and its history, especially Boyd Owens of Owens Pottery, Richard Gillson of Holly Hill, Pam and Vernon

Owens of Jugtown, Sid Luck of Luck's Pottery, Ben Owen III of Ben Owen Pottery, Samantha and Bruce Gholson of Bulldawg Pots, Beth Gore and Johannes Mellage of Cady Clay Works, and David Stuempfle. David Garner of Turn and Burn let me get my hands dirty and that lump of recalcitrant clay taught me greater respect for the potters who make it look so incredibly easy.

Nancy Gottovi and Anne-Kemp Neely took me down rutted lanes and introduced me to potters I'd never have found on my own.

District Court Judges John W. Smith, Shelly S. Holt, and Rebecca W. Blackmore of the 5th Judicial District Court (New Hanover and Pender Counties, North Carolina) once again gave me invaluable courtroom advice.

Any errors I have made probably came from not taking it.

THE SUPREME COURT
OF NORTH CAROLINA
OFFICE OF THE CHIEF JUSTICE
ORDER AND COMMISSION

As Chief Justice of the Supreme Court of North Carolina, by virtue of authority vested in me by the Constitution of North Carolina, and in accordance with the laws of North Carolina and the rules of the Supreme Court, I do hereby enter the following order(s):

The Honorable J. H. Corpening II, one of the Regular Judges of the District Court is hereby commissioned and assigned to preside over a session or sessions of District Court in the District Court Judicial District Three A, to begin April 7 and continue One Day or until the business is completed.

The Honorable T. Yates Dobson, Jr., one of the Regular Judges of the District Court is hereby commissioned and assigned to preside over a session or sessions of District Court in the District Court Judicial District Eight, to begin March 27 and continue Four Days or until the business is completed.

The Honorable Deborah S. Knott, one of the Regular Judges of the District Court is hereby commissioned and assigned to preside over a session or sessions of District Court in the District Court Judicial District Nineteen B, to begin April 6 and continue Two Days or until the business is completed.

In Witness Whereof, I have hereunto signed my name as Chief Justice of the Supreme Court of North Carolina:

The Honorable Henry E. Frye
Chief Justice of the Supreme Court of
North Carolina

CHAPTER

1

The high-fired stonewares . . . although far stronger and more vitreous, were less likely to withstand thermal shock and could crack when heated or cooled too rapidly.

— Turners and Burners,
Charles G. Zug III

April is the cruellest month.
Who said that?
— mixing memory and desire.
(Oh, yes indeed, ladies and gentlemen of the jury. We know all about desire, don't we? And hurtful memory, too.)
— breeding lilacs out of the dead land.
Walt Whitman?
No, Whitman was *When lilacs last in the dooryard bloomed.*
There's a lilac in my own dooryard.

Maidie Holt, who keeps house for my daddy, gave me one last fall. It's a sprout off her bush that was itself a sprout off the bush her great-grandmother brought from Richmond after the war.

The Civil War.

There were three fat purple blossoms on it this year even though Maidie didn't think it'd bloom so quickly after being transplanted. I cut one of them, gathered daffodils from the ditch bank and scarlet honeysuckle from the woods, added a few white dogwood blossoms, and stuck them all in a brown earthenware jar that used to hold butter in the springhouse when my daddy was a little boy eighty years ago. The flowers look and smell like Easter.

— and stands about the woodland ride, wearing white for Eastertide.

My mind was looping through all the poetry I ever read in college lit courses a million years ago, anything to paper over the memory of last weekend when I'd gone hippity-hopping down to New Bern just like a horny little bunny. I'd even carried along a whimsical basket of erotic goodies, an early Easter treat for Kidd Chapin, the decidedly sexy game warden who had me seriously thinking about marriage for the first time in six years. I had thought I wouldn't be able to get away till Saturday noon, but then things changed and I found myself impulsively heading east on Highway 70 Friday night, smiling as I thought of how surprised he'd be to see me twelve hours early.

— *like a guilty thing surprised.*

That's Wordsworth.

Talking about some bastard like Kidd.

It was almost two a.m. when I reached New Bern that night. I cut my lights and engine at the top of Kidd's driveway and just let gravity carry me the rest of the way, coming to rest beside his Dodge Caravan. To my relief, there was no sign of Amber's Mustang.

(Kidd's daughter turned sixteen last fall, and having her own car had loosened some of the reins she kept him on, but this didn't mean she disliked me less or had given up hope her parents would eventually get back together.)

One of his caged rabbit dogs farther down the slope let out a few yips when it heard my car door open. It barked again as the door latched, then fell silent. The waning moon was lost in the trees that rimmed the western sky and no lights shone from the cabin windows. A floorboard creaked as I walked across the porch. I opened the screen door that he'd left unhooked, inserted my key in the lock of the heavy cedar front door, and quietly let myself into the dark house. The main room — a combination living room, den, and dining room — runs the full width of the house, with a glass wall at the far end that opens onto a deck overlooking the Neuse River.

There was barely enough moonlight for me to make out the shadowy shapes of furniture as I crossed the room and I stubbed my toe on the runner of an oak rocking chair. From the master bedroom came the sound of Kidd's soft snores rising and falling. Shivering with anticipation, I shed my clothes, draped them over the nearest chair, and felt my way silently down the short dark hallway.

The bedroom was almost pitch-black, but I was so familiar with the layout that my bare feet didn't stumble as I tiptoed over to the king-size bed. A careful sweep of my hand told me that he lay almost in the center of the bed. I lifted the sheet and coverlet and eased in beside him.

He didn't move.

I gently worked my way closer till I could feel the warmth of his smooth shoulder, then in one fluid motion, I cupped my body to his back and slid my arm over his to clasp his chest.

And touched a woman's bare breast instead.

Both of us jerked apart with shrieks that could have waked the dead. They certainly waked Kidd, who'd been dead to the world till that moment.

Lights came on. She clutched at the sheet, I grabbed the coverlet as I hit the floor, Kidd dived for his pants.

"What the hell is this?" I asked angrily, pulling the coverlet tightly around my nakedness.

She glared back at me. "Who the heck are you?"

Then we both glared at Kidd, who was still blinking in the sudden light.

"Uh — Deborah? Um, this is Jean," he said sheepishly.

"Jean?" I snapped. "As in the former Mrs. Chapin?"

I don't know why I hadn't seen this coming. After the hurricane flooded them out last fall, she and Amber had camped in with Kidd for a couple of weeks. He'd sworn to me that it was nothing more than Good Samaritanism and that there was absolutely no spark left between him and his wife.

If these were the ashes, damned if I wanted to see the fire.

And she, now in full possession of the bed,

pushed the pillows into a heap and lay back with a smug look.

"So pleased to meet you, Judge," she cooed.

With as much dignity as I could muster, I swept from the room in my coverlet, retrieved my clothes, and ducked into the hall bathroom.

"Look, you said you weren't coming till tomorrow noon," Kidd said when I emerged, fully dressed.

Shirtless and barefoot, his hair tousled, his tone was half-apologetic, half-accusing. I heard only the accusation.

"This is my fault?" I snarled. "Because I didn't give you enough time to let your bed cool off before showing up? How long have you been sleeping with her again?"

"Aw, come on, honey," he said coaxingly.

"Screw it!" I said coarsely. "And screw you, too."

With the lights on, I saw their empty glasses, a pair of blue jeans on the hearth, a black bra dangling from the back of the couch, a handful of CD cases —

"Patsy Cline? Willie Nelson? You made love to her with *my* CDs?" Somehow that made it even worse.

I mashed the eject button on his player and scooped them up, along with a half-dozen more that I'd brought along with me

16

over the last few months.

"You can send me the rest of my stuff," I said, heading for the door. "And yours'll be on the next UPS truck."

He followed me outside to my car, oblivious to the chilly night air on his bare feet and naked chest.

"Look," he said. "I'm sorry. I really am. I was going to tell you tomorrow. It just happened. Jean and me — and what with Amber and all. I mean, it's like we've got all this history, you know? And getting back together would make everything easier, somehow. But I never meant to hurt you, Deb'rah. Honest to God, I didn't."

"Go to hell!" I shoved the car in gear and backed out so fast Kidd had to jump away to keep me from running over his bare toes.

I must have been doing fifty when I hit the top of his drive and the car fishtailed so hard when I turned onto the road that I almost lost control and flipped it. All I needed, right? Having to get him to come haul me out of the ditch.

That was five days ago. As I drove west toward Asheboro, I still felt a hot flush of mortification every time I thought about crawling into that bed, snuggling up to his wife. That I could have been so stupid. Left myself open to

17

such humiliation. Allowed a game warden to trifle with my emotions just because he was good in bed. When was I going to quit letting my hormones rule my head and start —

A sharp horn blast off my left shoulder jerked me back to the present. Even though I had set the cruise control, I'd overtaken the car ahead and was automatically starting to pass without checking my blind spot to see that a pickup truck was about to pass me. If I didn't quit stressing over Kidd and get my mind back on my driving, I was going to be roadkill right beside the possums and gray squirrels that littered this stretch of U.S. 64.

I had no business driving over fifty-five anyhow, what with all the construction going on. They've been trying to four-lane this highway forever, but seems like they only got serious about it these last couple of years. Some of the bits had been graded so long ago that they were fully grassed over and small trees were starting to grow up again. But lately, yellow bulldozers and backhoes had been busy here. Wide strips of land lay open in bright red gashes against the new green grass of spring. Over in Colleton County, our soil has so much sand in it that it's almost like the beach, beige to black in color. Here in the piedmont, the

18

heavy earth of eastern Randolph County was nothing but bright red clay.

With all this raw material lying free for the digging, it's no wonder the area has produced so many potters, potters like the — I glanced at the tab of the folder on the seat beside me — like the Nordans. Sandra Kay Nordan, Plaintiff, versus James Lucas Nordan, Defendant. Both potters, married for almost twenty-five years, and now the marriage was completely over except for a judge putting the final stamp on the equitable distribution of their marital property.

Me.

CHAPTER

2

Virtually all the folk potters in North Carolina have resided in the Piedmont.

— *Turners and Burners*,
Charles G. Zug III

From Manteo on Roanoke Island to Murphy out in the mountains is more than five hundred miles, and Asheboro comes pretty close to being North Carolina's geographical center. They even built the state zoo here so it could be accessible to all our schoolchildren, coastal or mountain.

I've never been much interested in zoos myself. Too much television, I suppose. When you grow up on a working farm with cows and horses, goats, pigs, and chickens, it's easy to extrapolate from all those *National Geographic* and nature specials. My appetite for elephants and zebras and hippopotami is more than satisfied by panoramic views of animals living wild on the Serengeti with a David Ogden Stiers voice-over to explain their habits and eccentricities. I don't need to get within smelling distance of African wildlife, even in a state-of-the-art "zoological park."

No, for me, the main attraction of Asheboro is that it's only a few miles north of Seagrove, home to more than a hundred potters bunched along the Randolph/Moore County line. This trip out, I was hoping to find a big serving platter for my new house.

The potters have a festival every year on the weekend before Thanksgiving and I've been over a few times with my Aunt Zell or some of my sisters-in-law. Pottery makes a great Christmas present, and some of the prettiest pieces in the world are created up these narrow rural lanes and down graveled drives, often at kilns that haven't changed much in the last two hundred years. I've bought fat little piggy banks for various family babies from Owens Pottery, sturdy white Christmas candlesticks from Holly Hill, and a charming cat-head jar from Pam Owens at Jugtown.

I'd even bought a set of green-and-gray soup bowls for a friend in New York from the Nordan Pottery last year. They were expensive, but next to Jugtown, Nordan's is the second most famous pottery outside the area. It's certainly one of the oldest. Their ware is exquisitely made — relatively thin and beautifully glazed and painted. The lids fit snugly and their three-legged pots sit squarely without a wobble.

None of the Nordans had been in the showroom the day we were there, which had disappointed my brother Adam's wife. (Adam's the success story in our family: Ph.D., electronic whiz, enjoying the good life in Silicon Valley, and partner in a new software company of his own.) Karen's not really a professional southerner, one of those Dixie belles whose drawl becomes more pronounced each year they're away, but living on the West Coast *has* turned her into something of a North Carolina history buff. Her most recent enthusiasm that year was a book about the "turners and burners" of the state, and there'd been many references to James Lucas Nordan's father Amos and grandfather Lucas. They had been famous for their glazes, especially their cardinal ware, so called because its bright clear red exactly matched the adult male plumage of our state bird.

I've forgotten the details, but I do remember Karen reading me snippets about some secret family formulas that Amos had improved upon and passed along to his son. She had wanted to touch a bit of that history, talk to Amos's son, perhaps try to buy a piece of Amos's glowing cardinal ware that was in the museum section of their showroom and labeled "Not for Sale."

The clerk, a middle-aged woman with wiry brown hair, Birkenstocks over thick brown socks, and paint flecks on her cheek, had been standoffish until she saw the address printed on the check Karen wrote for the set of wonderful gray-and-purple plates, and then she'd become downright chatty in her homesickness for California. She confided that James Lucas did occasionally let a piece of old Amos's work go for the right price, but she wasn't authorized to sell any and he was at a folklife conference out in the mountains. "I'm afraid he won't be back till Monday night."

"I'll be on a plane back to California by then," Karen had said regretfully.

"Wished I was going to be in the seat next to you," the woman had sighed.

So Karen had come away without a piece of Amos Nordan pottery and now, a year later, the whole collection would no doubt be listed on one of the inventory sheets of this ED.

An ED — the equitable distribution of marital property — comes after the divorce is final and is the last fence to be jumped before the two parties are finally, legally, quit of each other. It can also be the most exasperating thing a district court judge has to adjudicate.

If there's no marital property or if both parties agree on who's to get what and there are no minor children involved, no problem. The headaches come when he says, "My mama gave me that cedar chest. It was her grandmother's," and she says, "Your mama gave it to both of us for a wedding present."

She says, "We bought them scale-model race cars together and they're worth five thousand dollars."

He says, "I bought most of them out of my own paychecks and they're only worth three thousand."

Except for their personal clothes and maybe their toothbrushes, everything of value in a couple's possession on the date of their separation — every piece of real estate, every vehicle, every set of silver, crystal, or Tupperware — *everything* has to be written down, with notations of how much it's worth, who has it, and who wants it. These are broken down into eleven separate schedules, but the main five list marital property upon which both parties agree as to value and who's to get it, marital property upon which there is agreement as to distribution but not value ("Okay, he can have them model cars, but I want it marked down that they're worth more'n he says they are"), marital property with an agreed value but disagreement as to who gets them, marital property in which there's total disagreement both as to the value and the distribution, and a list of items where the dispute is over whether an item even *is* marital property in the first place (great-grandmother's cedar chest, for instance).

There are also lists of items that neither party wants (and yes, I've heard of a couple who tried to list their minor children here), lists of separate possessions of each party, lists of separate debts and marital debts. Finally there are the affidavits of the expert witnesses.

Sometimes the two parties will agree to use the same appraiser; more often, each gets his or her own and the evaluations will be no closer together than if the two had done the appraisals themselves.

That's where judges come in. Keeping in mind that "equitable" is not always "equal," it's up to us to decide what's fair.

Looking over the summations of the two

EDs I'd been assigned, I saw that the Nordan case had been dragging on for months. The judge who was supposed to preside at their final hearing had suffered a mild stroke and was now in a rehab center down in Southern Pines.

The other case, an attorney and his wife, also an attorney, were at the final pretrial conference stage. Nick and Kelly Sanderson. Two attorneys in a fight to the death in a small city where everyone knows everyone else and has probably already chosen sides?

No wonder I'd been specialed in.

I followed 64 all the way into Asheboro and pulled in at a Comfort Inn just before the 220/74 interchange. According to the map and directions I'd been sent by the chief district court judge's office, it was clean, convenient to the courthouse, and comparatively cheap — always a plus in a state that's not particularly lavish with its per diem.

I entered the lobby a minute or two after six and started to check in, but the clerk on duty hesitated before swiping my credit card.

"Deborah Knott? Judge Knott?" he asked.

"Yes."

He gave me back my credit card, along with an envelope that bore my name in a large spiky handwriting. "She said for me not to check you in before you read this."

She? I ripped open the envelope.

Hey, Deborah!

Judge Neely told me you were coming over to do some EDs. Why are you staying at a motel when I've got two empty bedrooms? I'll be in the office till 7, then at the house. Call me!

Fliss

Below were listed two phone numbers, one for work, the other home.

I knew she lived in the district but had almost forgotten that her law practice was here in Asheboro.

The clerk obligingly gestured to the phone at the end of the counter and canceled my reservation while I dialed.

She picked up on the first ring and her voice was as husky as ever. "Felicity Chadwick."

"Hey, girl!" I said. "How come you're working so late?"

"Private sector," she said in that throaty drawl. "An eighteen-year-old at Princeton who thinks money grows on trees. Billable hours, remember?"

I listened for sour grapes in her tone, but

there didn't seem to be any.

"Actually, I was just killing time waiting for you," she said. "I'll come right over and you can follow me home, okay?"

"You sure?" I asked. "I don't want to put you out."

"Don't be silly. See you in fifteen minutes, okay?"

It was actually less than ten when she arrived. We hadn't seen each other in several months and we each sneaked appraising glances even as we hugged and laughed.

She had a sleek new haircut, and the rich chestnut color looked so utterly natural that I'd have never guessed a bottle if I didn't know her real hair was mousy gray.

"Like it?"

"I do," I assured her truthfully. "It takes off at least ten years."

We went through the You're-sure-this-is-no-trouble?/Of-course-not routine a final time, then I was back in my car, following her lead as she made a suicidal left turn out of the parking lot, then an almost immediate right onto 220 south to Seagrove.

"You're only ten miles away from the best Bloody Marys in this part of the state," she had bragged.

As we drove through the wooded countryside, brilliant with bursts of dogwoods and flowering Judas trees, I had to smile, thinking again of our first meeting.

It was in a motel in Burlington.

New Judges' School.

New district court judges have to attend one sometime during their freshman year on the bench. It's how we learn about payroll options, ethics, decorum, and where to order new robes. We also get cultural sensitivity training, mediation pointers, and updates on laws governing the bulk of our cases: DWI, domestic violence, child support, child custody, etc.

Due to a booking error on someone's part, Fliss Chadwick and I wound up assigned to the same room. By the time we realized what had happened, all the motel's nonsmoking single rooms were taken. At least the room had two beds. Nevertheless, my heart sank when I realized I was stuck for a whole weekend with this tall, serious-looking woman, a woman at least ten years older, whose dark hair was streaked with gray. It didn't help that she seemed to be a total slob, to boot. Already her belongings were strewn across both beds and both sides of the dresser, as if some secret agent had torn her luggage apart looking for a microchip.

"Sorry," she said, scooping up lingerie

and tank tops and dumping them on the floor on the other side of her bed. "I couldn't find my corkscrew. Chardonnay or Merlot? Or would you rather have a Bud?"

She was funny, earthy, and totally serious about the law, yet ready to kick back at the drop of a black silk bra (witness that ice chest in the corner stocked with beer and wine). Our room became party central that weekend and probably wrecked any hopes I might have had of building a reputation for sobriety and wisdom among my new colleagues. On the other hand, I noticed that very few of those new colleagues had to have their arms twisted. In fact, that was the weekend I finally understood, once and for all, the irony implicit in "sober as a judge."

Overall, a very educational two days.

Like me, Felicity Chadwick was a Democrat appointed by the governor. Unlike me, she lives in a heavily Republican district and was not reelected last November, which was why she was back in private practice.

I had called her to sympathize when I heard she lost, but this was the first time we'd seen each other since a conference up in the mountains before the election. We'd roomed together then, too, and this time I brought the corkscrew, but it didn't help. Two minutes after Fliss walked in, the room was a cheerful shambles.

I could just imagine what her house looked like. Still, so far as I knew, she was happily married. Maybe he was a slob, too.

A mile or so outside of Seagrove, she gave two quick blinks of her left-turn signal and abruptly turned into a long narrow driveway lined with blooming cherry trees. A quarter of a mile off the hardtop, she stopped at the back of a modern stone house framed in drifts of dogwoods, upright mountain laurels, and sprawling pink azaleas.

Fliss hopped out of her car and grabbed my overnight bag while I gathered up my purse and the files that had spilled across the seat.

She held the back door open for me and led the way into a kitchen with clean and shining countertops. No dirty dishes in the sink, no clutter of pans on the stove. Beyond was an equally tidy family room.

"Call the cops," I said. "You've been burgled."

"What?" Her eyes quickly scanned the rooms. "Where? I don't see anything out of place."

"Exactly," I said. "No way could you have left your house this neat. Someone's obviously been here. Unless the world's best cleaning person just left?"

Fliss laughed and led me down the hall to a pristine guest room. "June's good, but she only comes once a week. Monday's her regular day."

That was three whole days ago. The Fliss Chadwick I knew could've trashed the place in three hours.

"You're telling me this is the new you?" I dumped my things on the bare dresser. "Along with a new haircut, you got a personality adjustment and turned into Martha Stewart?"

She set my bag on a chest at the end of the bed and smiled. "Better. I finally got rid of the junk in my life. Starting with Winslow Prentice Chadwick the Fourth."

I suddenly realized how very little I knew of Fliss's personal life. We'd recognized each other as compatible spirits, but she probably knew more about me. Yes, she'd talked about her practice before she'd been appointed to the bench and she'd talked about her son Vee, so nicknamed because he was the fifth Winslow Prentice Chadwick, but her mentions of WP-Four had been fleeting and incidental, the way of long-married couples when they've been together for so many years that everything's taken for granted, like the ground underfoot or the sky overhead.

Still, I usually pick up on bitchy remarks and if she'd dropped any about her husband last October, they'd gone right past me. I wasn't hearing any regret in her tone, though. More like smug satisfaction.

"What'd you do?" I asked. "Bag him up and set him out by the curb?"

"Actually, I stuck him in a recycling bin and got started on the legalities," she said cheerfully as she pulled towels and wash-cloths from a linen closet in the hallway. "He's not a bad man. I expect someone will come along one of these days and get a few more miles out of him."

"Not another woman already out there waiting?" I asked, thinking of Kidd's soon-to-be-former Mrs. Ex.

"Nothing that interesting," she assured me. "Come on. Let's get that Bloody Mary I promised you."

In the kitchen, I watched her pull out bottle and jars and a tall aluminum shaker.

"When Vee went off to Princeton last fall, I realized he was the only thing holding Winslow and me together. I also realized that he and Vee had been making me crazy all these years. Believe it or not, I'm not a nat-ural slob — at least, no more than normal — but those two are such neat freaks that messi-ness became my passive rebellion against their aggressive attempts to control my whole life."

She grinned. "Least, that's what my therapist said. Made sense to me."

"You're in therapy?" I was surprised. She always seemed so at ease with herself.

"*Was.* I got really depressed last November. At first I thought it was a combination of Vee going off to college and then losing the election — I just couldn't face going back into private practice. So Winslow insisted that I go see a therapist over in Winston. Two sessions were all it took to put everything in proper perspective. He still doesn't know what hit him."

She mixed together tomato juice, Texas Pete, Worcestershire sauce, lime juice, and God knows what else with a healthy shot of vodka, then added an even healthier stalk of celery to each glass and lifted hers in a toast of welcome.

"So what's happening with you these days? Still seeing that game warden? What was his name? Kip?"

"Kidd," I said, cautiously sipping. Despite the chilled tomato juice, a tingle of chili warmed my tongue and throat all the way down. "Ummm. This is delicious."

We carried our drinks into the den that had probably belonged mostly to WP-Four

34

but which now was all Fliss's. A nicely pro-portioned space. One wall was nothing but windows and a pair of French doors that opened onto a deck shaded by dogwoods and maples. The other wall was covered floor to ceiling with white-enameled shelves behind gleaming glass doors. The shelves were mostly empty except for a few pieces of pottery.

At the far end of the room, a large clut-tered desk had been angled to face the door, and white azaleas in a dark blue jug shed their petals over a desk calendar and pencil mug. Here, finally, was a trace of the old Fliss I knew. The low bookcase behind the desk was filled with reference books. On top were a couple of small face jugs, those idio-syncratic pieces of glazed stoneware shaped to look like scowling faces. Bits of white por-celain formed misshapen teeth inside the open mouths. Newspapers and magazines lay heaped on the low table in front of a new-looking pale gray leather sofa with squishy pink and gray pillows. The couch was made for lounging and Fliss kicked off her shoes and sank into it with a contented sigh, gesturing me to an equally comfort-able chaise sprigged in spring flowers.

As I slid off my own shoes and leaned back against the pillows, Fliss said, "Now, what about that guy of yours?"

I shrugged, but hey, it was a good story and I hadn't brought a house present, so I told her all about my midnight drive, drawing out the suspense of getting into Kidd's house without waking him, his soft snores, stubbing my toe. Law school trains us to unfold dramas for a jury's edification and Fliss listened as raptly as any jury I'd ever addressed. She smiled in all the right places and when I described exactly *how* I'd discovered another woman in his bed, she fell back into the pillows laughing. I took another swallow of my Bloody Mary and laughed, too.

Laughed, and then found myself getting angry all over again at how he'd done me dirt.

"To think I let a game warden — a rabbit sheriff, for Pete's sake! — get to me like that," I said, working up to righteous indignation. "An overgrown Boy Scout — that's all he is. Give him a dog and turn him outdoors and he's happy as a beagle with a treed possum. If he's ever read a book that wasn't about hunting or fishing, I couldn't tell you what it was. When I suggested a movie, it had to have at least one car chase and one huge explosion or he'd grumble about it the whole way through. He's not even all that good-looking, so what the hell did I ever see in the bastard besides maybe that goofy smile of his?"

"Goofy sex?" Fliss suggested softly.

"Well, yes," I admitted. "He's really good in bed, can't deny that. Those slow hands. And we laugh at the same things and I can — *could* talk to him about anything, and —"

To my absolute horror, I realized that tears were stinging my eyes.

"I don't cry," I told Fliss, choking back a sob. "I *never* cry. Not over men anyhow. And even if I did, it wouldn't be for a sorry snake's belly like Kidd Chapin."

Then she was there beside me, taking the glass from my shaking hands and hugging me while my heart finished breaking.

Eventually I pulled away and with a mumbled "Sorry" I bolted for the nearest bathroom and put a cold wet cloth on my face till my nose quit looking so pink and some of the red was gone from my eyes.

"Feel better?" Fliss asked sympathetically when I came back.

"Yes, thanks."

Surprised, I realized I actually did. I'd been so angry all week over Kidd's betrayal that I'd blocked out my genuine grief at losing him. For the first time in my life, I'd actually begun to think of white organza and bridal showers and whether he'd ask for a transfer over to Colleton County or if I could commute from New Bern. I'd thought about puttering in the kitchen together, of spoiling his grandchildren if Amber ever came to accept me. Hell, I'd even begun to try out the phrases in my mind — "My husband thinks . . . my husband says . . . let me check with my husband and get back to you."

I felt myself tearing up again, and to divert the hurt and loss welling up inside, I paused by the nearly empty shelves and looked at the few pieces of pottery. "Local work?"

Fliss got up and came over. "I've finally started my own collection."

"Do all these bare shelves mean your husband had a collection?"

"And thank God he wanted it," she said fervently with a smile as bright as her new red hair. "He had these cabinets specially built so they wouldn't collect dust. Can you believe it? Living in the middle of the richest lode of folk pottery in the country, Winslow collected Meissen porcelains — delicate little sandwich plates and teacups hand-painted with flowers and English motifs. And all of it having to be washed once a year by hand in a towel-lined sink. No wonder I was a slob.

The floor was just about the only surface in the house that didn't have his fussy little china doodads on them."

I shuddered at the thought of having to live amid so many accidents waiting to happen.

"These you can hold without feeling that they'll shatter if you breathe on them," Fliss said.

She opened the glass door and put a beautiful lidded bowl in my hand. The grays and purples were a dead giveaway.

"It's Nordan pottery, isn't it?"

She nodded. "And here's a piece I've had packed up for years."

It was a homely old earthenware pie plate. The burnt-pumpkin glaze was chipped around the rim and showed the red clay beneath. I turned it to look at the marks on the bottom, not that they meant anything to me. It wasn't particularly beautiful, so I guessed that its value to Fliss lay in its age.

"Actually, it's not all that old," she said. "You know the story of the Busbees and Jugtown?"

"I know the Jugtown name, but who are the Busbees?"

"Well, to give you the condensed version, between the Prohibition movement that did away with the market for whiskey jugs and the arrival of cheap glass jars, potters were getting pretty thin on the ground around here in the 1910s. The Busbees were a wealthy young couple with artistic aspirations from over in Raleigh. He was a failed portrait painter and she was a frustrated photographer who sublimated by doing good works in the state's federation of women's clubs. Supposedly, she was arranging a display of fruit at a county fair down in Lexington and sent someone out to buy a pie tin to put the fruit on, only they brought back an earthenware plate like this one. Or maybe it was Davidson and a farmer already had his apples on it. Take your pick. There are lots of minor variations on the details.

"Anyhow, everybody agrees that Juliana Busbee saw an orange pie plate exactly like this one and went bonkers over it. She rushed over to the hardware store that carried them, bought every one she could find, then brought them back to Raleigh and got her husband just as excited. They decided that pottery was an indigenous craft worth studying and preserving. They also realized there was a big folk art market in New York."

There was more than a touch of cynicism in her voice.

"You sound as if you don't much revere the Busbees."

Fliss shrugged. "I think they were dilettantes looking for something to give meaning to their lives. He was a mediocre painter, she was a young society matron in a presuffragette South. The whole craze for folk arts and crafts was just hitting New York and they were smart enough to realize this was a way to get their ticket stamped and to be part of the avant-garde.

"To make a long story short, the Busbees moved over here and built a pottery — Jugtown — and they hired local potters to come turn pots for them. And, to do them justice, they introduced a lot of oriental art forms that rejuvenated the whole area. They were probably almost as important as they thought they were, although the wealthy tourists who'd started spending their winters at Southern Pines probably helped a lot, too."

"Is this one of the original pie plates Mrs. Busbee bought?" I asked, carefully setting the dish back on the shelf.

"No, but it's from that era, made around 1917, back when they still used pure red lead for glazing. These were common as the red mud clay the potters dug out of the creekbanks here. In fact, this was called a

41

mud dish and sold for about ten cents." She straightened it with a connoisseur's fond caress. "Of course, it cost me a bit more than a dime when I wheedled it out of old Ben Owen more than twenty years ago."

Next to the plate was a modern-day Jugtown piece, a whimsical rooster created by Pam Owens. A graceful Rebecca pitcher turned by Nell Cole Graves stood on a shelf by itself. It was beautiful. I'm not a collector, but for a moment I almost coveted that pitcher.

"What about these down here?" I asked, stooping to get a closer look at two pieces that were almost hidden on the bottom shelf next to the floor.

"You tell me," Fliss said, lifting them up so I could see them better.

Both were gray-and-purple bowls, about the size of two loosely cupped hands. They were almost identical except that the glaze on one was a clearer color. That one was heavier, though, with thicker sides and a slightly chunkier feel. The other had a more pleasing thinness to the sides, but the glaze had a muddy tone to it and the purple had been applied in less-artistic swirls.

"The purple on this one makes me think of the Nordan wares," I said hesitantly, glancing at the gray-and-purple Nordan

42

vase nearby, "but it doesn't feel right. This other one feels right, but the color's off."

"Very good." She touched the lidded Nordan bowl I'd held earlier. "This one's from when they were still working together. These others were fired this year. James Lucas turned the thin one and Sandra Kay mixed the glaze and painted that one at the pottery where she's been working ever since she filed for divorce."

My equitable distribution case. Of course.

Fliss shook her head regretfully. "This really is a case of the parts being a lot less than the whole. Too bad."

If this was the result, she was certainly right. He could turn elegant, thin-walled pieces, but his glazes were muddy. Her colors were rich and vibrant and as wasted on this clumsy piece as a tutu on a mule. In a no-fault state like North Carolina, it really doesn't matter why a couple seeks a divorce, but I was curious. "Why'd they split?"

"She thought he was trying to kill her."

"What?"

"Personally, given her temper, I always thought that if anyone was going to get killed in that marriage, it'd be her doing him."

Fliss slipped the two unfortunate bowls back on the bottom shelf and closed the glass door. "I heard most of the actual divorce proceedings," she said. "Let's go get some supper and I'll tell you about it."

CHAPTER

3

Clay is one of the most versatile materials known to man. It is soft, flexible, plastic, almost infinitely variable in its natural state. . . . This "mud," as the potters refer to it, is abundant, easy to locate, and cheap. But when it is burned with fire, it undergoes an irreversible transformation.

— *Turners and Burners*,
Charles G. Zug III

I changed my jacket for a turquoise cotton sweater, slipped out of my heels into flats, and freshened my lipstick, while Fliss went from uptown attorney in a navy blue suit to good ol' girl in faded jeans and a long-sleeved green silk shirt that turned her hazel eyes sea green.

It was a short drive to Seagrove proper. There's not much there — the remains of an old lumberyard, a couple of newish furniture factories, the relatively recent North Carolina Pottery Center up the hill, a grocery, and a hardware store. Mainly, Seagrove is a cluster of small pottery shops at the intersection of two state highways. Three blocks from the intersection in most directions and you're back in the country again. The Crock Pot sits at the edge of town and is the sort of place I always slide into when I'm on the road — a comfortable, old-shoe place where you seat yourself and the tea comes iced and sweet unless you specify differently. It's down-home cooking and waitresses old enough to be your grandmother, who wear cotton print aprons over their own clothes instead of look-alike uniforms.

I suppose that similar mismatched chairs and tables and blue-checked tablecloths can still be bought by the yard at any flea market or yard sale. What can't be bought by the yard are all the pickups and the old Ford and Chevy sedans in the parking lot. They usually tell me clearer than any advertising what the locals think about the cooking inside.

At least two-thirds of the twenty-five or so

tables were taken when we entered the big main room. Fliss seemed to know most of the people, so our progress toward a table back against a side wall was slow.

On the wall over the cash register, a board listed the daily specials. Tonight's was meatloaf.

I took a good look at the tables we passed by and was ready to order without looking at the menu our waitress brought over.

"Meatloaf with a double side of steamed cabbage, please, and hold the mashed potatoes."

The waitress gave an exaggerated cluck of disapproval as she efficiently slapped down bundles of flatware wrapped in paper napkins with one hand and filled our water glasses with the other. "Skinny as you are, honey, you ain't doing one of them low-carb diets, are you?"

"I love this lady," I told Fliss. "You be sure and leave her a big tip, hear?"

Fliss laughed. "Me? I thought *you* were treating."

"Or one of y'all could pay the bill and the other one leave a nice tip," said our waitress with an absolutely straight face, "and then you'd both come out even."

Given that the most expensive entrée was less than five dollars, she wasn't necessarily joking. She brought us our iced tea and Fliss raised her glass to renewed friendship and another welcome to Judicial District 19B. "But you might just want to borrow a bullet-proof vest tomorrow."

"For what? Stoneware mugs and cream pitchers at twenty paces?"

"You laugh, but that's almost what it came to last fall."

Technically, judges aren't supposed to receive any *ex parte* information that could influence a judgment, but there was nothing left to influence in the Nordan ED. As Fliss had reminded me on the short drive over, the divorce was finalized early last fall. All the fault hearings were over, support issues had been worked out, the scheduling and discovery conferences had already taken place.

The only thing left for me to do was add up the figures they'd agreed on and make the final adjustments so that whatever they'd acquired together could be equitably divided. If everything went as it should, the Nordans would be completely quit of each other by the time I adjourned tomorrow, and nothing Fliss told me about either combatant would make the slightest particle of difference.

Not that she'd said much, having gotten sidetracked by the history of Nordan Pottery.

"A lot of potters around here will talk about how their forebears used to turn a little mud so you'll think they learned their skills at their granddaddy's knee."

"They're lying?" I asked, thinking of the many signs I'd seen in previous trips that implied unbroken lines of tradition.

"Well, not lying, exactly. Just sort of stretching the truth a little. Look, my own paternal great-great-grandfather used to turn the crockery his family needed after the Civil War. Didn't cost him anything but time and labor to dig some clay out of the creekbank behind his house and make his own. Cheaper and easier than struggling out of these backwoods on roads that weren't much more than pig trots. But neither my grandfather nor either of his sons ever messed with it, though you wouldn't know that to hear my cousin Patty talk. She and her husband have a little pottery over at the old homeplace and their card says, 'A tradition begun in 1874.'

"Many of the old families did work the local clay back in the 1800s. But most of their descendants today — including my cousin Patty — wouldn't even know which end of a pug mill to put the clay in if they hadn't gone over and taken courses at the community college. They'll brag about being fourth- or fifth-generation potters, when everybody knows there were only about five or six families still potting regularly before the Busbees came. Hell, even as late as 1970, you could probably count all the active potteries on two hands."

"And the Nordans were one of those families?"

She nodded. "Amos's father was one of those too set in his ways to try the new forms. He just kept turning out the old wood-fired earthenware plates and bowls along with salt-glazed stoneware — churns and crocks and demijohns. Amos, now, he took a look at what the Jugtown potters were doing and adapted it to his own things. And his glazes were something else. Beautiful clear reds. It's a shame he can't throw those tall, thin-walled vases anymore."

I was surprised to hear that Amos Nordan was still numbered among the living. "The way my sister-in-law went on about how collectible his work is, I thought he'd been dead for ages."

"No, but he did have a stroke a couple of years ago that affected the left side of his body, especially his left hand," Fliss said, squeezing lemon into her tea. "His other son had just died — that's what brought on the stroke. He was the one found Donny's body.

It left him so sick and discouraged that he deeded James Lucas a lifetime right to the pottery and laid his own body down to die."

"Only it didn't?"

She shook her head. "When he was better, he tried to get James Lucas to renounce his right, but it didn't happen. Even before Donny died, James Lucas had been doing most of the grunt work and I guess he was tired of having to clear everything with Amos. Amos was mad enough to spit nails and he still sulks about it, but he's gone back to his old wheel. About all he can manage, though, are small bowls and plates. Nothing like the jugs and vases he used to turn."

Our own plates arrived, and yes, they were local earthenware, a bright blue to match the blue-checked tablecloths.

"Okay?" asked Fliss, who'd opted for the fried shrimp.

I nodded happily, my mouth too full of ambrosial meatloaf to speak for a moment. "But why a lifetime right? Why not deed it to his son outright?"

"Some say it's because James Lucas and Sandra Kay don't have any children, but others say he's had it in for Sandra Kay ever since she threatened to turn him in if he didn't follow all the rules about his glazes."

"Turn him in? To whom? Why?"

51

"FDA, Department of Commerce, you name it," Fliss mumbled, her mouth too full of fried shrimp to answer clearly. She swallowed, then dabbed her lips with her napkin. "There was a big deal about lead poisoning back in the late sixties, early seventies. I forget all the details, but I remember my mother's uncles fuming about it. They did a little turning and they liked the old glazes and didn't see why the state had to come meddling in just because some kids out West somewhere got lead poisoning from drinking juice every day out of ceramic cups made in Mexico. Nevertheless, there are still random tests, state *and* federal, to make sure everything meant to hold food is lead-free. It's against the law to use lead glazes for anything except purely decorative pieces, and even those have to be clearly labeled."

She sipped her tea and ate another shrimp. "Amos Nordan was one of the few who was stubborn enough to keep using it. There's just no other way to get that bright red that he was famous for. He's an ornery old cuss. James Lucas doesn't like to mess with it much, but his brother Donny did. Sandra Kay made them build new kilns to keep their cardinal ware separate from the tableware because of the fumes. If you burn a load of pots in the same kiln that you use over and over for lead-glazed things, they can test positive for lead. Amos still doesn't fully believe it. He thinks Sandra Kay was just being bitchy."

Fliss paused in midbite. "Well, damn!" she said. "You know, I never thought about it before, but wonder if Amos had anything to do with her accidents?"

"What accidents?"

"I don't remember all the details, but things like shelves and bricks falling on her, buckets left where she'd trip and fall. Any one thing could have been a pure accident, but these seemed to come in a series thick and fast. Then she caught James Lucas putting a footstool in her way. Least that's what she says he was doing. He swore he didn't know how it got there and that he was only moving it out of the way so she wouldn't trip again. Maybe he was telling the truth. Maybe it was Amos instead."

"Why? Was he trying to break up the marriage?"

"Who knows? Anyhow, as soon as Donny died —"

She broke off to smile at someone behind me. "Hey there, Connor. Fern and the girls not with you?"

"Naw," said a deep male voice. "They're having a lingerie party tonight and I was told not to come home before nine-thirty."

I turned and saw a man of medium height and solid build. Early to mid-forties maybe, in a dark blue windbreaker and a white shirt over chinos. The end of a green plaid tie dangled from his jacket pocket. He had police officer written all over him, but that's not why I took a second look. Pale reddish blond hair? Eyebrows and eyelashes that were almost white against the fair skin of his face? I'd seen him before. Not in court, but where?

"Deborah, this is Connor Woodall of the Randolph County Sheriff's Department. Connor, Judge Deborah Knott."

"Connor Woodall?" I asked. "The same Connor Woodall that graduated from West Colleton with Adam and Zach Knott and used to come out to the farm once in a while with Dwight Bryant?"

Now it was his turn to take a closer look, and his fair skin flushed with delight as he grabbed my hand and started shaking it. "Deborah? Deb'rah Knott? Well, I'll be darned! Last time I asked about your brothers, must've been about four years ago. Dwight did say you were a lawyer now, but I never heard you'd made judge. How's ol' Dwight doing? I haven't seen him since we did a computer seminar together over in Greensboro."

"He's fine," I said. "But how'd you wind up in Seagrove?"

"Aw, I went and married me a Seagrove gal and she said she couldn't live where the dirt wasn't red clay, so that pretty much let out Colleton County, didn't it? And I had some family over here, too, so it all worked out."

"Sounds like old home week," said Fliss. "You might as well sit with us, Connor, if you're by yourself."

"You sure I won't be butting in?"

Even as he spoke, he was already pulling out a chair.

"Not a bit," said Fliss. "Deborah's over here for the Sandersons' pretrial conference and to finish up the Nordan ED. I was telling her about all the accidents out at Nordan Pottery a couple of years ago. Didn't Sandra Kay call you to come about them?"

"Not me, one of the other boys. And I believe she wanted to put a restraining order on poor old James Lucas. Keep him out of his own house and pottery. Her brother talked her out of that. Course, I hear she's still mad at Dillard 'cause he wouldn't let her go back to the Rooster Clay."

I smiled at the name. "Does that mean Sandra Kay Nordan was born a Hitchcock?"

55

"You know them?" asked Connor.

"Not personally. Adam's wife bought a face jug there and we did hear a scatological story of how Hitchcock Pottery became Rooster Clay."

"Yeah, well, did you know that brother and sister married brother and sister?" he asked me. "Her brother, Dillard Hitchcock, married James Lucas's sister Betty. Thing is, when Sandra Kay and James Lucas split up, Betty naturally took her brother's part, so Dillard wasn't exactly free to invite Sandra Kay to come work with them even if she was his sister. Least that's what I heard. Fern knows these people better than I do and she says it's because there's not really enough room for another full-time decorator. Especially not with their own three kids starting to take hold in the business."

"If your sister-in-law's seriously into pottery, Deborah, you ought to get her one of Libbet Hitchcock's Rebecca pitchers," said Fliss.

"Libbet?" I asked. "That's an odd name."

"She was named for her mother," Connor explained. "They started out calling her Little Betty and Libbet's what it turned into after a while."

"Only fourteen years old," said Fliss, "but that child really has an uncommon talent for

56

clay and she's going to get better when she grows up and gets a little muscle on those arms. Even her decorations are good, right, Connor?"

"Fern says so," he agreed. "But you know Amos."

"Worst chauvinist you'll ever meet," Fliss told me. "You were asking why Amos only gave James Lucas a lifetime, right? He wants to leave Nordan Pottery to Betty's younger son so that the older one can get the Rooster Clay outright. Amos thinks those two boys hung the moon."

"But what about the girl? If she's so talented . . . ?"

"She's a girl," said Connor with a what-can-you-do? shrug. He must have given his order when he came in the door, for our waitress arrived with a plate of meatloaf for him and a pitcher of tea to top off our glasses.

"Lingerie, huh?" asked Fliss. "I can't believe your girls are old enough to be interested."

"Thirteen and fifteen," he said, proudly pulling out his wallet to show us pictures. The older one had his fair coloring and her long straight hair was so flaxen, it was almost silver. The younger one was more of a sandy blond. "Looks like her mother," he said, which meant I then got to see a picture of his pleasant-faced wife.

"That's Miss Fern! She's nice." The words were so thick as to be almost incoherent.

Unnoticed by us, another person had joined us, looking over our shoulders at the pictures.

I glanced up to see a head too big for his body. At first I thought he was a shorter-than-average adolescent, then the awkward movements combined with the thick speech made me realize that here was the mind of a not very bright three-year-old confined in the small body of someone around thirty. He had straight black hair and dark brown eyes that glanced away as soon as they met mine.

"Hey there, Jeffy," Connor said easily, putting his arm around the childish form. "Did you see Miss Fern today?"

He nodded enthusiastically. "We went to her place today. We made bunny rabbits. Wanna see mine?"

Without waiting for an answer, he pulled a lump of clay from the bib pocket of his denim overalls. It may have begun as a rabbit, but the ears had squished down and the cotton tail now looked like a fifth paw. Jeffy displayed it proudly on his small open hand. "See, Miss Fliss?"

"That's some rabbit," said Fliss, "but weren't you supposed to let Miss Fern fire it in her kiln so it'd get hard?"

"No!" The boy-man closed his hand defensively around the blob of clay. "It's mine. Miss Fern said."

"Of course she did," Connor said soothingly.

"Jeffy! Come back and quit bothering those — Oh!" said the woman who'd come over to get him. "Hi, Connor. Fliss. Didn't see it was you two sitting there."

By this time, Connor Woodall was politely on his feet and introducing me to Jeffy's mom. From the things said, I soon realized that she was the same woman who cleaned for Fliss every week.

June Gregorich was probably mid-fifties, which shouldn't have put her in a high-risk age group when she was pregnant with Jeffy. About my height, she was more sturdily built, and when we shook hands, her palm was hard and callused, her clasp strong, which I always like. (A limp handshake is a real turnoff for me.)

Everything about the woman spoke of strength and vigor. Her shoulder-length hair was dark brown, beginning to go seriously gray, but it was so thick and wiry that it seemed to have a life of its own, which was barely restrained by a large wooden clasp at the nape of her neck. Even without the Birkenstocks and denim skirt she was wearing, I would have remembered her by her hair and her West Coast accent. This was the salesclerk out at Nordan's the day Karen tried to buy some of old Amos Nordan's pottery last spring.

"My sister-in-law was going back to California," I reminded her, "and you said you wished you were going, too."

She laughed, but of course she didn't remember us. "I'm afraid we get too many California tourists to remember them all. Will you be staying in North Carolina long this trip?"

"Oh, I'm not from California," I said hastily. "I live here. Or rather, I live over in Colleton County, about ninety minutes from here."

"She's over to finish up with James Lucas and Sandra Kay's divorce settlement," Connor said. "She's a judge."

"A judge?" Distracted, she cast a quick eye across the restaurant's crowded length. Her son had wandered away and was now sitting at a table with an elderly man, who gestured to her impatiently. "I'd better go. Mr. Amos looks like he's ready to leave. Nice meeting you, Judge. 'Bye, Fliss.

Connor, tell Fern that Jeffy and his group really did have fun today, okay?"

I shifted my chair so that I could watch the legendary Amos Nordan get slowly to his feet. He had a walking stick, and he seemed to lean on it heavily as he shuffled across the floor to the cash register by the door. It was more like a processional than an exit because people spoke to him from every table that he passed.

"He's something else," Connor agreed. "Fern calls him one of the living legends."

"I take it your wife's a potter, too?" I asked.

He nodded. "She went and worked for free at Nordan Pottery when she was in high school, just to watch Amos turn those big vases. She's so short that, even doing it in three or four sections, she could never make one that size without using a ton of clay. See how tall he is? How long his arms are?"

I did.

"You don't really need to be a strong man with a long reach to throw tall pots, but it sure doesn't hurt."

He watched June Gregorich pay the cashier and send Jeffy back to their table with a couple of dollar bills for a tip. "How long's June been with Amos?"

"About two years now, wouldn't you say?"

Fliss answered. "Right about the time Sandra Kay moved out. Or maybe a little before? James Lucas needed somebody to stay with Amos after his stroke and she'd just started cleaning for him, remember? The Nordans were good about letting her bring Jeffy. You know what the Keefers were like."

Connor nodded and Fliss explained to me that the Keefers had hired June Gregorich when she first came to the area two or three years ago looking for work as a shop assistant, cleaning woman, anything to earn enough to live on that would let her keep her handicapped son with her during the day. "The Keefers didn't want Jeffy to set foot in the showroom. Didn't want to make their customers 'uncomfortable.' Can you believe that?"

I could.

We turned back to our food. Fliss and Connor gossiped about local people, and he told me a couple of tales on Dwight Bryant I'd never heard before. Dwight's the deputy sheriff over in Colleton and almost like another brother. I'm always glad to collect a little spare ammunition to keep in reserve for when he gets on my case.

We were finishing second cups of coffee, watching Connor enjoy a generous serving of fresh peach cobbler hot out of the oven, when there was a crash of china from the back room.

"Uh-oh," Fliss said.

Stomping through an archway labeled "Smoking Section" was a taller, younger, and ten times angrier edition of Amos Nordan. He wore clay-stained jeans, a tan jacket, and high-top, lace-up work boots, and he carried a thick manila folder that he must have slammed shut in a hurry, because papers were dangling from both ends.

Close on his heels was a short blond woman in red slacks and a black T-shirt. She clutched her own manila folder of papers and was even angrier. "Yeah, run away, you — you thick-fingered clodhopper!" she cried.

"*Me?* Thick-fingered?" He snorted derisively as everyone in the place stopped eating to watch. "And what do you call that bastard you shacked up with? Takes him ten pounds of clay to make a half-gallon jug," he sneered.

"Well, at least he's a hell of a lot more careful with heavy-metal glazes than you've ever been. And you'd never see *him* faking stuff."

That brought him up short and he glanced around the room as if suddenly aware of all the watching faces. "Shut your mouth, you hear me?"

"You don't get to tell me that anymore, mister. If I want to talk about what you and Donny were doing with the stamp —"

"Yeah, well, I didn't hear you talking back then, did I?" he snapped, drawn back into their fight. "You damn well kept your mouth shut long as it was putting clothes on your back."

"*My* back? Huh! Don't you mean the clothes on Donny's back?" There was such mocking acid in her voice that he whirled around to face her.

"You keep your filthy tongue off my brother's name."

"At least he found a way to get it up!"

He gave her a malevolent glare and headed for the door.

"You could've taken lessons from him," she taunted him. "Or maybe you did."

He turned back with such venom in his face that she almost stumbled backward as she raised her folder to ward off a blow.

"You say another damn word," he snarled, "and I'll smash every pot you own. Right now. Tonight."

"Yeah? You do and I'll tell everybody in Seagrove your other filthy little secret."

For a minute, I thought he really was going to smash her in the face. Connor must have thought so, too, for he stood up and started over.

Instead, the man spun on his heel, slapped some money down by the cash register so hard that it was a wonder the glass counter-top didn't crack, then pushed past some people in the doorway. The woman followed. A moment later, we heard two vehicles screech out of the parking lot, headed in different directions.

I let out the breath I'd been holding. "Don't tell me."

Fliss nodded. "Yep. That's your ED."

CHAPTER

4

It is generally asserted that the salt glaze
first appeared in Germany, possibly as
early as the fourteenth century. . . . In
any case, there is no hard evidence of any
ancestor to the long, low groundhog kiln
that came into use in the early nine-
teenth century.

— Turners and Burners,
Charles G. Zug III

Next morning, I left Fliss's house earlier than
I would normally because she'd warned me
that parking might be tricky. Over the years,
Randolph County had turned its courthouse
into a warren of haphazard add-ons. Now
they were in the process of getting a unified
structure, and everyone was sure the new judicial complex was going to be great once it

was finished, Fliss told me.

"In the meantime, the construction work's driving us all crazy. Every time it rains, the parking lot becomes a clay muck. I've already wrecked three pairs of shoes this spring."

Since April had given us showers night before last, I finessed the whole thing and parked beside the nearby county library so that I could walk across the street and up an unmuddy sidewalk. Once inside, I had to find the clerk of court's office, introduce myself, and pick up the file for *Nordan v. Nordan* and *Sanderson v. Sanderson*. A clerk showed me into an office behind Courtroom D, where I changed into my black robe.

When I entered the courtroom, the bailiff quickly said, "All rise," and launched into the familiar "Oyez, oyez, oyez" ritual, ending in, "Be seated."

Besides the gray-haired courtroom clerk, a hefty bailiff, and me, there were only four other people in the courtroom: two middle-aged male attorneys in neat blue suits and white shirts, and the two people I'd seen yelling at each other in the Crock Pot last night, looking none the worse for wear — no bandages, no bruises or cuts, despite all the threats that had been hurled and the reckless way their cars had left the parking lot.

This morning, they sat side by side at tables that were separated by less than six feet of space and stared at me in stony silence.

As Kidd and his wife must have once sat when their marriage came unglued.

As he and I might have sat one day if we'd ever gotten as far as a wedding ceremony, given Amber's hostility to me. Never under-estimate a child's power over her parents.

Congratulations, Amber, honey. You won after all.

I pulled my thoughts back to the case at hand.

Looking at least ten years older than his ex-wife, James Lucas Nordan appeared ill at ease here in a courtroom, with papers spread on the table before him. He re-minded me of most of my brothers, men who'd rather be up and doing with their hands instead of their tongues. In his gray sports jacket and tie over dark gray slacks, Mr. Nordan looked like an old plow horse that had been specially washed and brushed for the occasion. His graying hair had been combed while wet, the comb marks still vis-ible above his strong brow.

Sandra Kay Hitchcock Nordan seemed to have taken just as many pains with her ap-pearance — muted red lipstick, discreet eye shadow, and a mere hint of blusher. Her bright blond hair fell in soft waves and she wore a spring pantsuit of forest green with a crisp white eyelet shirt, gold studs in her ears, and a thin gold chain around her neck. Since they'd been together twenty-four years before separating, I had to assume she was at least mid-forties, but she certainly didn't look it today.

To my bemusement, she was represented by Nick Sanderson, soon to be standing before me as the plaintiff in his own pretrial conference.

Opposing counsel for defense was Wallace Frye, another attorney I'd never met before.

I explained my ground rules to both attorneys. "In this final proceeding, there's no need for the usual formalities. We'll just swear each of your clients in and let them testify from their seats at the table. Will there be any expert witnesses?"

"None for our side, Your Honor," said Sanderson. He had a deep resonant voice and would have been quite handsome except for a weak chin. A small beard as dark as his straight black hair would have helped his face a lot.

"None for ours, either," Wallace Frye sang out quickly. He was shorter, bone-thin, and possessed enough chin for two men. I had an impression of sharp intelligence and an impatience with routine procedures in the way he riffled through the papers before him.

"Fine," I said.

While both parties swore on the Bible that they would each tell the truth, the whole truth, and nothing but the truth, I opened up my laptop and clicked on to the spreadsheet program I use for EDs so I can keep a running total of the values assigned to each party.

"Everybody have a copy of the schedules?" I asked.

Murmured agreement.

Schedule A was six pages long and listed everything from a car up on blocks behind the pottery, through Christmas decorations and kitchen utensils, to the marital home where Mr. Nordan still lived, but since both sides agreed on their value and distribution, we passed immediately to Schedule B. There were only twelve items here. Both agreed on who was to get them, but not the value. On the d.o.s. — their date of separation and our benchmark for all valuations — she had taken their Grand Am and subsequently traded it in on a Lumina. Mrs. Nordan said she'd recently gotten a twenty-seven-hundred credit toward the newer car; Mr. Nordan claimed that old car had been worth six thousand.

That was a fairly simple matter to decide.

All I had to do was look up the retail price of a three-year-old Grand Am in the NADA book that covered the year they separated and rule that the worth of the car had been four thousand on that date.

"But I didn't get anywhere near that much," Mrs. Nordan protested earnestly.

I explained that I was obliged to go with the retail price. "It's not what you could sell the car for, but for what it would've cost if you'd tried to buy it at the date of your separation."

The leather chairs and couch were a little trickier. She said the "leather" was some sort of plastic and worth only three hundred dollars.

"They were nicer than regular plastic," Mr. Nordan said indignantly when it was his turn to speak. "We paid two thousand dollars for those three pieces when they were brand-new, and we'd only had them about two years when she walked out and took them with her. Real high quality. Looked like what you'd find in a lawyer's office," he added earnestly. "They had to be worth fifteen hundred at least."

If I was going to start cutting some Gordian knots, it was time to let them know I don't play games.

"Before we go any further," I said, "are

both parties willing to stipulate that I can find a value in between the two if the parties disagree? Otherwise, the law requires me to choose one of the values you've listed."

Mrs. Nordan didn't wait for Nick Sanderson to answer. "I trust Your Honor's fairness," she said, giving me what I suppose was a woman-to-woman look of solidarity.

"So stipulated," Wallace Frye said crisply after a quick consultation with his client.

"Now, Mrs. Nordan, you say the furniture is worth only three hundred dollars?"

"Yes, ma'am."

"So, if I awarded it to Mr. Nordan, who sounds as if he wouldn't mind having it back, and valued it in his column as only three hundred dollars, you would still agree that's fair?" I asked with a pleasant smile.

Her look of cozy solidarity turned to chagrin.

"Let's call it nine hundred and fifty dollars," I said.

"And I still get to keep it?" she asked sheepishly.

"To the plaintiff," I agreed.

Wallace Frye smiled broadly as he entered the new figures.

I went right on down Schedule B, hearing their testimony as to why I should agree with their valuations. Naturally I didn't forget that it was to each one's advantage to come out with the least dollar value on their individual possessions. Nordan was going to wind up with most of the big-ticket items connected with the pottery, as well as the marital home, which he'd inherited from his grandparents before the marriage but which still carried a hefty marital equity from all the improvements they'd made over the years. That meant he'd be trying to keep everything valued low on his side of the ledger and high on hers so that he wouldn't have to pay her a huge lump sum at the end to make the division equitable.

As objectively as possible, I tried to hit the middle ground on the thirty-year-old tractor Nordan used to haul firewood for the groundhog kilns ($1,500), the inventory pottery that was there on the d.o.s. and had since been sold by him ($1,900), her collection of Barbie dolls ($800).

The only item on Schedule C was the pottery they'd collected together. Each had brought separate pieces to the collection from their own heritage and there was no question of ownership on those, but together they'd amassed a collection that was almost museum quality in its range and depth. Both agreed it was worth approximately thirty thousand dollars at today's auction prices. Both wanted all of it and neither was prepared to budge.

When it was clear that there was no hope of compromise, I said, "Then let's leave C for now and move on to Schedule D."

D contained two riding lawn mowers neither party wanted and eighteen Hallmark Christmas ornaments that both did want even though their estimates of value were a couple of hundred dollars apart. After some bickering back and forth, they agreed to divide them. Since she particularly wanted the 1997 ornament, I let her take the odd years and gave him the even. I valued the orphaned lawn mowers at a hundred dollars each and split them, too.

Schedule E listed two groundhog kilns, a car kiln (whatever that was), and three turning wheels that Mrs. Nordan contended were marital property, since they'd been built before the d.o.s. with materials she'd helped pay for. Mr. Nordan testified they were part of the real estate, which his father technically owned, since he himself only held a lifetime right to the pottery.

"What's a car kiln?" I asked, curious to know if it was shaped like an automobile or big enough to put a car inside or what.

Both attorneys and Mrs. Nordan deferred to the expert.

"Well," said James Lucas Nordan, gesturing with his hands, "it's like a little three-sided house built out'n firebricks. Ours is about eight foot tall and five or six foot deep. You've got three gas burners on two sides with baffles so your flames don't hit directly on your pots. Then you've got a ware cart on steel wheels that run on two little steel tracks." He held his thumb and forefinger apart to show me the narrow gauge. "That's your car. The back end of it's made out'n firebricks, too, like the fourth wall of your little brick house. So you load your setters with your glazed bisque ware, then push it in like a railroad car. Clamp it shut real tight and fire it up. You can get a higher temperature. We use the car kiln for stoneware and the groundhogs for salt glazing."

He looked at me doubtfully. "You do know about salt glazing, don't you?"

I've been told and I can speak glibly enough about it. I know that oral tradition traces the practice back to the Middle Ages when German potters threw some barrels that had held salted fish or sauerkraut into a kiln's firebox and discovered it gave the clay an impregnable skin, but I've never really understood how common table salt can turn a plain clay surface into something hard and glassy. This looked like my chance to have it explained by a professional.

"Pretend I don't," I told him.

"Well, your groundhog kiln's dug right into the ground with a rounded brick roof. Looks just like a big mole run. You've got about six or eight salt ports in the sides. They're holes exactly the size of your bricks. When the temperature inside your kiln is hot enough, you pull your bricks out and throw your salt through those port holes. Your salt vaporizes, the chlorine burns off, and the sodium acts like a flux to melt the silica on the surface of your wares. That's how you get your hard glassy coating like your old potters did it. You still got to stock salt-glazed earthenware. Folks like that old-timey look, but believe me, Your Honor, it's a lot easier to load your ware cart and push it in than it is to crawl around inside a groundhog kiln to set your pots."

He spoke with an owner's pride in a piece of efficient equipment, his big hands demonstrating the push/pull of moving a loaded cart in and out of the kiln proper. In animation, especially when he smiled, his eyes crinkled and his leathery face looked younger. The Nordans must have been a very attractive couple in their youth. After lasting nearly a quarter of a century, it was too bad they couldn't have made it all the way. Not my business, though. My job was to stay neutral and finish the division they'd begun.

"Are all three of these kilns permanent structures?"

"Oh, yes, ma'am."

"But you built them before you and your wife separated?"

"Well, we rebuilt the old one that was there before she come and my brother and me did the work on the two new ones, but my daddy paid for all the material."

"Out of profits I helped make," Mrs. Nordan argued.

After listening to both sides, I ruled the two newer kilns and the turning wheels marital, but valued them at a somewhat lower figure than Mrs. Nordan's.

Schedules F and G were their separate contentions for an unequal division. He presented evidence that he'd been paying all property taxes for the last two years, along with paying down the marital debt, and that he'd also incurred maintenance and upkeep expenses on their property during this time. Her counterclaim cited his control of her income-producing property, namely her place of work, and her marital claim on income produced as a result of his lifetime right to Nordan Pottery.

After ruling on the marital debt and allowing the defendant credit for an unequal distribution for his payment of property taxes, I further ruled that the division of the marital property as both had agreed upon would effect an equitable distribution. Since a distribution in kind was impractical — there's no simple way to divide a kiln — I granted a distributive award to the plaintiff.

Then we (or rather my laptop and the attorneys' calculators) added up all the figures. When the numbers quit flying around, it looked as if Mr. Nordan would owe his ex-wife a little over forty thousand dollars.

"But what about our pottery collection?" asked Mrs. Nordan. "You didn't tell us who's going to get it."

I looked again at the photographs they'd submitted for my examination and felt a little helpless. This was way outside my realm of expertise. If it were twelve place settings of mutually acquired silverware, I could simply split it down the middle and give six place settings to each. If he had been the collector and she were claiming it simply because she knew how much it would grieve him to lose it, then I'd accept their evaluation and give it all to him. But both of them argued with heat and passion and it was clear that each would be devastated to lose.

I heard them out, then sat there silently, trying to decide. Again, I looked through the pictures. Even as an outsider, I knew that both of these people had roots that went deep into the red clay of Randolph County. Hitchcocks and Nordans had been making pottery here in a continuous line since the Revolution and both of their descendants wore their ancestry proudly. These simple jugs and pots were the visible symbols of their heritage. How could I ask either to take the monetary value and give up a claim to those symbols?

With a sigh, I realized there was nothing to do but go for the Beanie Baby solution, which is what I'd started calling it after I learned what a judge in another state had done in a similar situation. He'd had some three hundred of the couple's stuffed toy animals hauled into court, then tossed a coin. The wife won the coin toss and got first choice, the husband got the next two picks, and then the two alternated till the entire pile was divided.

"But that's not fair," both Nordans protested.

"You've got an eighteenth century storage jar here that's worth twice any other piece," said James Lucas Nordan.

"Then whoever chooses that one, the

other gets to pick two," I said.

They still muttered mutinously to their attorneys.

"Look," I said finally. "You people have had two years to sort this out. You've tied up your lives, you've tied up the courts. One way or another, this is going to be settled today. You can either divide it as I've suggested or I'll split the whole collection straight down the middle based strictly on the appraised value on the date of separation."

That got their attention.

"But we can't bring them all in today," said Mrs. Nordan. "They'll have to be carefully packed up and —"

"How many pieces are we talking about?" I interrupted.

"About fifty?" Mr. Nordan hazarded, speaking directly to Mrs. Nordan for the first time.

"Not counting what belongs to him and what belongs to me, there's forty-three pieces."

"Permission to approach, Your Honor," said Wallace Frye after a furious thumb-through of the piles of paper in front of him.

I nodded and he handed some papers to Nick Sanderson and to me. They were a set of inventory sheets with comprehensive descriptions of each piece of pottery, when and how acquired, and their current value. Several had been highlighted in red and were initialed SKN, others were marked in fluorescent yellow and initialed JLN. I counted the rest. She was right. Forty-three.

"Does this agree with your client's perception of the collection?" I asked Sanderson.

"Yes, Your Honor. She already had a disk copy. This is an abstract of the records they kept on the pottery's computer."

Of course. Low-tech meets high-tech. One of their groundhog kilns was eighty years old, the computer was only three (and, as I recalled, awarded on Schedule A to the defendant).

"Where's the collection right now?"

"Out at the house," said James Lucas Nordan. "Or rather at the shop. We built like a museum on the side with lighted shelves and all."

"And it's all there, easily viewed?"

"Yes, ma'am."

"Very well," I said, glancing at the clock on the rear wall. "It's almost twelve-thirty. We'll finish up here, take a lunch recess, and, if everyone agrees, we'll reconvene at your shop at two-thirty and get this done."

They agreed. As did the bailiff and the

clerk, who were also required to be present.

My action would be unusual, but not unheard of.

I finished filling out the Memorandum of Judgment form and went through the ritual of asking both parties if their consent to the agreements we'd reached was informed and voluntary. After they agreed and signed, I dated and signed it, too, making it an official court order which I handed to the clerk to process.

The bailiff offered me a ride down to Seagrove after lunch, but I declined. There'd be no need to come back into Asheboro after we'd finished, so I could go straight on to Fliss's house.

"Court will be adjourned until two-thirty," I said.

"All rise," said the bailiff.

CHAPTER

5

Most small family potteries could not support the needs of grown men as well as other members of the family. As each son reached about eighteen years of age he usually left home to find work elsewhere.

— *Raised in Clay*,
Nancy Sweezy

Tommy Hitchcock slammed his senior English textbook down on the low wall that edged the school's parking lot. "Old Lasater's rode my ass for the last time," he snarled. "I'm quitting."

"No, you're not," said Brittany Simmons. Her long blond hair gleamed in the spring sunshine as she reached for the lighted cigarette in his hand and took a small ladylike drag.

"Oh, come on, Brit! What the hell I need Shakespeare for?"

"You need it to graduate," she said calmly, lighting a cigarette of her own.

"I don't need no high school diploma to turn pots."

"If a jackleg pot turner's all you aim to be, working for your daddy and your brother all your life —"

"I won't be working for them. Nordan Pottery's going to be ours someday."

"*Someday,*" she said scornfully. "Someday when your uncle's dead and gone. It's his till he dies, remember?"

"Well, yeah, but he's old."

She shook her head. "My mom was in school with him and she's only fifty-two. Your granddaddy's seventy-five. If James Lucas Nordan lives as long, you'll be forty-two years old before the pottery's ours. And you keep pissing him off, you won't see a penny out of it as long as he's alive."

"You saying you don't want to marry me?"

"I'm saying I don't want to marry a loser with no options. It's only a month and a half till graduation. You quit school now, all you can do is turn pots for somebody else the next twenty-five years. With a diploma, you could go to Winston-Salem or Greensboro. Get a real job. Make some decent money."

"Potting *is* a real job! Look at all the money Ben Owen must be making," he said, citing one of Seagrove's most successful craftsmen.

"Yeah, like you're a Ben Owen," she said scornfully as the bell rang for their next class. "He's gone to college, studied pot-making all over the world, and you can't even suck it up for a month?"

She dropped her cigarette on the gravel, crushed it daintily with her sandal, picked up her textbooks, and handed him his. "You quit school, we're finished."

"Yeah? Well, if that's all you think of me, maybe we're finished now!"

"Fine," she said, dropping his book on the ground before turning to walk inside.

"Fine!" he said, and kicked the book halfway to Christmas.

When he peeled out of the parking lot two minutes later, the tires on his old white Toyota laid down twin strips of rubber.

"She's not getting my Runcie bird jar," James Lucas said tightly as he towered over Wallace Frye on the sidewalk outside the courthouse. "I'm the one heard about it and tracked it down, and I'll be damned if she's getting it."

"You'll get it," his attorney said soothingly. "If you win first pick, you'll have it. If she wins, she'll take the 1798 storage jar and you'll still get your bird jar, plus the next-best piece to boot."

Wallace Frye had grown up in Charlotte and he'd moved to Asheboro as soon as he passed the bar exam. The slower pace suited him and he liked having the zoo close enough that he could slip off with the kids whenever he wanted. In the eight years he'd lived here, he'd met a lot of potters, but he'd never fallen under the spell of their wares and he didn't really believe clay pots of any vintage were worth as much as some of his colleagues were willing to pay. A couple of attorneys here in town had practically turned their homes into museums and would lecture on long-dead indigenous potters versus modern practitioners at the drop of a coffee mug, so he recognized a collector's passion when he saw it and he was exasperated though not surprised by Nordan's response to logic.

"But I want that one, too," his client protested.

"Then you're just going to have to figure out which pieces she particularly values and pick enough of those that she'll trade you for them," Frye said. He glanced at his watch. "Lunch?"

James Lucas shook his head morosely. "No, I'll grab a burger and head on back."

"Fine," Frye said briskly. "I'll see you out at your shop at two-thirty."

The back door of the sales shop opened and Amos Nordan's stooped length almost filled the frame. "Ain't it about time James Lucas was getting home?" he asked for the second time in the last hour.

He was getting as bad as Jeffy waiting for a clock's little hand to reach a certain hour, June Gregorich thought irritably. It annoyed her to think his mental faculties might be going, that he might be entering second childhood this soon. She wanted to tell him to get a grip, that he was only seventy-six, with at least another ten years ahead of him if he'd just set his mind to it.

Instead, she kept her voice patient. "Soon as he comes in, I'll send him on down to the shed. Isn't Bobby back from lunch yet?"

"Naw, and it gets lonesome down there by myself," the old man grumbled as he watched her wrap the bright red vase a happy tourist had just bought for her Florida home.

Even before she went to work for Amos Nordan, June had been told that Donny was his favorite son, but she'd only seen them together twice before that November day two years ago when she'd called 911 after Mr. Amos found him dead. She didn't know if he'd been as emotionally dependent on Donny as he'd become on James Lucas since his stroke, but he'd certainly grieved enough. Hardly a day passed without mention of Donny. Some people thought it was morbid, but June understood exactly what he'd lost. She knew what it was like to keep on mourning for unrealized potential. Wasn't Jeffy a constant reminder of the hopes and dreams she and his father had envisioned when she was carrying him thirty-one years ago and the future spread out brightly before them?

Not that she ever talked about her losses the way Mr. Amos did his. What was the point of weeping on somebody's shoulder? She hadn't done it in California, even after Ted walked out on them with all their assets, condemning her to a life of menial labor that would let her give Jeffy a life outside the walls of an institution, so why burden the new friends she'd made here? With their soft southern accents and quick sympathies, they could only offer assurances she didn't need and no longer wanted. She knew very well that Jeffy's condition wasn't her fault. She'd done everything her obstetrician advised — vitamins, diet, organic foods, exercise. If only —

June's mental treadmill of weary if-onlys was interrupted as the customer in front of her noticed Amos Nordan's clay-stained rubber apron.

"Are you the one who made my vase?" she asked brightly.

He gave her a grudging nod.

"I'd sure love to see your wheel," the woman chirped.

Most potters were amenable to giving mini-demonstrations. They even sold their wares right out of the pottery where they worked.

Not Amos Nordan.

More than once she'd heard him complain to James Lucas, "I ain't no performing monkey. I'll sell 'em my pots, but bedamned if I'll put on a show for 'em to stand around taking pictures with their stinking cameras."

Fortunately, he was too savvy to say it to a customer's face.

"Sorry, ma'am," he said blandly, "but I've stopped for dinner. If you're set on seeing somebody throw a pot, though . . ." He mischievously reached for her map and pointed to a spot a few miles across the Moore County line as the crow flies. "Luck's Wares. Sid Luck used to be a teacher and he pure enjoys showing folks how it's done. You ask him real nice and he might even show you how to turn a ring jug. Don't tell him it was me sent you, though. I don't want him to feel he owes me anything."

June gave him a disapproving look as the customer hurried out the door, to catch a potter at work.

"One of these days Mr. Luck's going to take a shotgun to you," she warned her employer.

All this time, Jeffy had been sitting on the floor at June's feet, playing with some miniature clay animals Amos had made for him in an unwonted burst of generosity this past Christmas, but the mention of lunch roused him from his absorption and he tugged at his mother's denim skirt. "I'm hungry, Momma."

She looked at Mr. Amos. "Want me to close the shop and fix lunch?"

Before he could answer, James Lucas opened the door and the old man's face lit up. "It's all done? You're completely shet of her now?"

"Not quite," he said. "We still have to divide the collection."

Jeffy went to him and held out a clay dog, but James Lucas was too distracted to notice. Nothing new there, June thought. He

90

had never been mean to Jeffy, but in the two years they'd lived there, he'd never taken any time with her son, either, which was about as much as you could expect from most folks. At least the Nordans had never asked her why she didn't stick her son in an institution, as if he were an awkward inconvenience who needed to be warehoused out of sight and out of mind.

"They're all coming out after they eat — the judge, the lawyers, Sandra Kay," he said.

As Jeffy butted up against him like a friendly puppy, James Lucas tousled his hair as if he were indeed a puppy. His own hair had gone a shade grayer in the two years she'd known him and the lines in his face were so deep now he could have passed for Mr. Nordan's brother instead of son, even though she knew he was almost exactly as old as she. While she was a carefree young wife in California, he was already carrying a man's workload here at Nordan Pottery, helping to turn out the pottery's famous cardinal ware.

"Bobby finish loading the car kiln?" he asked.

Amos shook his head. "He swears he'll finish this evening, but you know him."

"Want me to set a plate for you?" June asked as she paused in the doorway with Jeffy.

"No, I already ate a hamburger. Y'all go ahead, though."

"Come on over and set with us," urged his father.

But James Lucas shook his head. "You go on and eat and have your rest, Dad, and I'll see you after this is over. I just want to look at everything one more time while it's all together, okay?"

When he finally eased them out of the showroom, James Lucas walked over to the addition they'd built on years before the separation. Till then, the pieces had sat haphazardly around their house, but one day he and Sandra Kay heard Dorothy and Walter Auman speak on the significance of old pots.

The Aumans were self-taught historians, potters just like the Nordans. They had loved and collected old family pieces, too, and sought out the stories behind them, and their enthusiasm sparked his and Sandra Kay's and gave them a rationale for the old chipped and cracked pieces they kept lugging home.

These homely demijohns, chamber pots, and butter jars were a tangible link to generations past and, lacking children and that link to the future, the two of them had become almost obsessed with finding things their grandparents and great-grandparents had made and used.

Now the Aumans were dead, their collection gone to the Charlotte museum, away from the clay pits of Seagrove. And soon this collection, too, would be broken up. He alternated between rage and grief as he moved from one glass case to another. He remembered the excitement when they found this jug etched with his great-great-grandfather's initials, the glow on Sandra Kay's face when she brought home that storage jar. They used to laugh together in those days. How could it have gone so wrong between them?

The bloom was long since off the rose by the time Donny died, yet they still worked well together, were easy in each other's company, with no thought of divorce.

But the minute Donny died, seemed like their marriage just flat went to hell.

Dad got it in his head that Sandra Kay had been having an affair with Donny and for some reason blamed her for the way Donny died.

Did she sleep with his brother? He still didn't know. She swore there was nothing between them, but where there's smoke . . . ?

And Donny wasn't there to answer his questions.

Not that he would've. Or not that he'd have told the truth if he did answer.

Sometimes, thought James Lucas, he could well understand why Joseph's brothers had thrown him in the pit and sold him into slavery. The Bible made it sound as if the brothers had acted without a bit of provocation even though the younger brother was old Jacob's pet, the one who got all the praise and all the consideration.

Just like Donny.

He didn't have a doubt in the world that Dad would have willed the pottery to Donny alone if his brother hadn't gone and killed himself when he did.

Well, that was water under the bridge now, he told himself, and switched off the lights in the glass shelves as a couple of customers came in.

They proved to be browsers only and left a minute or so after June returned to mind the shop.

"I'll be down at the sheds if anybody needs me," James Lucas told her as she sat down at the computer to finish entering the last kilnload of ware in their inventory records.

Better to be busy than to be brooding on what can't be helped, he thought as he walked along the path through a bed of rhododendrons that were now taller than he. Their large pink or purple blossoms were prettier to him than any lilies or orchids he'd ever seen. He and Sandra Kay had once talked about designing a set of tableware around rhododendron colors, but Dad and Donny had vetoed the idea — "Gray and purple are our colors," they said. "That and our cardinal red" — and after Donny died, there was no working with her.

Bobby hadn't made much headway on loading the car kiln with a new batch of bowls and plates, and James Lucas set to work. His hands were full when a white car eased slowly through the rutted lane that led from the road out front over to Felton Creek Road.

Sandra Kay. On her way to her double-wide on the other side of the Rooster, no doubt.

Hitchcocks had used the shortcut since the horse-and-buggy days and she couldn't seem to break the habit. Weren't for his sister Betty being married to Dillard Hitchcock, he'd put a chain up and close the lane once and for all, James Lucas thought.

Through the rhododendrons, he caught a glimpse of his ex-wife's face as she slowed for a particularly deep pothole and he deliberately turned his back on her. Time enough for phony politeness when the others arrived.

He continued ferrying the wares from the drying shelves inside the potting shed to the car kiln and was half-finished when he heard his name.

"Yeah?"

He turned to see a shard of pottery held out to him.

"What's that?" he asked, but before his fingers could close around it, the shard fell to the ground.

He stooped to pick it up and a crushing blow smashed his head.

Something cool and wet splashed on his face and hands and he groggily opened his eyes.

The pain was so intense that it took a moment to register that he was lying amid broken bowls and plates.

He looked at his hands. At the sleeves of his shirt.

Red. Bright red.

Blood?

Then he felt himself moving and his world went dark again.

CHAPTER

6

As Joe Owen points out, the potter's first task was to get the kiln to full heat.

— *Turners and Burners*,
Charles G. Zug III

Fliss had planned to meet me for lunch at Zoo City, a café that sits a half-block down from the courthouse where Worth Street tees into Fayetteville, but when I buzzed her office, I found she'd left a message with her secretary that she was going to be tied up in a deposition and would see me back at the house.

"And Mrs. Chadwick told me to ask if you wanted to go with her to the bar association dinner at the country club down in Troy tonight."

"Sure," I said.

Okay, so a bar association dinner isn't usually a barrel of laughs, but since there was nothing more exciting on my docket, why not network a little?

In the meantime, lunch.

When I came down the steps of the courthouse, I saw Mrs. Nordan and her attorney take leave of each other. She seemed to be heading for Zoo City, while Nick Sanderson veered off toward one of the perfectly charming offices that lined Lawyers Row and fronted onto the courthouse square. I could understand why neither Sanderson would want to relinquish such desirable quarters.

Although connected, each row house had its own distinctive architectural charm, from leaded windows to discreet gingerbread trim. Together, they breathed an automatic tradition and solidity that no modern office complex could ever match. Whichever Sanderson lost, that Sanderson would be losing more than the usual goodwill owned by most firms. He (or she, let us not forget) would be losing status, convenience, and income, too, no doubt. Anyone charging out of the courthouse with the sudden urgent need of an attorney would surely head straight for this row of legal saviors.

I thought of the law offices over in Dobbs, where I had practiced before becoming a judge. The white clapboard house had been built in 1867, half a block from the courthouse, by my maternal grandmother's grandfather, and it had been hard to leave even though it was my own choice to run for the bench. What if my cousins and I had dissolved the partnership under acrimonious terms? I would have felt bereft and dispossessed.

Maybe the Sandersons would be able to reach a civilized agreement on their own, but if they didn't, my next hope was that Judge Ferris would recover from his stroke in time to render the final findings of fact and conclusions of law.

Rather than risk the awkwardness of lunching in a small place where one or other of the Nordans or their attorneys might also be eating, I decided to pick up an apple, a handful of raw string beans, and a bottle of water at a grocery store on my way out of town. I could munch my way down to Seagrove, pick up a map of area potteries, and look for a serving platter that would go with the casual lifestyle I'd adopted since building my own house out by one of the farm ponds.

Summer was coming and with it would

come hordes of nieces and nephews to swim off the pier I'd had built. Most of my eleven older brothers still lived in Colleton County and they and their wives would be out, too. I was probably going to need two platters to hold all the sandwiches or grilled chicken it would take to feed them. Just thinking of it made me smile as I browsed the exhibit hall at the Pottery Center.

Not that any pottery is sold there. Fliss had told me that many of the potters originally opposed the center because they feared that a gift shop would end the custom of buyers coming out to the potteries, which would, in turn, cut down on their impulse buys when surrounded by so many goodies. So there's no gift shop in the usual sense. Instead, the center displays representative pieces from most of the surrounding potteries, each keyed to a simplified map of the area. "Which doesn't stop people from whining, 'Oh, but I just loved your sample at the Pottery Center,' " says Fliss. "It's a joke how often the potters come in to take away the old sample and put in a new one, but you'll never get them to admit that they're selling from the center."

Since no one at the center can let you buy a sample outright, you're encouraged to go foraging on your own. Potteries are found on both sides of Highway 705 as well as along the branching roads. Most are right on the road, but others are up narrow dirt lanes, hidden from casual view by stands of cedar and pine, with only a small sign to tell you you've arrived. I found a half-dozen pieces whose style and color appealed to me, marked my map, and was on my way by one-fifteen.

At that, I barely had time to check out three or four places in the next hour, because you can't just go in and look only at platters. There's so much tactile variety, so many intriguing shapes, all demanding to be touched and held. The shops themselves were interesting, too. Some had regular museum pedestals with single pieces displayed like works of art, others stacked up rough planks and bricks and loaded the planks down like a discount warehouse. Some of the shops were separate showrooms, some were tables and racks at one end with the potter and his wheel at the other end, up to his elbows in wet clay as the wheel spun around and bowls magically emerged from the lump beneath his hands.

Although I didn't find my platters, I bought a grotesque face jug at one place and a large flower pot at another. At still another, I stood mesmerized as the potter turned out several cereal bowls in a row without a hair's worth of difference between them.

"Practice does make perfect, doesn't it?" I marveled. "I don't see how you can make them so uniformly."

The potter chuckled and wet his hands again before cupping them around the next ball of clay. "Things don't always come out of the kiln as identical as they went in. I've had many a customer fuss 'cause they couldn't find six juice cups that matched precisely. One woman was so picky, I finally told 'er to go on over to Kmart. Every one of their cups match."

I would have enjoyed talking to him longer, but a glance at my watch showed a quarter past two. Even though Nordan Pottery was less than a half-mile away, I didn't want to be late.

Built of rough clapboards stained a dark brown, the pottery complex nestled in a grove of dogwoods and pine as if it'd been there forever, or at least for the whole two hundred years that Nordans had owned this section of land. It was far enough back from the road to have a graveled parking area that could accommodate six or eight cars, yet it was partially screened by a weathered split-rail fence and head-high azaleas and rhododendrons. Here in early April, everything was pink and green and earth-toned. No grass, just a thick carpet of pine needles and leaf mold.

To the right of the shop was the house James Lucas Nordan had inherited from his grandparents and where he still lived alone since the separation. To the left was Amos Nordan's house, which the old man shared with June Gregorich and her son Jeffy. Fliss had told me that she kept house for him in exchange for their room and board and that she was free to work elsewhere for wages as she chose.

"She works in the shop on weekends, decorates part-time for them and for Grist Mill Pottery," Fliss had said, ticking the jobs off on her fingers. "Cleans for me on Mondays and for a friend of mine on Fridays."

"When does she rest?" I'd asked.

"I'm not sure she does. But she's trained Jeffy to help a little. He can use a broom, run the vacuum, or scrub down a shower stall. You just have to keep it real specific."

When I arrived, Jeffy was rocking in the porch swing with Mrs. Cagle, the matronly, gray-haired recording clerk, who probably had grandchildren. They were singing a *Sesame Street* song about friendship and taking turns.

The bailiff, whose name I kept forgetting, was leaning against the porch post to smoke a cigarette. His toe unconsciously tapped along with the rhythm of the songs. The two attorneys were talking together under a dogwood in full flower and as I got out of my car, three unfamiliar women came through the shop doorway with brown paper sacks that bulged with newspaper-wrapped pottery.

June Gregorich saw them down the porch steps, then turned the OPEN sign on the door around so that it now read CLOSED.

"Oh, goodness!" exclaimed one of the tourists. "We got here just in time, didn't we?"

Her friend gave the attorneys and me a look of commiseration. "Too bad they're closing on y'all. Their stuff is so wonderful! You simply *have* to come back."

Wallace Frye smiled and assured them we certainly would.

They started to drive out of the parking lot and had to wait while a shiny white Lumina turned in. Sandra Kay Nordan. She drove right up to the edge of the porch and parked.

"Am I late?" she asked as she hopped out of the car. She had changed into khaki slacks, sneakers, and a short-sleeved bright red cotton sweater. There were smudges on the sides of her pants, as if she'd wiped her dusty hands there.

"We still have five minutes, according to my watch," I said. "Is the collection in this building?"

She nodded and led the way up the porch steps with a mixture of awkwardness and familiarity. Mrs. Nordan had spent thirty years of her life here, yet now she came as a truculent visitor.

June Gregorich held the door open for us.

"Hey, June," she said. "Where is he?"

"Out back somewhere. Didn't you find him before?" The housekeeper's wiry brown hair was standing almost straight on its ends like some sort of fright wig and as she spoke, she smoothed it back with her hands and tied it with an orange ribbon that matched her faded and paint-splattered T-shirt.

"Before? I just got here."

"Oh? I thought I saw your car when —" She broke off with a shrug and gestured for us to come in.

The others waited for me to enter, then followed me into the long room. The ceiling was open timbers and had been set with clear glass skylights. Natural sunlight fell upon the purple-and-gray pieces of pottery like spotlights aimed on expensive jewelry.

There were no windows in the rear wall, but more light came from windows along the front, where a glistening row of Amos Nordan's trademark cardinal tableware sat behind a placard that warned, "Not for sale — Don't even ask."

Mrs. Nordan went straight past the sale displays, back to where the ceiling lowered and there were no windows or skylights. The shadowy space was clearly a home-built add-on.

"Want me to get the lights?" asked June Gregorich.

"That's okay, I'll do it," said Mrs. Nordan. She opened an inconspicuous panel in the wall, flipped a series of switches, and the pottery collection sprang into view. The small open room was lined with glass-fronted shelves from floor to ceiling and each shelf had its own concealed strip of lighting so that every piece could be seen and appreciated.

I hadn't paid that much attention to it when I was here before with my sister-in-law, and I had to remind myself that I wasn't here to sightsee. Instead, I turned to Mrs. Gregorich. "Would you tell Mr. Nordan we're ready to begin?"

"Certainly," she said, and went out through the rear door.

While we waited, I took a closer look at

the collection. The pieces were arranged chronologically and most of the early ones were simple and utilitarian shapes. Among them was a salt-glazed stoneware grave marker that was poignantly incised in crude lettering:

Chas Nordan
Dyed • Oct. 1st • 1832
Aged • 13M°.

"Oh, for heaven's sake," said Sandra Kay Nordan, looking at her watch impatiently. She started for the rear door, but as she put out her hand to turn the knob, it opened and Jeffy came shuffling back in, followed by his mother.

"Watch out for that table, Jeffy," she warned.

The boy — given his small physical size and mental capacity, it was hard to think of this thirty-year-old as a man — backed away from a display table of stoneware candlesticks with exaggerated care as June Gregorich stepped around him and picked up the telephone on the counter.

"James Lucas must be out at the house," she said. "I'll just call and remind him you're here."

After a couple of moments, it was obvious

that no one was going to answer.

She frowned and speed-dialed another number. "Mr. Amos? Is James Lucas over there with you? . . . He's not? . . . Well, did he say he was going anywhere? . . . No, no, that's all right. He's probably out back and didn't hear me call. I'm going to send Jeffy over to watch television with you, okay?"

"Mr. Rogers?" her son asked.

"Almost, sweetie. It'll be on in just a few minutes. You go sit with Mr. Amos, okay?"

Jeffy nodded and shambled out the back door.

"I'll check down at the house," his mother told us. "Maybe he was in the yard and didn't hear the phone ring."

"If he was in the yard, he must've seen us drive in," huffed Sandra Kay Nordan. "He's probably got his head stuck in one of the kilns."

It was too pretty a day to wait inside and I followed Mrs. Nordan outside. Two workshops were back there, about twenty yards from the rear door of the shop, and the new kilns were under tin-roofed shelters beyond, half-hidden by those flowering bushes. Graveled driveways linked the houses and main buildings, and dirt lanes led off up the hill through oaks and pines, probably to the wood lots that supplied firewood for the old-time kilns or possibly even to clay beds on the downslope beyond the rise. Nowadays, most potters prefer to buy their clay, I'd been told, but some of the traditionalists still like to dig and pug their own.

The smell of yellow jasmine floated on the spring air and somewhere someone was rushing the season by barbecuing outside, reminding me that it would soon be time to plan a summer pig-picking.

Mrs. Nordan opened the door and called, "James Lucas? You in here?"

The pottery shed was long and poorly lit and every surface seemed covered in powdery gray clay dust. The floor was nothing but dirt, and bare light bulbs dangled at the end of extension cords over the work areas. Steel utility shelves held the greenware that hadn't yet been fired; behind them were barrels of clay, buckets of glazes, and other supplies of the potting trade.

Both wheels stood motionless, though. No potter here.

I tagged along as Mrs. Nordan passed straight through and out a side door and there were the two newer kilns, each under its own tall tin-roofed shelter. To the left was the nonmarital groundhog kiln, a low, domed, brick-lined burrow with a firebox in the front and a chimney at the back. I looked at it with new eyes after Mr. Nordan's recent testimony. It must be tedious as hell to load one of those things. You'd have to crawl through a small door on your hands and knees and, if you were lucky enough to have help, those helpers would hand in the various pots and crocks and churns, which you would space in rows according to size and glazes. I guess you really would look like a groundhog entering and leaving a burrow.

To the right was a more modern construction of creamy white firebricks and gas lines hooked up to heat dials along the sides — Mr. Nordan's car kiln.

"That's why he's late," said Mrs. Nordan. "He's got the dogged kiln fired up." Impatiently, she called, "James Lucas! What the dickens are you —"

"What is it?" I asked, seeing the puzzled look on her face as her words broke off.

She pointed to the far side of the kiln, to a heap of shattered pottery and scattered debris.

The kiln was clamped shut, but some sort of red liquid had puddled on the concrete floor between the runner tracks.

"That's Amos's glaze and it's still wet," said Sandra Kay Nordan, "but the burners are running wide open. What the heck's he thinking? He's not supposed to use this kiln for cardinal ware."

She grabbed a pair of heavy leather gloves from a nearby shelf, pulled a brick out of the nearest peephole, and looked through.

"What on earth?" she said to herself, and then in sudden horror, she dropped the brick as if it'd burned through the glove. "Oh, my God! Oh, my God," she moaned, and began turning off the gas valves as fast as she could.

I stepped up to look through the hole myself. At first, all I saw was a dark shape beyond the tongue of fire that leaped in front of me. Then I saw a ghastly toothy grin in red-glazed features. At first, I thought it was a particularly gruesome face jug made to represent the devil. As I watched, the hair burst into flames.

That's when I realized it wasn't a pig that I'd smelled cooking and almost lost the string beans and apple I'd had for lunch.

CHAPTER

7

Unquestionably, there was some danger involved in this operation.

> — *Turners and Burners*,
> Charles G. Zug III

Okay, it was completely unprofessional of me. I do know better than to watch someone tamper with a crime scene.

Theoretically, anyhow.

In practice, in the grisly horror of the moment, there was no way I could've stopped Sandra Kay Nordan from turning off the gas, unclamping the bolts, and with unimaginable strength, pulling on the heavy apparatus until it rolled out of that broiling kiln.

James Lucas Nordan, or what was left of whoever it was — and who else could it possibly be? — lay crumpled amongst broken pots and mugs on a platform of plate setters that teetered precariously. His clothes had burned off and his flesh was charred black, but the bright glaze that coated his head and hands hadn't heated high enough to start melting into glass. It had certainly dried, though, and as the cooler air hit the body, the thick glaze began to crack and powder while we watched helplessly.

Sandra Kay's screams brought the others running to the kiln shelter.

"Oh, dear God!" said Wallace Frye.

"How . . . ?" faltered Mrs. Cagle.

Wide-eyed, June Gregorich said, "He was just talking to me an hour ago."

"Who could've . . . ?" asked Nick Sanderson. "Dammit! Who *would've?*"

Shock and morbid fascination had us all babbling.

"Here, now. What's going on?" said Amos Nordan, who moved so slowly, he'd probably set out as soon as June Gregorich called over to his house.

He reminded me of my own daddy, in his bib overalls and a long-sleeved blue chambray shirt, except my daddy still walked the earth with strength and vigor. This old man needed the support of a homemade staff cut from wild cherry as he walked unsteadily across the gravel drive and peered nearsightedly under the shelter. "That you bawling, Sandra Kay? What ails you, girl?"

Motherly little Mrs. Cagle, who seemed to know him, hurried over and took his arm. "Come away, Amos. You don't want to see."

"The hell I don't!" He shook off her hand and kept coming. "Some damn fool tourist go poking his nose too close to a peephole? Get his eyelashes burnt off? James Lucas! Where you at?"

"You really need to go on back to the house, Mr. Nordan," the bailiff said firmly.

Too late.

Before he could be turned back, the old man brandished his staff and June Gregorich stepped aside, giving him an unobstructed view of the grisly scene behind her. Amos Nordan stared at the charred, still-smoking figure lying on the kiln's car and wrinkled his forehead in bewilderment. Suddenly, in one heart-wrenching moment, I saw comprehension flood his face and contort his features till he, too, looked like a face jug turned by a demented potter.

"James Lucas? No!" His legs collapsed beneath him in instant, heart-shattering grief. "Say that ain't him! That can't be him."

Half-kneeling, half-sitting, he pounded the dirt with his gnarled hands until they came up bloody from the sharp-edged chips of past kiln breakages. "No, no, no, no! Not my boy? Please? Not my last son!"

Sanderson and Frye retrieved his staff and tried to help him up, but he wouldn't rise, just sat there on the ground like some Old Testament Jeremiah, shaking his head and howling in anguished protest.

With tears in her eyes, Sandra Kay Nordan went to him, knelt down on the broken shards, and tried to speak.

"Goddamn you to hell and back," he snarled, almost spitting in her face.

She drew back, shocked.

"This is your fault, you horny bitch! You killed him sure as you put him in that kiln. Won't for you and this mess you brought on my family" — his bloody hand swept the yard to encompass all of us — "this wouldn't have happened."

"You're a mean old man," his ex-daughter-in-law said, rising angrily, "and when I get what's mine, I hope I never have to see your greedy face again." She turned and stomped back toward the shop.

Galvanized by the anger that momentarily blanked his grief, Amos Nordan gestured to Mrs. Gregorich and let her help him stand. His bloody hands streaked her arm.

Jeffy, meanwhile, had edged closer to the

kiln car, unnoticed by us. I saw him just as he put out his finger, then jerked it back with a whimper. "Hot!" He stuck his burnt forefinger in his mouth. "All red, Momma. He got a boo-boo?"

The bailiff reached for the cell phone clipped to his waist and said, "Folks, I think we all oughta move on up to the shop."

It was close to five-thirty before I made it back to Fliss's house. The two attorneys had convoyed out from Asheboro and they got to leave shortly after Connor Woodall arrived. Mrs. Cagle had ridden out with the bailiff and they, too, were soon allowed to go. But since I'd been there when James Lucas Nordan's body was discovered, Connor said he'd really appreciate it if I'd wait in the shop a little longer. His "little longer" lasted a full two hours, so I heard everything the others had to say before they left. And yes, I asked questions of my own while we waited for the sheriff's department to get to us.

Wallace Frye said he and his client had parted in front of the courthouse. "He told me he was going home and would see me here."

"Did he mention that he was meeting anyone?"

116

Frye shook his head. "Far as I know, he didn't have any special reason for hurrying back."

The bailiff — *Anderson, Anderson, Anderson,* I chanted mentally, trying to fix his name tag in my brain — and Mrs. Cagle had gotten there a few minutes before either attorney.

"Customers were in the shop with June and Jeffy," said Mrs. Cagle. "I didn't see James Lucas, though. You, Andy?"

He shook his head.

"Any other cars drive in or out?" I asked.

"Not that I saw. Course, now, if a car was already there and they drove out the back way, we wouldn't've seen them, would we, Andy? There's lanes that go over past the Hitchcock place and come out on Felton Creek Road. Quicker than going 'round."

Mrs. Nordan said she'd planned to eat lunch at Zoo City, but it was so crowded, she decided to go on home, home being a double-wide she'd had set up on Hitchcock land inherited from her parents.

"Betty Nordan might've kept me out of the Rooster," she said bitterly, "but she couldn't keep me off my own land. Thank goodness the trees are thick enough on my side that I don't have to see them going and coming every time I turn around."

117

"Poor Amos," Mrs. Cagle said sadly. "This is just going to kill him. First Donny, now James Lucas. I reckon this'll be the end of Nordan Pottery."

"Donny?" I asked, half-remembering that Fliss had mentioned a Nordan son who died.

"James Lucas and Betty's brother." She cast a guilty glance toward Sandra Kay Nordan. "He . . . um . . . he died — over a year ago, was it?"

"Two and a half years," Mrs. Nordan said. Her voice held a quality I couldn't quite decipher. "The fair-haired son with the magic fingers."

Before I could get her to elaborate, a deputy stepped through the back door and told the other four that they could go.

June Gregorich came back about then. She said that Amos Nordan wanted to be alone for a while, "but I left Jeffy watching television. He knows how to press the shop button on the telephone if Mr. Amos needs anything."

She had brought with her a plastic milk jug full of chilled sweet tea. Sandra Kay plucked three tall stoneware mugs from the display shelves, wiped out any dust with paper towels, and we drank thirstily.

Once the bailiff, the clerk, and the attorneys left, the three of us were pretty much on a first-name basis within ten minutes. There seemed no need to keep up formalities when it was clear to me that any division of the Nordans' collection would involve probate.

"What *does* happen now?" Sandra Kay asked, wandering restlessly back and forth in front of the glass shelves that housed the pottery collection she'd shared with her ex-husband. "Do we have to start the dogged thing all over again?"

"The ED, you mean? No," I said. "Both of you signed the Memorandum of Judgment, so everything you and he agreed to this morning is still binding. Whoever represents Mr. Nordan's estate will substitute for him in dividing the collection. Everything else stays the same."

"That'll be Betty, probably," she said. "If he still has a will. I made a new one after we split up."

"If he died intestate, his father would be the next of kin. Unless there were children?"

"No children," she said abruptly. "Not even any bastards."

"Oh?" I was sensing all sorts of unspoken undercurrents. Sometimes an innocuous "Oh?" will loosen tongues itching to speak. Not this time, though.

So I asked June Gregorich, "Did you see Mr. Nordan when he came home? Was anybody with him?"

She shook her head. "Far as I know, he was by himself. That was a little before one, I think. He told me to go on to lunch, that you and the others were coming out to split up the collection and he wanted to have another last look at it while it was still all together."

Sandra Kay rolled her eyes.

"Well, I'm sorry, Sandra Kay, but that's what he said and that's how he said it. Not mean or anything. More sad-like."

"What about Bobby Gerard?" Sandra Kay said. "Was he working today?"

"Supposed to be. He was here this morning, but nobody's seen him since lunchtime. It's been a couple of weeks since he went on one of his benders, so . . ." She made a face and Sandra Kay nodded in understanding.

I asked who Bobby Gerard was and they explained that he was the pottery's kiln helper. Not a very reliable one, I gathered.

"So lunchtime was the last you saw of James Lucas?"

"No. He'd changed clothes when I got back around one-thirty, and he said he was going down to the pottery and for me to put up the closed sign soon as you got here.

There were a couple of people looking around, but they didn't buy anything. Weekdays are usually pretty slow. But the next ones — well, I guess you saw them because they were still here when you came."

"How did they pay?" I asked.

"One with a check, the others with cash." She hit the key that opened the computerized cash register and took out the check. "Winston-Salem. And there's a phone number. But they didn't go out back and I'm sure they never saw James Lucas."

"Who hated him that much?" I asked.

Sandra Kay shook her head helplessly and June said, "Nobody that I knew of. But then I probably wouldn't. We've only lived in Seagrove about three years."

"I don't understand trying to glaze his face," said Sandra Kay. "It was awful to put him in the kiln, but to paint his face and hands first? That doesn't make sense."

"Another potter?" I wondered aloud. "Somebody jealous of his standing in the field?"

Sandra Kay ran both hands through her blond hair with a bewildered frown. "But he doesn't have that much standing. Not since we split up."

She glanced apologetically at June Gregorich. "I'm sorry, June. I know you've tried."

The older woman shut the cash drawer and closed down the computer. "You don't need to apologize for speaking the truth. I told James Lucas I didn't know anything about mixing glazes and Mr. Amos only knows red. I can dip ware into a glaze barrel and I can paint simple flowers and vines and things like that — that's just common sense. But the stuff you do? That's talent."

Sandra Kay started to demur, but June wasn't having it. "Yes, it *is* talent. And nothing to brag about or be modest either. It's straight from the genes and you either have it or you don't."

She faced me forthrightly. "She's got it. I don't."

"And neither did James Lucas," Sandra Kay said sadly. "He could turn as good as his daddy, almost as good as Donny, but he didn't have their feel for slips and glazes and the way they work over different clays. No, if professional jealousy was reason to kill a Nordan, it's Donny they'd have killed. If he wasn't already dead."

Again that odd awkwardness hung in the air and I remembered Fliss saying that Amos Nordan's stroke was brought on by finding his son's body.

"How *did* he die?" I asked bluntly.

"An accident," she said, her face closing

down. "We don't like to talk about it."

"Sorry," I murmured, and backed off. I'd soon be seeing Fliss. She'd certainly know, and if not, there was always Connor Woodall, who ought to be getting around to taking my statement sometime before dark. If we went one on one, he might be persuaded to gossip a bit with the nosy younger sister of old boyhood friends.

All this time, various official vehicles had come and gone through the yard, including the ambulance that would be taking Nordan's body over to Chapel Hill for autopsy. As the minutes dragged on, we became more and more restless. June went back to the house to check on Jeffy and Mr. Amos and that left Sandra Kay and me casting about for something safe to talk about, since I could hardly ask her why her ex-father-in-law called her a horny bitch or why June thought she'd driven her white car through the yard before any of the rest of us arrived.

Their pottery collection was good for another fifteen minutes, then I asked about the set of bright red tableware with the emphatic NOT FOR SALE sign.

"That was Nordan Pottery's biggest seller for years. They shipped it all over the country," she said, picking up a dinner plate and flicking a bit of dust from its shining glassy surface. It was that rich clear hue that balances perfectly at true red. No touch of yellow to tip it toward orange. No hint of blue to tip toward violet.

"It's a shame Mr. Nordan quit making it," I said. "I'd love a set of plates and mugs for family barbecues."

"No, you wouldn't," she said firmly. "This is a low-fired lead glaze. The minute it crazes or chips, the vinegar in barbecue would leach the lead right out. Same with the mugs and anything as acidic as hot coffee or tea. It —"

Her lecture was interrupted by a loud car horn from out back just as June Gregorich pushed open the door. She looked back over her shoulder and we saw a white van splashed with red mud come tearing through the lane that snaked down from the wooded hill behind the kiln sheds. When it became clear that the patrol car blocking the lane wasn't going to move, the van quit honking and pulled up sharply. Two of the three doors were open before it came to a full stop and out tumbled a tall woman and two tall kids, a boy and a girl. He was almost a man, she looked to be early teens. They were immediately followed by the driver, a shorter, middle-aged man in mud-stained khaki work clothes and a John Deere cap.

An officer moved to intercept them.

"I'm sorry," June told Sandra Kay again as she stepped on through the door, "but Mr. Amos called her a few minutes ago."

Her California voice might have held sympathy, but her brown eyes flashed with universal interest in drama and I didn't need a printout to realize this was the Hitchcock clan — James Lucas's sister Betty and Sandra Kay's brother Dillard Hitchcock with two of their three children.

They were too far away for me to make out her words and a few of the bushes blocked our view, but Betty Nordan Hitchcock was clearly crying as she spoke to Connor Woodall, who had stepped forward to meet them and turn them away from the kiln where all the activity was centered. I heard her voice raised in tearful argument, but Connor's voice was a steady rumble and her shoulders slumped as she gave up. Supported by her son, she stumbled up the path that led directly to her father's house. Her daughter started to trail along behind them, but when Dillard Hitchcock took the path that led to the shop door where I stood looking over Sandra Kay's shoulder, she came with him.

As soon as he saw Sandra Kay, he

stretched out his arms and she ran to him with a low moan. Whatever her problems with her sister-in-law, Sandra Kay was clearly ready for a brother's comfort. "Oh, Dilly, it's awful. So awful."

The girl, the super-talented Libbet that Fliss and Connor had discussed the night before, watched without speaking. Tall as all the Nordans seemed to be, she was so thin that there was almost no sign of breasts or hips inside her oversized T-shirt and straight-legged jeans. Her long brown hair was plaited with a single braid that hung halfway down her back and was secured with a plain rubber band. Her dark blue eyes flicked from her aunt to June and me, then back again. All the fourteen-year-olds I knew would've been babbling, but she just listened silently till Sandra Kay finished telling how she'd found James Lucas's body in the kiln, then said, "If you hadn't gone and left him, you'd be in charge here now and I could've come and turned for you."

"Libbet!" said her father, sounding appalled.

The girl shrugged. "Well, it's true. Now Granddaddy'll give it to Tom and he'll just run it into the ground. You know he will."

"Now, see here —"

"Soon as he hears, he'll probably head

straight to Brittany and pop the question. You and Mom won't be able to stop him this time."

"That's enough, Elizabeth!"

" 'Soon as he hears'?" Sandra Kay pulled back and looked at her brother. "Where *is* Tom, Dillard? Why isn't he with y'all? And where was he right after lunch?"

CHAPTER

8

It is commonly believed that glaze seals a pot against liquid penetration. With the exception of . . . slip gazes, this is not always the case since many glazes do not fit a pot perfectly and therefore are under tension, causing the glaze to yield and develop fine crazed lines (sometimes discernible only with a magnifying glass) either immediately or over time.

— Raised in Clay,
Nancy Sweezy

It was almost five-thirty before I got back to Fliss's house. She met me in the doorway with a drink we'd concocted together and christened a Carolina Cooler: half orange juice and half tonic water in a twelve-ounce glass with enough gin to suit whatever the occasion. Since she'd be driving, hers was almost a virgin. Mine was not.

"You sure you still want to go with me?" she asked when I'd finished telling her about James Lucas Nordan's death. "I'm one of the officers, so I have to be there tonight, but if you'd rather skip it . . . ?"

Even a bar association dinner seemed preferable to spending the evening alone at Fliss's house. Besides, it'd give me the chance to ask her some of the questions I hadn't been able to ask Connor Woodall.

After all that waiting, he'd barely asked for my name, rank, and serial number before letting me leave. "I'll catch up with you tomorrow," he'd said, turning his attention to Sandra Kay and June.

So now I took a quick shower and changed into a silky, ankle-length, sleeveless shift. It was olive green with a random scattering of black leaves around the neckline. Over it, I wore a short, fitted black jacket. When I stood perfectly still, I was a demure and proper judge. When I moved, a thigh-high side slit suggested other adjectives.

As befits an officer of the association, Fliss wore a rust-colored linen suit the exact same shade as her new hair.

Once we were on 134 heading south to

Troy, I settled back in my seat and described the weird vibes given off in the Nordan shop when Donny Nordan's name came up.

"How did he die?" I asked Fliss.

"Truth to tell, I'm not a hundred percent sure," she said, passing a tractor that had a bewildered-looking cow tethered in the railed flatbed it was pulling. "First they said it was suicide, then they said it was an accident. He'd remodeled the loft over his potting shed. Called it his bachelor's pad, and that's where it happened. They found him hanging from one of the rafters. No one could figure out why. His work was selling well — a lot of serious collectors were starting to say he was the most gifted potter Nordan Pottery's ever produced."

"That's what Sandra Kay said, only she was sort of snide about it. She called him the fair-haired son with the magic fingers."

"I wouldn't read too much into that. Yeah, Amos favored Donny over James Lucas, but Nordan Pottery wouldn't have been profitable if it hadn't been for her and James Lucas's steadiness. Donny was gifted, but he was erratic as hell and lazy, too."

"When he was good, he was very, very good?" I suggested.

"And when he was bad?" She smiled.

"Well, he'd just found out he was a father."

"Huh?"

Without taking her eyes off the road, Fliss nodded. "He never married. Lot of girlfriends, but none of them ever got pregnant. And since Sandra Kay and James Lucas didn't have children, I guess Donny assumed that he and his brother were both sterile. Then, out of the blue, he got a letter from a woman who'd been in a pottery class he gave over in Raleigh years ago. She'd been married at the time, but now she was divorced or her husband died, I forget which, and she wanted Donny to know that he was the father of her younger son. I heard he was happy about it, happy but so surprised that they were going to do a blood test. That's why suicide seemed so unlikely."

"You think he was murdered?"

"Oh, no," Fliss said as I fiddled with an air vent that was blowing on my face. "About a week after the funeral, word seeped out that it was an accident. Though I don't know why that should be something the Nordans would want hushed up, I couldn't say. Seems to me an accident is better than killing yourself, but that's when my dad was going into a rest home over in Charlotte and I was back and forth a lot about the time they changed Donny's cause of death, so I missed whatever talk there was. But the Nordans still don't want to talk about, so it must've been a real dumb accident. Like drowning in the toilet bowl or something."

"Was Amos the one who found him?"

She nodded. "And right after that, he had his stroke."

We drove in silence for a few minutes while I thought about ways to accidentally hang yourself.

"What happened to the boy?" I asked. "Was it his?"

"Who knows? Donny died owning nothing but a few pots, a car, and the clothes on his back, so it's not as if he had much to leave to an illegitimate child."

"But if Amos Nordan was so crazy about Donny, wouldn't he want to help raise Donny's son, his own grandson?"

"We're talking a teenager here," she said. "Not an infant. And remember I told you that Amos went and signed a lifetime right over to James Lucas when he had his stroke? So it's not as if he had much extra money to toss around even if he wanted to."

"Didn't James Lucas care about his brother's son?"

"Evidently not. But then he and Donny weren't all that close, either. Now that he's dead, too, maybe Amos will change his mind."

"His granddaughter — that Libbet Hitchcock you were bragging on? She seems to think her brother Tom's going to step right in and take over the works. That he's been waiting for an opportunity to get married and strike out on his own."

Fliss snorted. "If he thinks working for Amos is going to be easier than working for his parents, he's in for a shock."

"The old man's got a real temper, hasn't he?" I said, and told her how he'd reacted to Sandra Kay's attempt to comfort him down at the kiln. "Why'd he call her a horny bitch, do you think?"

She shrugged. "Believe it or not, Deborah, I really don't keep up with every jot and tittle of gossip that swirls through Seagrove. Half the time, things go in one ear and out the other, and — Oh, damn!"

With no warning blink of her signal lights, Fliss swerved to the right, barely missing the ditch as she pulled into a dirt parking lot under some tall oaks.

"I always miss this turn," she said.

Unnecessarily.

CHAPTER

9

In this dynamic, shared memory, incidents of twenty-five and fifty years ago are kept so vivid that they are often related as recent happenings.

— *Raised in Clay*,
Nancy Sweezy

June Gregorich tiptoed to the door of Amos Nordan's bedroom and was relieved to hear the old man's light snores. It had been a stressful afternoon and early evening for all of them and she was glad when Betty and Dillard Hitchcock cleared the house of friends and neighbors who'd heard the grisly news and wanted to hear all the gory details. Amos had sat stunned, his eyes wide and unseeing, until Betty persuaded him to drink some of the hot chicken broth left over from lunch. Then she and Dillard had helped him up to bed.

"I gave him one of his sleeping pills," she said when they came back down.

The phone rang shrilly and her older son Edward answered it before it could ring a second time. Another concerned neighbor wanted to know how Amos was or if there was anything they could do to help.

"I'm going to cut off the phones," Betty said, "or they'll keep y'all awake all night. Call me in the morning, though, and let me know how Dad is, okay?"

"Certainly," June said.

At the door, Betty had hugged her impulsively. "Thank goodness we have you here for him, June. I don't know what we'd do without you."

June had made a deprecating sound. "You'd have managed."

"You sure you don't want me to stay the night with you, Miss June?" asked Libbet Hitchcock.

"No, we'll be fine, thanks," said June.

It was still early evening — barely dark, in fact — but Jeffy was already asleep, worn out by so many people. As she checked on him and then went around locking up, June wondered how much longer the two of them could stay here and where they would go when everything was over. Mr. Amos swore he'd live under his own roof and die in his own bed. That's why James Lucas and Betty asked her to move in two years ago after his stroke. And it'd worked out even better than she'd hoped. He tolerated Jeffy well enough and he was easy to clean and cook for. But if the pottery closed or changed hands, Betty might insist on his going to live over there. And then there was Tom Dillard, heir presumptive to the pottery. If he married that Simmons girl as gossip predicted, he and his bride might move in here to take care of his grandfather.

June brushed her thick wiry hair and braided it into a single plait for the night, then slipped on the oversized T-shirt she wore as a nightgown, brushed her teeth, and got into bed.

As she had feared, she couldn't stave off the ghastly image of James Lucas on that kiln car, hair burnt, his face and hands coated with dried red glaze. She saw again the utter shock and grief on Mr. Amos's face when she realized who it was. It was a wonder he hadn't had another stroke then and there.

Her thoughts moved on to the white car that had driven through the lane while James Lucas was down at the kiln. She had thought it was Sandra Kay and that's what she'd told Connor Woodall, but lying there, staring into the darkness, she remembered that Tom Dillard drove a white car, too.

And where had Bobby Gerard been at the time?

Twilight was fading into darkness as Dillard Hitchcock switched off the van and looked over at his wife.

"You okay, hon?"

In the seat behind them, their firstborn, twenty-year-old Edward, already had the door open and was halfway out, but their fourteen-year-old daughter lingered, as if to hear Betty's answer.

"Mom?"

"I'm fine, sweetie. Why don't you go on in and get started on your homework?"

"I'm not going to school tomorrow," she said mutinously.

"Don't argue with your mother," said Dillard. "Whether it's tomorrow or Monday, your schoolwork's got to be done sometime."

"And what about Tom? He's not here doing his."

"You want to get left back a year, too? Fine. Forget about schoolwork. You and Edward can see to putting some supper on the table for us."

137

"Go ahead, Libbet," said Betty. "We'll be there in a minute."

Reluctantly, the girl went.

"You okay?" Dillard asked again. His face and voice softened and he reached out to clasp his wife's hand.

"No." Her eyes were red from all the crying she'd done at her father's house and they filled with tears again as she spoke. "No, I'm not okay."

She cupped his big square hand between her thin ones. "My last brother's just been killed, my daddy's half out of his mind with grief, Tom hasn't been seen since his first class this morning, and your sister's acting like he's the one killed James Lucas."

"Aw, now, honey, you know Sandra Kay don't really mean that." With his free hand, he brushed back a lock of hair that had fallen over her cheek.

It always came as a mild shock to realize that she was going gray. In his mind's eye, she would always be the teenage girl he'd fallen in love with on the school bus when her straight dark hair blew back in his face from the open window beside her. They had known each other from childhood. She was just another Nordan, one of several kids who lived and played together along the rutted back lane that ran from Nordan Road to Felton Creek Road. Until that day, he'd taken no more notice of her than he'd take of the flat rock that served as home plate in their summer afternoon ball games.

Then her hair brushed against his face, soft as a morning fog, smelling of spring sunshine and lilacs, and something intense and yearning had grabbed his heart and never let go. He had leaned forward and tapped Sandra Kay on the shoulder — she and Betty were friends back then and usually shared the same seat. "Change places with me, okay?"

Thinking he only wanted to talk to the boys in the seat ahead of hers, his sister had complied. For the next month, from that day till his graduation, he and Betty sat together every morning, every afternoon. When she graduated two years later, they were married.

Her hair was still soft, still smelled like spring lilacs, he thought, as her head drooped on his shoulder. And her tears still tore him up when she cried. He knew that a lot of his friends thought he was pussy-whipped, just as he knew there'd been times when Betty used her tears to get her way, like when she'd cried to keep Sandra Kay from coming back to Rooster Clay after her marriage to James Lucas went bust.

He didn't care what people thought or said.

Even though he knew he'd done wrong by his sister, even though he'd hated to deny her a place back here at the pottery where she'd stood on tiptoes to turn her first pot on an old kick wheel, he knew he'd do it again if it was a choice between his sister and his wife.

"Tom couldn't do such a horrible thing," Betty said, as if trying to convince herself. "He has a temper. I know he can fly off the handle, but put his own uncle in a kiln and turn on the burners? He'd never do that!"

"No," said Dillard, trying not to remember the times Tom had blown up over some trifling matter, not caring whose pots got smashed in his rage. All those smashed plates and bowls around James Lucas's body —

"It wasn't Tom," Betty said again, burying her face against his shoulder.

He held her tightly, as much for his own comfort as hers. "Of course it wasn't," he said.

CHAPTER

10

Without a full consideration of the cultural context, it becomes all too easy both to romanticize and to depreciate the achievements of the folk potter.

> — *Turners and Burners,*
> Charles G. Zug III

The Montgomery Country Club wasn't much more elaborate than a circa 1930 spacious country house that had been remodeled to have a large meeting space and a smaller kitchen. Circular tables for six had been set up for about sixty people and Fliss introduced me to members of this three-county bar association. Some of the judges I'd met before, of course, but many others, especially the attorneys, were strangers.

I like hanging out with lawyers. Yes, arguing both sides of the law can lead to cynicism at times, but as a rule, lawyers are smart and funny, too.

Word of James Lucas Nordan's murder had already reached Troy. Not surprising, since both attorneys from the Nordan ED were there. Speculation flowed as freely as the wine.

And not just about the murder.

Sanderson's wife was at the opposite end of the room and people were glancing covertly from one to the other. I guessed that neither intended to give an inch professionally, but they were making it awkward for those colleagues who wouldn't want to appear to be taking sides. Since I was still scheduled to preside over their final pretrial conference tomorrow morning, I kept to the middle of the room after paying my respects to Bill Neely, who was the chief judge of the district court over here.

Fliss seemed to have decided I needed a little diversion and immediately introduced me to a newly appointed judge from Carthage. He looked to be about five years older and a couple of inches taller than I am, with curly brown hair, brown eyes, and a trimly muscular build. Amusingly, his name was William Blackstone, just like the famous eighteenth century jurist.

"Don't laugh," he said with an infectious smile. "My people were blue-collar mill hands. They never heard of Sir William. My mother named me William Cobb after the doctor that delivered me. I still don't know if it's because she'd used up all the family names on my four older brothers or if she hoped I'd become a doctor."

"You have four older brothers?" I said. "I'll see your four and raise you seven."

"Really? You have eleven brothers? How many sisters?"

"None," I admitted.

"Got you there, then." He smiled. "I have three."

"Any twins?"

He shook his head.

"Two sets," I bragged.

"Deborah was there when James Lucas's body was found in the kiln," said Fliss.

"I heard." He shook his head sympathetically. "Rough on you. And poor old Amos. This could be his death blow."

"Will used to be Amos Nordan's attorney," Fliss explained as someone pulled her away with a question.

"I guess he wasn't too happy that you became a judge," I said. A little bit of butter never hurts.

"Oh, he fired me quite a while ago," Will said easily.

He scooped up two glasses of wine from a passing tray and we moved out of the flow of traffic.

"So why did he fire you?" I asked.

"Because I drew up the papers that gave James Lucas a lifetime right to Nordan Pottery. I tried my best to talk him out of it. He was hurting so bad after Donny died and James Lucas was talking about pulling out and moving over to Sanford. He was afraid that the pottery was going to die, too. I told him to make the trust revokable, but he thought it wouldn't be enough to hold James Lucas here. He's a real pigheaded ol' cuss. Wants what he wants when he wants it and doesn't want to hear the advice he's paying you to give. So I did what he asked and then, sure enough, it was barely a year before he wanted to retract it. When I told him it was too airtight, I thought he was going to pick up one of his pots and crown me.

"He's part of a dying breed, Amos is. When he's gone, a lot of Seagrove history will go with him."

At the head of the room, the association's president was asking us to be seated and Fliss waved to us that she had seats at her table.

As we made our way over, I thought how much Amos Nordan reminded me of my own daddy, another facet of that dying breed.

Will Blackstone must have been reading my mind because we were no sooner seated than he said genially, "Deborah Knott. Fliss says you're over in Colleton County. Not any kin to the famous Kezzie Knott, are you?"

I'm sure he expected me to say no, as do most people who ask that question in that particular tone of amusement.

"My father," I said austerely, and watched as he tried to rearrange his face — a very attractive face, let me stipulate — into something more appropriate to the discussion of a judge's father. Hard to do when the father in question is notorious for his bootlegging past.

(At least I *hope* it's firmly in the past.)

(And if it's not, I don't want to know it.)

A very unjudgelike giggle escaped me. "Did you mean famous or infamous?"

He looked at me cautiously and then relaxed. "Are you really his daughter?"

"Oh, yes. And that reminds me. He had a sly look on his face last week when I said I was coming over to Seagrove. Told me to say hey to a Miss Nina Bean if she was still alive. Who's Nina Bean?"

Will Blackstone laughed out loud, a deep rolling laugh that made others at our table smile even though they didn't know what we were talking about. "It would take a book. Let's just say that Nina Bean — the late Nina Bean, unfortunately — was probably a colleague of your daddy's. Or competitor. And old Amos probably helped with the distribution, for all I know. He certainly made whiskey jugs and demijohns when he was a boy. In fact, I have some *his* daddy made. There were times when Amos paid me in pots instead of cash, so I have a pretty good collection, if you're interested."

He paused and looked directly into my eyes.

I smiled. Hell, I even dimpled. "Oh, I'm interested."

"These dinners never run very long," he said, his voice too low for anyone else to hear. "If you'd like to stop by for a drink after, I'd be glad to show them."

"Is a collection of pots anything like a collection of etchings?" I bantered.

"Would you like it to be?" he asked, arching an eyebrow at me.

Kidd might not want me, but it was gratifying to see that there really were other fish swimming in North Carolina's ponds. Right about then, the preacher who lives in my head and monitors my impulses gave an exasperated sigh. *You call this curbing your hormones?*

Right.

"I'll have to take a rain check tonight," I said regretfully. "Early court tomorrow. But if I'm back in a couple of weeks . . . ?"

"Anytime," he assured me.

On the drive home, Fliss tried to pump me about how I got along with Will Blackstone, even though I kept telling her there was really nothing to pump.

"He's certainly cute, though," I conceded. "And fun to talk to. Is he really as available as he led me to think?"

"He led you on?" she teased. "That's encouraging."

"Forget it," I said firmly. "I'm not ready to jump into another relationship."

"But if you were, Will might be a good jumping-off place. And yes," she said before I could ask again, "he's extremely available. Divorced three or four years ago. No kids. It must've been fairly amicable, since nothing much was said about it at the time. I gather that he hasn't exactly been celibate since then, but he's discreet. Actually, there's not a lot of gossip about him. Some of the younger clerks try to get assigned to him, but he never asks for anyone in particular. Just takes whoever's in the rotation."

"Good judge?"

She shrugged. "Competent. Keeps the calendar moving. A bit on the conservative side, but that's normal in these parts. What can I tell you? You don't think I'd try to fix you up with an ax-murderer, do you?"

I grinned. "Hey, good men are hard to find these days."

CHAPTER

11

Perhaps he was no scientist or techni-
cian, but [the folk potter] approached his
work in a direct, pragmatic manner and
displayed an admirable competence in
all he did. It is essential then to view the
realities of his world with openness and
understanding.

— Turners and Burners,
Charles G. Zug III

Next morning, I carried my bag out to the car
because I planned to drive on back to
Colleton County directly after court. I
thanked Fliss for her hospitality and promised that I'd stay with her again if I came back
for the Sandersons' next hearing anytime
soon, a distinct possibility, since Judge Ferris
wasn't expected back for six months.

At the courthouse, clerks and bailiffs were still abuzz when I arrived. Grandmotherly Mrs. Cagle and portly Mr. Anderson took their places with the slightly embarrassed self-consciousness of people unused to being so squarely in the spotlight. Because both of them had been at Nordan Pottery when James Lucas was found, they had been asked to describe and speculate on his death so many times that I think they were grateful for the anonymity of a courtroom.

Fliss had warned me that the Sandersons were arguing their own cases, so I was not surprised to take my seat on the bench and find only two people facing me.

"Don't they know the first rule of law?" I'd asked Fliss.

"That a lawyer who represents himself has a fool for a client? Of course they do. But once the first one announced their intent, the other felt as if it were a challenge," she'd answered, carefully avoiding the use of gender-specific pronouns so as not to influence me.

"I take it that one of them considers himself or herself a better courtroom attorney than the other?"

Fliss had smiled as she shook her head. "You didn't hear that from me, Your Honor."

As I opened the session, dark-haired Nick

Sanderson didn't presume upon his acquaintance with me from the day before, just gave me a polite smile and a "Good morning, Judge," when I nodded to him.

Kelly Sanderson was small-boned and tiny and looked as Irish as her name. She had strawberry blond hair that covered her head in short ringlets, green eyes, and an exceedingly freckled face. Her wrists and hands were also freckled. Indeed, she was probably freckled all over her body. Despite the shortness of her hair and the severity of her navy blue suit, she was such a Little Orphan Annie look-alike that I almost expected her to start singing "Tomorrow, Tomorrow" when she rose to respond to her ex-husband's opening remarks.

There were two minor children involved and while Mrs. Sanderson still lived with them in the marital home, both parents shared equal custody. I didn't know how messy the divorce had been. That wasn't any of my business. I was here strictly to preside over the distribution of the marital property acquired during their marriage.

Happily, they seemed to have opted for civility. Almost everything they owned was listed on Schedule A, marital property upon which there was complete agreement as to value and distribution. No argument over who got the silver or how much it was worth, no bickering about granny's hand-stitched quilts or the value of a car at the date of separation. In short, no Schedule B, D, or E.

Schedule C was the sticking point — marital property upon which there was agreement as to value and disagreement as to distribution — and the single item there was their law office. My eyes widened at the value they'd placed on it, but both assured me that had been the going market rate for an address on Lawyers Row at their date of separation.

"I strongly advise you to try to reach a compromise," I told them.

"I couldn't agree more, Your Honor," Mrs. Sanderson said crisply, displaying the first bit of animus I'd seen between them, "but we appear to be deadlocked."

I listened to their contentions as to whether or not an equal division would be equitable and they both expressed a desire to proceed to trial as soon as possible.

"We both want this settled," said Mr. Sanderson.

I conferred with Mrs. Cagle and compared her calendar with mine and the Sandersons'. We agreed on a court date for week after next and I adjourned court.

"Lieutenant Woodall asked me to see if you'd come by and see him after you finished," said Mr. Anderson, following me into the room where I removed my robe and retrieved my jacket. "It'll be easier to show you where he is than try to tell you."

The bailiff hadn't exaggerated. The old courthouse was such a warren of mismatched additions that I'd have never found the sheriff's detective on my own. With renovations in full swing, I wasn't real sure I'd ever find the main entrance and the path back to my car again, since I hadn't left a trail of breadcrumbs, but I thanked Anderson and said I hoped I'd see him when I was next over.

"Maybe they'll have Mr. Nordan's killer in jail by then," he said, turning me over to a deputy.

Connor Woodall was on the phone when I reached his doorway and he waved me in and gestured to the chair in front of a tidy desk.

"One of my men with the preliminary findings from the ME's office over in Chapel Hill," he said after hanging up. "James Lucas was still alive when he was rolled into that kiln."

An involuntary shudder swept over me.

"What a horrible way to die."

"Yeah," Connor said with a heavy sigh. "There's a possibility that he wasn't conscious, though. He seems to have sustained a heavy blow to the back of his head. Fractured skull and massive intercranial bleeding."

It was nice to talk to a deputy sheriff you didn't have to pull every bit of information out of.

"So who do you like for it?" I asked.

"Well, now, it's still early days," he said cautiously. And then spoiled it by flushing bright red.

This was somebody I'd love to get in a poker game. How could the poor man ever bluff? Or lie to his wife, for that matter?

Looking at his fair hair and those eyes rimmed in straw-colored lashes, I was struck by an irrelevant thought. "Are you any kin to Kelly Sanderson?"

He nodded. "First cousin. Why? Oh, yeah, that's right. You're doing their property division."

"You didn't say anything about her Wednesday night when Fliss told you why I was here."

"Nothing to say. Kelly and me, we don't run in the same circles."

No flushing, just a matter-of-fact statement. Watching as he cued up a tape recorder, I wondered if Cousin Kelly was a snob.

"You don't mind if I tape your interview, do you?" he asked.

"Half the courtrooms I work in use tape recorders," I told him. My voice always sounds dumb on tape, but then I don't have to listen to it.

So he asked his preliminary questions and I answered as concisely as possible, then described everything pertinent I could think of from the day before.

When I'd finished, he asked, "What was Mrs. Nordan's reaction when Mrs. Gregorich said she'd seen her car go through the lane past the kilns?"

"I didn't notice any particular reaction. Sandra Kay said that she'd just arrived and that she hadn't seen James Lucas since I adjourned court."

"Those were her specific words?"

"Well, I wouldn't swear specific, but certainly close enough. Sandra Kay asked where James Lucas was. June said, 'Didn't you see him before?' and Sandra Kay said she hadn't been there before. Then June said she thought she'd seen Sandra Kay's car earlier, but she didn't make a big deal out of it. I guess there are a lot of white cars around, though, and I myself can't tell one make from the other." I reached over and pressed the recorder's pause button. "Can June?"

Connor shrugged. "All she could tell us was that she'd caught a glimpse of a white car out of the corner of her eye and that she'd assumed it was Mrs. Nordan, but she wouldn't want to swear to it."

"And what does Sandra Kay say?"

"She says it wasn't her."

"Is she telling the truth?"

"I didn't ask to see her tongue." He grinned, remembering how my brothers used to tease me.

Whenever Mother doubted our word, she'd say, "Let me see your tongue." She assured us it would have a black spot if we were lying to her.

We were never quite certain if she really did see black spots or not, but she nearly always knew. Once when I was around five or six, I had to put out my tongue for inspection and there actually was a black spot on it, which Mother triumphantly showed me in the mirror. (I think I'd probably eaten some blackberries a little earlier.) For years afterwards, if I'd shaded the truth by even a hair, I wouldn't show my tongue and the boys rode me unmercifully.

I laughed and, hoping that the shared

memory had relaxed his own tongue, asked, "Was Sandra Kay Nordan sleeping with her brother-in-law before he died?"

His face turned bright red. "You heard about that? I didn't think Fliss was that big a gossip."

I was delighted to have tricked him into confirming my guess as to why Amos Nordan had cursed his ex-daughter-in-law. "She didn't tell me. I asked, but she didn't know."

"I don't think anybody does," Connor said. "Amos got it in his head that something was going on between them. I questioned Mrs. Nordan when Donny died, and she denied it, but she would, wouldn't she? And then she and James Lucas split up right after that."

So he'd asked questions after Donny Nordan's death, had he? A verdict of suicide that had been changed to accidental death? A death no Nordan wanted to talk about? I had a theory about that, too.

"Another thing Fliss doesn't know," I said meaningfully, "is the precise nature of Donny Nordan's so-called 'accidental' death."

I thought I'd seen Connor's whole range, but even his ears turned red on that one. *Bull's-eye!*

"Jesus, Deb'rah! You've been over here

how long? Two days? And you've picked up that much."

"Judges learn to read between the lines," I told him kindly. "Was it a self-inflicted sexual accident? Autoerotic asphyxiation?"

He shook his head and I knew he wasn't going to tell me whether Donny Nordan had been dressed in black leather or black silk when Amos found him.

"At least tell me this much," I said. "You're convinced it really was an accident and not murder? I mean, nobody's out there killing Nordans for the hell of it, are they?"

His color was returning to normal. "And waiting two years between times? Not hardly." He frowned. "On the other hand . . ."

I waited in hopeful silence, but he didn't complete the thought aloud. Instead, he pushed away from his desk and offered to walk me back to the main entrance.

"You'll have to come over for supper and meet Fern and my girls when you get back," he told me. "And don't forget to say hey to Dwight for me."

CHAPTER

12

As Auby Hilton wryly put it, "Working with clays is like dealing with human nature — you have to work them as they are . . . for trying to force them beyond their nature you make a failure."

— Turners and Burners,
Charles G. Zug III

When I got home early Friday afternoon, the first message on my answering machine was from my brother Herman's wife Nadine, reminding me that I'd promised to attend church services and then take dinner with them on Sunday. The second was from Kidd Chapin: "I've UPS'd your stuff . . . and, Deborah? I'm sure sorry it ended like this."

Yeah, right.

My brother Andrew was third, telling me

that if I didn't get a load of gravel to put around the drip lines of my house, the rain was going to wash gullies there this fall. "Gravel don't cost all that much if you do the raking yourself and you can probably use the exercise."

Thanks, Andrew. I really needed to hear that you think I've put on weight.

Next came Dwight Bryant. "They didn't have that video you wanted, but it's just as well. I'm off to stay with Cal this weekend while Jonna goes to Virginia Beach with some of her friends."

There went my Saturday night. Dwight's not seeing anybody special these days, either, and we both like old movies, but he's crazy about his son and hops up to Virginia anytime Jonna offers him extra time with Cal.

After four downers, it was a relief to get Portland Brewer's voice.

Portland's Uncle Ash is married to my Aunt Zell, but our long friendship began with a mutual loathing of a tattletale in our Junior Girls Sunday School class. In fact, we've been sworn best friends ever since we got kicked out of the class for hiding all the yellow crayons so that a tearful Caroline Atherton had to color Jesus' halo orange. Nevertheless, I didn't much trust the excitement that bubbled in Portland's voice as she commanded me to come by her office no later than five o'clock. I'd told her all about my breakup with Kidd within hours of the incident and I had a feeling she'd been beating the bushes all week looking for someone to distract me. I wasn't anywhere near ready for that yet, but the only way to keep Por off my back was to go take a look.

Accordingly, I slipped into an all-purpose black pantsuit, wound some gold-and-turquoise beads around my neck, took a few pains with my makeup, and drove over to Dobbs. The sun was still halfway up the sky, but the grandfather clock in the outer office of Brewer and Brewer, Attorneys at Law, was just striking five as I stepped inside the door.

"Well, hel-*lo*, gorgeous!" said Avery Brewer, who seemed to be rummaging beneath the receptionist's deserted counter for manila folders. He gave me a huge smile, then came around the counter and gave me a kiss on the cheek together with a warm hug.

And I'd only been gone two days.

"Seen Por yet?" he asked, still beaming at me.

"Just got here. She in her office?"

He nodded happily and dumped the folders to lead the way. I was starting to get unnerved. Who in God's name had Por found for me that had her husband grinning like this? One of their newly single friends? An LL.D. from the law school over at Duke or Chapel Hill? A movie star on location in Wilmington?

"Deborah!" Portland rose from her desk and embraced me with a similar goofy smile. She has tight black curls and a little round face. Today her face seemed a tiny bit rounder and her hair looked like Julia Lee's poodle when CoCo's in need of a good clipping. Her white jeans and lime green sweatshirt did not spell an evening at La Residence.

"What's up?" I asked, sinking down on the leather chair adjacent to a matching couch and glass-topped coffee table that comprised an informal setting designed to put nervous clients at ease. It wasn't doing a thing to help me, other than reminding me of James Lucas's comment on the furniture Sandra Kay had taken from their house ("Real high quality — like what you'd find in a lawyer's office"), but we seemed to be alone here in the office, so I was safe for the moment.

They sat down, too, side by side on the couch, holding hands like a pair of excited teenagers.

"We wanted you to be the first to know," Portland said. "We're going to have a baby!"

I was stunned. They've been married nine years, but when she stopped taking her birth-control pills four years ago and nothing happened, she hadn't acted like it was a big deal.

"A child would be great," she'd told me only six months ago, "but we aren't going to jump through any fertility hoops. If it happens, it happens."

Looking at their blissed-out grins, I knew it was a very big deal.

Not about me at all.

About them.

I moved over to sit on the coffee table so I could hug them both. "That's so abso-fricking-wonderful! When?"

"Por's birthday," Avery said. "That bottle of champagne you gave her."

Portland giggled and punched him in the ribs. "Idiot! She wasn't asking when the baby was conceived. She's asking when's the due date."

"Not that I wouldn't be totally fascinated with a blow-by-blow account of your technique, Avery." I laughed, already counting on my fingers from her early March birthday. "December? A Christmas baby?"

"Definitely before the first of the year,"

said Avery. "We might as well get the deduction."

"Once a tax lawyer, always a tax lawyer," Por said happily.

"Well, why are we sitting here?" I asked. "We need another bottle of champagne to celebrate."

"No champagne," Avery warned me. "No alcohol of any kind for the next eight months. Everything she eats or drinks goes right across the umbilical cord."

One month pregnant and now he was an expert.

Por made a face. "I couldn't drink anything anyhow. You wouldn't believe the morning sickness. If I don't eat a couple of soda crackers before I lift my head off the pillow, I wind up barfing my head off. And I stay so damn sleepy I actually dozed off during Ed Whitbread's summing up this morning."

"Ed's summations always put me to sleep, too," I said, "and I've never had your excuse. But I'm serious about celebrating. Let me take you guys to dinner. Avery and I can drink your share of the champagne."

"Sorry," he said. "We're on our way down to Wilmington to tell my mom and dad. They're beginning to think they're never going to have any grandchildren and we want to see their faces when they hear."

So there I was. All dressed up and nowhere to go. Nowhere in Dobbs anyhow. It's a real Noah's Ark town — everything from McDonald's to the country club is on a two-by-two basis. But I hadn't stopped in at Miss Molly's in a while, so I headed on over, knowing I'd probably catch the after-work crowd.

Miss Molly's is on Raleigh's South Wilmington Street and is the watering hole of choice for many state and local law enforcement agents on their way home from work or as an interlude before dinner.

As I pulled into the parking lot a little after six, the car in the next space cranked up to leave. I gave the white-haired driver a cursory glance, then we both did double-takes and he had a wide grin on his weatherbeaten face as he let his window down.

"What are you doing this far inland?" I asked him. "I thought you were going to retire and write position papers from a laptop on the beach."

When I first met him, Quig Smith was a detective with the Carteret County Sheriff's Department down in Beaufort, just counting the days till he could retire and become a full-time watchdog for the Clean Water Act.

"Didn't change your mind, did you?"

"Naw," he said. "I'm up here to try to lobby the legislature out of some more relief money."

Last fall, down east suffered a major hurricane disaster. There was unprecedented flooding that swept away whole towns and communities, businesses and churches, crops and livestock. Hog lagoons overflowed into the rivers. Dead pigs and poultry floated across the flat land. Buildings and houses weren't just underwater, they were under filthy, nasty, polluted water. Damages ran into the hundred millions. In what everybody agreed was a hundred-year storm, the poorest section of the state was devastated.

So how did Raleigh react to this emergency?

As politicians, not statesmen.

Instead of a onetime tax to which the whole populace would have consented in compassion for the thousands of victims, our legislators are so scared of the T-word that they've tried to raise the necessary aid by cutting social and cultural programs that were already underfunded. Down east should have gotten the economic equivalent of hospitals and ambulances. Instead they got a handful of Band-Aids, while overstressed programs all across the state now go begging, too.

It has not been North Carolina's finest moment.

"You really think you're going to pry loose another nickel for cleaning up waterways?" I asked him.

"Don't hurt to try," he said cheerfully. "The most they can do is say no and we're no worse off than we were, except I'm out a tank of expensive gas."

He started to put his car in reverse, then hesitated. "I was real sorry to hear about you and Kidd."

"He told you?"

He and Kidd had been friendly colleagues, but as Quig nodded, there was nothing — thank you, Jesus! — in his expression to indicate that Kidd had told him any of the juicier details.

"He only told me because I asked him if he was coming up this weekend." Quig gave me a puzzled look. "I thought he had his head screwed on better than to go back to that wife of his."

"Me, too," I said and tried for a smile that would imply it was more Kidd's loss than mine.

As he backed out, we agreed that the next time I was in Morehead, I'd call him for some of the best grilled sea bass on the whole coast. I waved goodbye, then the door of

167

Miss Molly's opened wide and I could hear the jukebox pounding out a rollicking salsa.

Inside, cigarette smokers still outnumbered nonsmokers. Toward the back of the big room, I immediately saw SBI friends K. C. Massengill and Morgan Slavin with their blond heads close together and Terry Wilson, who was about four boyfriends before Kidd and who is still a good buddy, something Kidd will never be. They welcomed me raucously and made room for me at a round table for eight that already held nine.

They were exchanging dumb bad guy stories and a Wake County sheriff's deputy was putting forth his candidate for dumbest.

Amid the general laughter, I ordered a light gin and tonic and heard about thieves who lock themselves out of their getaway cars, bank robbers who write their demands on the back of their own deposit slips, and insurance frauds who forget and wear their "stolen" rings to file their claims.

For some reason, though, my heart wasn't really in it.

Truth was, I was beginning to feel as if life were changing all around me, passing me by. Marriage to Avery hadn't altered my friendship with Portland, but I had a feeling this baby might. Babies complicate everything.

Not only do they require a lot of attention, previously carefree couples immediately morph into parents, anxious one minute, insufferably smug the next.

I was really happy for Portland.

Honest I was.

All the same, until the baby hit sixteen, there would be no more spur-of-the-moment trips to the coast or mountains, no all-night parties, no late afternoon cookouts at the lake. Everything would have to be scheduled in advance and geared around the baby's schedule.

I'd seen it happen to most of my friends and now it was happening to my oldest and best friend.

I looked around the smoky table, at Morgan and K.C. and Terry and the others. How many marriages and divorces between them? And why were we all still hanging out at Miss Molly's?

I was pretty much over Kidd, but I wasn't over wanting someone special in my life.

Easy enough for my brothers and their wives to keep nagging me to settle down. Hard to find someone with the right qualities.

I thought about that new judge over in Carthage.

Will Blackstone.

Maybe I *would* let him show me his pots next time I was there. Who knows? To quote my brother Haywood, "You can't catch a fish if you ain't got a line in the water."

Saturday I cleaned house and planted a flat of red petunias that Daddy brought me. "Your mama always liked these," he said. He also said that Maidie was rooting me some of the old roses from the family graveyard down from the homeplace.

On Sunday I did my duty by Nadine and Herman and went to church with them even though New Deliverance is my least favorite of all the houses of worship in the area. The minister's one of those borderline control freaks who preaches from the Old Testament more often than the New, more shalt-not than shall. There's not a single window in the sanctuary and nothing on the walls, not even a cross, to distract the congregation's attention from his joyless sermons. He manages to make heaven and salvation sound so dreary that I always leave more depressed than uplifted.

If my brother wasn't such a sweetie . . .

If Nadine's Sunday dinners weren't so delicious . . .

But he is and hers are and it's only once or twice a year, so I hold my tongue and go.

★ ★ ★

By Monday, I had my equilibrium back and was ready to sit my normal rotation down in Makely. It was the usual calendar of petty crimes and misdemeanors, traffic violations and such, until the middle of the week, when we got to the *State vs. Allie Johnson.*

Briefly, it was alleged that Ms. Johnson (nineteen, blond, blue-eyed, blue jeans, and many silver bracelets) had taken her car to the local car wash and there at the entrance of the Tunnel of Suds, she discovered that the car ahead of her was that of her not-then-ex-boyfriend Carl Judd. In the car ahead of Mr. Judd was his newest girlfriend, a Ms. Stauffer. Enraged by the sight of them, Ms. Johnson drove around to the car wash exit, blocked Ms. Stauffer's car, jumped out, and started trying to choke her rival.

Mr. Judd tried to intervene, at which point Ms. Johnson pulled a knife and tried to cut him.

She was charged with assault on Ms. Stauffer with a deadly weapon and she was the picture of outraged innocence on the stand. "I did *not* assault that bitch with a deadly weapon," she said.

I cautioned her about language suitable to the courtroom.

"Well, I didn't," she said stubbornly. "I only tried to choke her with my hands. *He's* the one I wanted to cut."

Amid barely concealed snickers from bailiff and attorneys, Mr. Judd (early twenties, flat black hair, chinos, and a red knit shirt) took the stand and my clerk chanted the formula. "Place your left hand on the Bible and raise your right hand. Do you solemnly swear that the testimony you're about to give shall be the truth, the whole truth, and nothing but the truth, so help you God?"

"No."

"Be seated," the clerk said automatically.

"Excuse me?" I said to the witness. "What did you say?"

Like a well-brought-up son of the South, Mr. Judd immediately corrected himself. "No, *ma'am*."

"Did you just say you would *not* tell the truth?"

"Yes, ma'am."

"I'm sorry, Mr. Judd, but that wasn't a polite question the clerk asked you. You're obliged to tell the truth or I'll have to hold you in contempt. Maybe even send you to jail. Do you understand?"

Mr. Judd nodded. "You do what you have to do, ma'am."

I leaned closer and tried to cajole him in a

low voice. "You really don't want to go to jail. Why don't you just tell us the truth about what happened?"

In a whisper so low that only I could hear him, he said, "Ma'am, you see those two women out there? One already wants to kill me. If I tell everything that happened that morning, both of them'll want to. I believe right now I'd rather go to jail, if it's all the same to you."

I had to agree it was probably safer and had the bailiff place him under arrest for contempt. I dismissed the assault with a deadly weapon since Ms. Johnson had been erroneously charged for the wrong person and I fined her for simple assault along with twenty-four hours in jail, suspended on the usual conditions.

Well, at least I hadn't tried to throttle Kidd's wife.

CHAPTER

13

The problem of continuity . . . resides in the potters and their families, in their subjective reaction to the loss of traditional culture. The craft may continue to be handed down within a family or younger generations may decide to enter a different career . . . although others are realizing the rewards of making pottery and are taking it up as their heritage.

— *Raised in Clay*,
Nancy Sweezy

Services for James Lucas Nordan were at four o'clock on Tuesday afternoon at the funeral home. The casket was closed, of course, which had made the "viewing" the night before more awkward than normal. After the interment, his extended family gathered at

Amos Nordan's house while June Gregorich put together a buffet supper comprised of leftovers from all the food various neighbors had brought in during the last three days.

"Times are changing," said a friend of Betty Hitchcock who had come by to help in the kitchen and who'd brought a basket of freshly baked yeast rolls and three plastic milk jugs full of iced tea.

"In what way?" asked June as she assembled one large platter of fried chicken from several Bojangles, Food Lion, and KFC boxes. Another platter held sliced ham.

"Two years ago, I'd never heard of green bean casseroles, yet here's four different ones. Nothing molded in Jell-O, though, is there?"

June smiled. "Not that I've seen."

"And time was, nobody'd bring store-bought fast food. Or if they did, they'd put it in their own bowls and pretend like they'd made it themselves."

"I think it's nice, however they do it," said June, looking around the comfortably shabby old kitchen. Her unruly hair was neatly tamed this evening by a black ribbon at the nape of her neck. A white bibbed chef's apron protected her dark green dress. "It shows a sense of community, how people care about each other. More than you'd ever get in California. Don't forget to write down your rolls in the food register there by the door. Betty asked me to make sure I got all the names so she can write thank-you notes."

"If that's one of Amos's bread baskets on top of the refrigerator, I'll go ahead and put my rolls in that and it'll be one less thing you have to return."

"Thanks. I've tried to keep track, but there's no name tape on the bottom of that cut-glass deviled egg plate and nobody wrote it in the register."

"Don't you worry," the neighbor said comfortably as she began to fill disposable cups with ice from a cooler chest. "Pretty as it is, someone'll come asking for it."

In addition to his father and his sister Betty's Hitchcock clan, James Lucas Nordan's three aunts and their assorted spouses and descendants overflowed the living and dining rooms and spilled onto the porch, where swings and rockers accommodated those who wanted to sit outside and smoke as the sun went down and darkness fell.

Bobby Gerard, completely sober and wearing a clean white shirt, sat on the steps with a cigarette in his hands, listening to all the speculation going on. No one paid much

176

attention to the itinerant kiln worker, nor did he seem to seek any. He nodded to those who greeted him perfunctorily but didn't try to engage them in conversation. Over thirty relatives were there, along with a half-dozen close family friends, and they ranged from a baby who was just starting to pull up on rubbery legs to its great-grandmother, who needed a walker.

As is usual at such times, emotions bubbled near the surface and went from tears to laughter to tears again. To this was added the baffled sorrow and anger over the way death had come to James Lucas. Everyone kept going over and over the known facts and there was endless theorizing.

"If the blow came from above," said one cousin's husband, "there's no way Sandra Kay could've done it, short as she is."

His brother-in-law nodded and the two cast furtive looks at Tom Hitchcock and his older brother Edward, both of whom had inherited the Nordan height.

"Besides, it takes a lot of strength to shift that car."

"I don't know about that," sniffed his sister, who'd never liked Sandra Kay. "She could've stood on a bucket or something to hit him, and don't forget she was the one pulled it out."

"Adrenaline'll do that," said the first man. "I know a guy, when his house caught on fire, he picked up their refrigerator and carried it outside all by himself, and he won't big as me."

Across the room, a trio of nieces were working on a different scenario. "Besides," said one, who'd always rather admired Sandra Kay's independent spirit, "what reason did she have to do him in? They were divorced and they'd just finished settling up their stuff."

"Well, I heard they had a big fight about Donny Wednesday night," said the second niece.

"Was it Donny?" asked the third. "I heard it was something secret about his pottery stamp."

"No, it was over their collection," said the first. "Maybe she wanted something real bad that she knew he wouldn't give up."

"Dumb," said her sister. "She has to know that Uncle Amos or Aunt Betty'd be picking for Uncle James Lucas and they'd know the collection almost as good as he did."

The first niece leaned in close and dropped her voice almost to a whisper. "I heard it wasn't Sandra Kay's car at all. Tom's car is white, too, you know. They say Tom broke up with Brittany and ditched school

Thursday morning and nobody knows where he was from then till bedtime."

"He and Brittany made up last night," said her cousin. "I saw them kissing in a back hall at the funeral home."

Out on the porch, one of the family friends said, "Half of Seagrove drives a white car. Besides, I heard that this Gregory woman don't know Fords from Toyotas."

"Gregorich," someone corrected him. "And she said herself she wasn't sure whose car it was."

"What the heck kind of name is Gregorich? Russian? Shame about that boy of hers, isn't it? Can't understand half the things he says. It'd drive me crazy being around a dummy like that all day. Doesn't seem to bother Amos, though."

"Aw, Jeffy's not so bad," said a good-hearted cousin. "He's a real sweet-natured little thing. Amos is lucky to have them. How else could he stay here if she wasn't around to cook and clean for him and be here during the night if he falls or something?"

"Yeah, but what's going to happen with Nordan Pottery now that James Lucas is gone? Amos can't keep it going by himself with just Bobby Gerard unless he hires somebody."

"Well, there's Betty and Dillard's second boy. Tom's young, but he'll season."

"If he lives that long. I was doing the speed limit the other day on that winding road past my sister's house and he passed me in the double-yellows like I was standing still."

"Yeah," said the cousin. "From the time he was a baby, he never liked to wait on anything."

Through all the swirling talk, Amos Nordan sat rigidly upright in his lounge chair. His red-rimmed eyes stared deep into his own private vision of despair, his hands clenching the ends of the armrests. Jeffy Gregorich was hunched on a low stool between the arm of Amos's chair and the wall, and his own eyes yearned after the children who eddied in and out of the room like a restless school of minnows. Occasionally he moved as if to follow them, but then he would look up at Amos and sink back onto the stool. That's when he would gently pat the gnarled hand nearest him as if he sensed and understood the pain and grief gnawing at the old man. Not by the flicker of an eyelash did Amos Nordan acknowledge his presence.

But he didn't move his hand away, either.

His son's friends and relatives paused by his chair to express their sympathy. His daughter Betty hovered like a sorrowful black shadow. Even Tom came over and tried to distract his grandfather. He could always make Amos smile. Not tonight.

"I heard you quit school," Amos said.

Tom shook his head. "No, I'm going back."

"Good. I don't like quitters. You finish and I'll —" He broke off. "Well, no point talking about lawyers yet. You graduate and then we'll talk."

A general shuffling toward the dining room indicated that supper was finally ready. The smell of hot bread and freshly brewed coffee drifted through the open kitchen door beyond. A hush fell as the husband of one of the elderly aunts asked the blessing, then the reverent silence was replaced by the clink of tableware against serving dishes.

June cut through the line and got Jeffy and took him out to the kitchen for his supper. He could feed himself, but he was such a messy eater that he couldn't be trusted with plate and glass except at a table.

Slowly, stiffly, Amos Nordan came to his feet.

"Oh, Dad, you don't have to get up," said Betty. "Let me fix you a plate."

"I'm not hungry." He fumbled in the pocket of his jacket for his cigarettes. "Too damn hot and stuffy in here anyhow. I'm going out on the porch awhile."

At first, it was like trying to swim upstream, but as those outside realized who wanted to come through, they all stepped back respectfully and let him pass out into the cool spring night. As the others went inside to eat, he walked down to the shadowy end of the porch away from the single low-watt light by the door, pausing to light a cigarette before easing his long length down on the swing. He had thought he was alone, but as his eyes adjusted to the darkness, he sourly realized that a skinny young man sat on the edge of the porch, his back against the post, his left knee drawn up, his right foot on the ground.

Although they were now facing each other, Amos studiously avoided eye contact. He'd come out here to be by himself for a minute and by damn he wasn't going to make small talk with one of his sisters-in-law's grandsons.

If that's who he was.

Didn't look like a Godwin. More like a Nordan, with those long arms and legs. Well, didn't matter who he was, as long as he kept his mouth shut.

The swing moved slowly back and forth as gently as a rocking chair. Amos smoked in silence except for a faint creak as the swing chains ground against the two metal hooks in the ceiling. He thought about his sons — first Donny, now James Lucas — and such pain shot through him that an involuntary groan escaped his lips.

Embarrassed, he tried to pretend it was only the opening of an extended cough. He darted a glance at the silent youth, but that one had his head back against the post now and seemed to be counting the stars.

The screen door banged and here came Libbet down the long porch with a plate of food and a plastic cup. "Mom says you really need to eat something, Granddaddy."

Anger churned like bile in his stomach. Women never left you alone one damn minute. They always thought that if they could feed you, you'd get over it. That food would make it easier. Help you get past it.

"Dump it in them bushes if it'll keep her quiet," he said harshly. "I ain't eating it."

She moved toward the edge of the porch and almost tripped over the young man sitting in the shadows. "Sorry! I didn't see you there."

"That's all right," he said.

"Aren't you eating, either?"

He turned his head away. "No, thank you."

"You sure?" She leaned closer, trying to see his features. "What about some tea?"

"Yes, please, if he doesn't want it?"

"Granddaddy?"

"Quit yapping and just give it to him."

She handed him the plastic cup and he drank thirstily. "Thank you."

The timbre of his voice stirred in Amos's memory.

His granddaughter sat down in the swing beside him. "I'm Libbet Hitchcock, Betty and Dillard's daughter. Who're you?"

"Glad to meet you, Libbet. I appreciate this tea." He drank again and ice rattled against the side of the cup.

Uneasily, Amos tried to remember how many grandsons his sister Miriam had. "You one of Clyde's boys?"

"No, sir."

He finished his cigarette and threw it in a glowing arc over the boy's head and out onto the gravel path. "Burl's, then."

"No, sir."

"I see," he said heavily, and leaned back in the swing, waiting for the iron bands that gripped his heart to ease up a little.

Libbet looked curiously from one to the other. "Who, then?"

"He's your cousin," said her grandfather.

There was such a roaring in his head that his voice was almost inaudible to his own ear. "He's Donny's boy."

CHAPTER

14

Perhaps the most important force for the continuity of these elements has been the way of learning — the passing of skills, knowledge, and attitudes from one generation to the next in an intimate context and over a long period of growth.

— *Raised in Clay*,
Nancy Sweezy

"What the hell you doing here?" Amos said when the roaring in his head stopped.

"I didn't come to cause trouble," the youth said. "You want me to leave?"

"Yes!" said Libbet, catching at Amos's good hand and squeezing it protectively.

He jerked it away. "I asked you a question, boy."

"I heard about your son. My uncle. It was in the paper. I thought the funeral would give me a chance to see this side of my family."

"We ain't your family," Amos said flatly.

"That's not what the blood test said." The boy went back to watching the stars.

The lift of his chin, his voice. There hadn't been any need of any fancy test. All you had to do was look at him, thought Amos. He was Donny all over again. Didn't make him his grandson by a damn sight, though. Tom and Edward, they were his grandsons. He'd held them in his arms when they were babies, made them little glazed animals to play with, watched them turn their first bowls.

Takes more than a squirt of jism up someone else's wife to make a person my grandson, he thought resentfully.

"What's your name?" Libbet asked.

"Davis. Davis Richmond. He said we're cousins. How?"

"My mom and your —" She hesitated, unwilling to grant him family status. "Uncle Donny and Mom were brother and sister."

"There were three children?"

"And now there's just one," Amos rasped.

His mind shied away from the image of James Lucas lying all red and burned on the kiln car, his clothes blackened, his hair singed off. Donny's death was bad, but this one was worse. Worse for how it was and worse for an end to his unvoiced dreams.

After Donny died, he had almost reconciled himself to the bitter knowledge that Betty was the conduit through which Nordan blood would flow into the future and he had pinned all his hopes on her son Tom, even though people in Seagrove were already taking bets on whether or not he'd make it to twenty, since he'd already wrecked two cars by the time he was seventeen. Then when James Lucas and Sandra Kay busted up, Amos suddenly realized that James Lucas was barely fifty. He could still marry again and if he picked a younger woman, he might even make a new batch of Nordan boy-babies.

Now James Lucas was dead. Today he'd been laid in a grave and it was back to Tom, all or nothing on a hotheaded boy who'd crashed a third car just last Christmas and wound up with a steel pin in his leg. It was almost like God was dealing off the bottom of the deck, he thought. Getting ready to call in all the chips and shut Nordan Pottery down for good.

God?

Or the devil?

Somebody, for whatever reason, had killed James Lucas, and ever since that hellacious moment, one son's death had made him think more and more on the other's. What if somebody'd killed Donny, too? Donny'd never had cause to do like how it looked. He had all the women a normal man could want — from this boy's mama to Sandra Kay and God knows how many in between. Won't no way he'd have dressed up like that or been doing what they said.

But why would somebody kill both his boys? They were so different. Different likes. Different friends.

Same enemy?

Sandra Kay'd had no reason to kill Donny even if she'd been sleeping with him. And yeah, she'd been awful mad at James Lucas when she walked out, but to wait two years, then splash red all over him and throw him in the kiln? That won't something a puny little woman did two years later.

No, it had to be man reasons. A man with a big hate could've rigged Donny up like that just so people would snigger about it behind his back, thought Amos.

But then why wait so long to kill James Lucas, too? What did it gain anybody? Keep on killing Nordans and it was going to shut down the pottery, but who the hell did that help? And if somebody out there *was* trying to kill off all the men that turned a wheel here, why was he still alive?

Because you're so old and one hand's so useless that he knows you can't keep it going on your own, he told himself mournfully. *All the same, maybe God slipped up when He dealt you this wild card.*

Fear and rebellion stirred within him. He might be old, but he still knew how to run a bluff. He'd have to play his cards close to his chest, though, not give anybody a peek.

Craftily, he looked at the boy seated on the edge of the porch. This Davis Richmond. This bait that would do to save his true grandson from a killer.

"You ever do any turning?" Amos asked.

"Not really. My mother used to have a wheel and she'd let me mess with it once in a while."

"You want to learn?"

"You saying you'd teach me?" The boy tried to sound casual, but Amos sensed an eagerness beneath his words.

"How old are you?"

"Nineteen."

"When can you start?"

"Friday?"

"Bring your things with you. You can

sleep in Donny's old place."

"*Granddaddy!*" Till then, Libbet had tried to keep quiet, but this was too much. "What about Tom?"

"Tom already knows how to turn," the old man said mildly.

"But he's ready to take hold and come work here."

"Ain't no reason he can't still come work here after school. Help teach Davis. Hell, you'n come, too, if you want. We got an order I'm not going to meet if I don't get more help than June and Bobby can give me. Half the stuff got smashed when James Lucas — when —"

He couldn't finish, and the girl laid her head on his shoulder and patted his stroke-drawn hand. "Don't worry, Granddaddy. We'll help you catch up. Mom's already said we would. You don't need any outsiders coming in."

For just an instant, Amos was tempted, but then he thought of what he'd be risking if he was right about Donny and he pulled himself straighter.

"Davis here ain't no outsider," he declared. "He's Donny's boy and that makes him just as much my grandson as Tom, and don't you forget it, missy!"

Libbet drew back as if he'd slapped her.

She and Tom were often at odds, but he was still her brother and it looked as if Granddaddy was getting ready to set this — this *bastard* in his place. When Tom had been *promised*.

The boy stood up. "Friday, then. With my stuff."

The door at the other end of the porch opened and his daughter called down their way, "Dad? Can I get you anything?"

"Yeah, Betty, I reckon you can." He tried to make his voice sound cheerful. "You can get yourself down here and meet your nephew."

"Nephew?" Betty Hitchcock faltered, peering nearsightedly through the darkness. As she came closer, she saw him standing there and caught her breath.

"You're Donny's son?"

"Yes, ma'am."

She shook her head at his likeness to her younger brother. "Why didn't you tell me he was coming, Dad?"

"Didn't rightly know it myself," Amos said dryly.

He'd never understand women. Here was Libbet acting like he was taking a snake to his bosom, and there was her mother hurrying past Bobby, who was back on the steps again, to shake the boy's hand, then give him a hug like he was her long-lost son.

"I've always felt so bad that we couldn't come find you after Donny died. But we didn't know your name or where you lived except Raleigh. I guess he felt like he ought not to say anything till . . ." She hesitated.

"Till he knew for sure I was his?" Davis asked.

"Till he found out if you wanted to know us," she said. "You're not going to run off so quick, are you?"

"He's coming back Friday," Libbet told her.

"Really? Oh, that will be so much better. Give us a chance to get to know you without so many people around. Can you stay for supper?"

Before Davis could answer, Libbet said, "Even better, Mom. Guess what? Granddaddy's going to teach him how to pot. He's going to live in Uncle Donny's place."

Betty finally became aware of the tension that thrummed the cool night air. "Oh?"

She looked from her daughter to her newly discovered nephew, back to her father. "Dad?"

"Might as well see if he's got a knack for it," said Amos, lighting another cigarette. "You better get moving, boy. You probably got a lot of ground to cover before Friday."

193

"Yessir. Nice meeting you, ma'am. Libbet."
At the edge of the yard, he hesitated. "Sir?
What do I call you?"

That was a question Amos hadn't expected, but in for a pig, in whole hog. "Your
cousins call me Granddaddy. You might as
well, too."

"Thanks. Well, see you all soon."

He threaded his way past all the parked
cars and disappeared into the dark parking
area out by the shop. A moment later, they
saw his car, a scruffy white Toyota that was
almost a twin of Tom's, pull out of the drive
and head toward Raleigh.

"That's good of you, Dad," Betty said.
"The way you talked after Donny died? But
there, now! I knew you'd be glad if you ever
met him. You can't go against your own
blood, can you?"

Amos leaned back in the swing and blew a
thin stream of smoke toward the porch
ceiling. "You never said a truer word, honey."

"And what about Tom's blood?" his granddaughter asked angrily. "Doesn't his count
anymore?"

Betty looked puzzled.

Behind her mother, people were beginning to drift back out to the porch, some
with plastic cups of tea, other with their cigarettes already out and lighters in hand.

Among them was her father, but Libbet Hitchcock didn't care. With all the harshness that only a teenager who knows herself in the right can voice, she asked, "What're you going to do? Make Davis change his name to Nordan when you give him the place?"

"Don't you speak to your grandfather in that tone," said Betty. "And what are you talking about? Everybody knows Tom's to have Nordan Pottery. Right, Dad?"

"Ain't nothing in writing yet," Amos said mildly.

CHAPTER

15

While Southerners seek and enjoy the boons of progress, they are also reluctant to abandon old ways.

— *Raised in Clay*,
Nancy Sweezy

Thursday was my brother Seth's birthday, so Minnie invited the whole family and a few friends over that night for cake and homemade ice cream.

Seth is five brothers up from me and I've always felt closer to him than to some of the others — probably because he cuts me more slack than they do. He doesn't spend half his life criticizing me or giving advice or acting like I'm still the baby sister, with emphasis on the baby part.

This makes birthday and Christmas gifts

something of a problem. I always want to give him the moon with a silver string around it, but I can't get too fancy for Seth or my other ten brothers will get their feelings hurt if the difference between his presents and theirs is too great. Not that most of them would notice, but their wives tend to keep score.

This year, I got sneaky and enlisted Haywood's son Stevie, who's in school over at Carolina. Seth's a huge Carolina fan and I'd scored a couple of tickets to the last home game of the basketball season from a fellow judge who's another Carolina alum. Stevie was more than willing to pretend that the tickets came from him and were practically freebies.

"How the hell'd you do that?" asked Will, who's three up from me. "I been trying to get tickets all season."

Stevie just grinned and murmured about friends in high places.

Haywood, Robert, Zach, Andrew, and Daddy had chipped in to get Seth a photocopier for his home office. Since Seth does all the bookkeeping for the farm, it struck me as a rather pragmatic (not to mention tax-deductible) gift.

Will gave him a gift certificate for dinner for two at a steakhouse in Dobbs, and

Herman, who's an electrician, gave him a paddle fan for the porch. (Annie Sue, Herman's daughter, promised to install it before summer.)

My official present, reservations at the Carolina Inn for the night of the game with a buffet breakfast next morning, slid right in among the others without sticking out too far, and Stevie gave me a thumbs up as he went out on the porch to help turn the crank on one of the two ice cream churns that Minnie had going.

In a family this big, it's impossible to get everyone here at the same time. Adam, Ben, Jack, and Frank live out of state and many of my nieces and nephews are married and off on their own, but that still left a lot of enthusiastic voices to sing "Happy Birthday" to Seth when Minnie brought in the cake, aglow with so many candles that Zach asked her if she had a permit from the fire marshal.

Through it all, Daddy sat beaming. He's not much for speech-making, but as he's gotten older, these times are precious to him. "Means a lot to me to see the family sticking together, prospering," he said, savoring the dish of strawberry ice cream I brought him. "Just wish the others lived closer to home."

"I'm working on Adam," said Karen, who

was back East this week to look after her mother. Mrs. Buffkin was recovering from a mastectomy, and her operation had suddenly made Karen realize just how far away she and Adam were from family out there in California. "Frank and Mae came up to see us last month. Janie's husband is being transferred to New Jersey and you know how crazy they are about those grandchildren. Wouldn't surprise me a bit to see them come, too."

Frank's my next-to-oldest brother and the one I know the least because he joined the Navy before I was born. He'd been stationed out in San Diego when his children started marrying, so that's where he and Mae retired. They get back every other year when Jack and Ben come, so they're certainly not strangers, but Daddy won't be completely happy till all his chicks are back under his wingspread.

"I hate to think that my funeral's the only time y'all will all be together," he grumbles, so Karen's words brightened his day.

I couldn't help thinking of Amos Nordan, a man who seemed even more patriarchal about his male descendants than Daddy. He'd begun with only two sons and now both were gone.

For good.

At least Daddy's missing sons were all alive.

The boys had brought their instruments, I had my guitar, Daddy picked up his fiddle, and those who felt like it sang along for over an hour. When we paused to retune, Karen's eyes were shining. "This is what I've missed out there," she said. "It's what our boys are missing."

With Karen tripping down memory lane, nobody had the heart to tell her that it's probably too late for her boys. She and Adam may not have gotten above their raising, but their sons have absolutely no interest in the life we live here. Too much money, too many expensive toys, too much private school snobbery, too little sweaty work — these things have made them very uncomfortable the few times they've visited Colleton County. As they've grown older, they've gotten more polite about it when Adam and Karen bring them south, but what roots they have are firmly attached to Silicon Valley's golden vistas and I see rough roads ahead if she tries to move them back.

We finished up with the favorite song of Robert's three-year-old grandson, the one about the preacher chased up a tree by a bear. He can carry a good tune now and he joined in lustily on the chorus:

Oh, Lord, you delivered Daniel from the lion's den.
And, Lord, you delivered Jonah from the whale and then
Three Hebrew children from the fiery furnace,
So the Good Book do declare.
But, Lord, Lord, if you can't help me,
For goodness sake, don't help that bear.

We broke for coffee around ten and some of the kids who had school the next day left with their parents.

Word had gone around most of my family about my ghastly experience over in Seagrove, but what with his being out of town last weekend and my holding court down in Makely all week, tonight was the first time I'd seen Dwight Bryant since I got back. It didn't surprise me, though, when he came over and said, "Getting to where you can't go anywhere without stumbling over a body. You okay?"

"I'm fine," I assured him. "And before you say it, yes, I'm minding my own business and not getting involved. If Connor Woodall called you, he must have told you that."

"Good. How's ol' Woodall holding up these days?"

"Woodall?" asked Will, who was standing nearby. "Con Woodall? Whatever happened to him?"

Which meant that I had to go through the whole thing again for Will, Dwight, and Karen, who had also known Connor when they were kids.

After they'd finished exclaiming over the way the murder happened and my part in discovering the body, Karen was interested to hear that Connor was married to a potter and instantly commissioned me to buy a piece of Fernwood pottery when I went back. "And if you can get Amos Nordan to turn loose a piece of his old cardinal ware, I don't care what you have to pay for it."

I had ridden over to Seth and Minnie's with Stevie, who'd already left to drive back to Chapel Hill, but since this was her first time out of the house since her mother's operation, Karen said she'd take me home. She hadn't seen my new house yet and she was interested in looking at the pottery I'd brought home from Seagrove.

We hugged the birthday boy goodnight and got more hugs from those still there, then cut across through the rutted back lanes that were a shortcut from Seth's house to mine. As Karen eased her rented car over the low humps that keep the lanes from washing out, I wondered again if Sandra Kay had been telling the truth when she said she hadn't driven through the lane past the car kiln at Nordan Pottery. Shortcuts become so automatic in the country that a person doesn't always consider bumps and holes.

My face jug didn't much interest Karen.

"I'm sorry," she said, "but they haven't been around all that long. They aren't really part of the true folk tradition, and anyhow, I can't help thinking that they started out as racist caricatures — those thick lips, bulging eyes, broad noses."

She conceded that mine didn't have any of those elements, that its expression of mild surprise was even charming. "All the same . . ."

Even planted with red petunias and blue salvia, my new salt-glazed flower pot took her fancy, with its understated sophistication and spare ornamentation. The maker, David Stuempfle, was unfamiliar to her, but she carefully wrote down his name and directions to his pottery. "Maybe I can get over before I go back. If not . . . ?"

"Sure," I said, laughing. "I'll get one for you."

She laughed, too. "Well, at least it's not furniture."

I'd held court last year over in High Point during their huge semiannual furniture market, and Karen knew that I'd wanted one of everything I saw, even though I was still living at Aunt Zell's then. I managed to restrain myself from buying anything except a bed.

Pottery was proving less resistible.

I offered Karen a glass of wine, but she shook her head regretfully. "It's been a lovely evening, but I'd better get back. Mother usually settles in for the night about now and I ought to be there to help her."

As I walked out to the car with her, stars were blazing overhead and the moon was nearly full. Spring peepers were loud down by the pond and somewhere a couple of dogs were barking back and forth at each other. I was still standing on the porch, watching the red taillights of her car disappear down the long drive that leads to the hardtop, when more headlights came through the lane from Seth's.

It was Dwight.

"You forgot your sweater," he said, as he got out of the truck. "Minnie thought you might want it."

I had to laugh as I took that old blue sweater and tossed it over my shoulders. The night air was cool, but not so cool that I had given its absence a second thought. Besides, I have lots of sweaters, as Minnie is very well aware.

"What's funny?"

"Oh, come on, Dwight! You know what Minnie really thought."

"Oh," he said, and grinned.

After all, it's not as if Minnie and Seth have been all that subtle about it since Dwight came back to Colleton County divorced and unattached.

"I'm sorry," I said. "You'd think by now they'd know it's never going to happen."

Until he joined the Army and went away, Dwight was always around while I was growing up, almost like another brother. Marriage, fatherhood, divorce — nothing changed that. Okay, there was that one nanosecond two or three years ago, a single experimental kiss that embarrassed the hell out of both of us, but all it really did was permanently confirm that there was nothing between us except a deep and solid friendship. He's handy when I need an escort for any couples-only thing, I'm here if he wants company watching old movies.

Dwight cocked an eye at the night sky. "You mean you're not going to be overcome by all this moonlight and hurl yourself into my manly arms?"

" 'Fraid not. Not tonight anyhow."

"Well, shucks." He smiled down at me. "On the other hand, it's probably just as good you don't. April's setting me up with a friend of hers and I couldn't handle two women at one time. Too out of practice."

"Oh, you'd soon remember," I assured him.

April is my brother Andrew's wife, a sixth-grade teacher with a flare for matching fabrics and wallpaper and now, it would appear, unattached deputies.

"A friend?" I asked. "Anybody I know?"

"I think her name's Sylvia something. Teaches at April's school. Know her?"

"Sylvia Clayton?"

"Yeah, that sounds right. What's she like?"

"I only met her once," I said. "She's not drop-dead gorgeous, but nice-looking, and she seems to have a good sense of humor."

In truth, it was her laugh I remembered best, a girlish giggle that seemed to be triggered by almost anything. I wasn't sure she'd be right for Dwight, but then I was the one who'd been plenty sure Kidd was right for me, and we see where *that* got me.

"Karen wasn't interested in anything to drink," I told him. "You?"

"You having one?"

We decided on bourbon and Pepsi and, since it was such a mild night, we sat on the porch awhile and then strolled down to the pond.

"Did Connor Woodall say anything about an arrest?" I asked.

"I thought you weren't going to get involved." He picked up some loose pebbles at the edge of the water and began plunking them out where the moon was mirrored on the surface. Around us, the little spring peepers went silent.

"I'm not. But I've met some of those people now and I can't help being curious."

I told him a little more about Amos Nordan and the pottery's long history as we walked out on the pier my nephews and nieces built for me. When we got to the end, we sat down on the edge, facing each other, our backs against the pilings, our shoes almost touching, as we sipped our drinks.

"How's Cal?" I asked.

"I don't know, Deb'rah." Dwight's back was to the moon and his face was in shadows, but I could still hear his sadness and frustration as he talked about how much he missed his son and how worried he was that Cal wasn't getting enough exercise and the right intellectual stimulation. "Sometimes I think I should move up there to Virginia, try to get a job in that little town. It wouldn't pay squat, but at least I'd get to see him more.

Get him out from in front of the television."

Jonna's elderly mother was Cal's baby-sitter and it was easier for her to watch him in the house than to take him to a park or enroll him in outdoor activities.

"Is Jonna going to let you have him over Easter?"

He nodded.

"Well, you be sure and bring him out here. Robert and Doris are going to have an Easter egg hunt for all the kids at church and I told her I'd help."

"Yeah, okay," he said, but his heart wasn't in it.

Small clouds scudded across the moon and a light wind began to blow from the northeast. We sat in silence and let the night sounds of frogs and crickets wash over us.

Dwight finished his drink, stood up, then gave me a hand to pull up and we headed back to the house.

"Sorry," he said. "Here I've dumped on you and never asked how you're doing. Will says you told him Chapin's going back to his wife. True?"

"Oh, yes," I said wearily. "Story of my life. But don't worry. It's no big deal."

"You sure?"

"Pretty sure. You never liked him, did you?"

Dwight shrugged. "He just seemed a little

lightweight. Like everything was a joke."

"You got that part right," I told him. "Only the joke was on me in the end."

"The guy's an idiot," Dwight said loyally.

"He missed his daughter as much as you miss Cal," I said, struggling to be fair. "You ever think of getting back with Jonna?"

"*Jonna?* Hell, no!"

"Not even for Cal?"

"Not even for Cal."

For some reason, I felt obscurely pleased.

CHAPTER

16

Most assuredly, memory can be a fickle
ally, subject to all types of distortions.

> — *Turners and Burners,*
> Charles G. Zug III

It was Friday morning.

Betty Hitchcock wrenched open the single
loft window as June Gregorich came up the
steps from Donny's old workshop below with
an armload of fresh bed linens. Jeffy shambled along behind carrying a broom and
dustpan.

Davis Richmond was expected by noon
and despite the hostility of her two younger
children and her own uneasy apprehen-
sions, Betty couldn't let him come into a
dusty, untidy place.

A thin drizzle still fell, the last remnants of

an early morning rain, but she could already see patches of blue sky to the west as the dark clouds moved eastward. Although the skylights overhead gave light, they couldn't be opened and the window over the bed was too small to be much help in clearing out the musty smell of disuse.

"I don't know why Dad doesn't just give him the spare bedroom in the house," she said. She had already stripped off the old quilt that served as the bed's dustcover and turned the double mattress in an attempt to freshen it. "This is going to be too much extra work for you."

"It's okay," June said. "Mr. Amos seems so anxious to have the boy here, it's worth a little extra work."

A clatter on the stairs made them turn in time to see the broom handle bang the railing as Jeffy attacked the dusty steps.

"Go easy, son," she called. "You're kicking up more dust than you're sweeping. Little short strokes, remember? And don't forget the corners."

Immediately, he slowed his tempo and earnestly concentrated on each step.

June fluffed the fitted white bottom sheet over the mattress and began tucking in the corners. "Besides," she told Betty, who came over to help, "he may not be here long."

"True," said Betty. "Learning to turn a pot or two is fun. Doing it day in and day out gets to be hard work real fast if you don't have the patience for it."

"No, I was thinking that he might give the boy James Lucas's house. If it all works out the way Mr. Amos hopes."

Betty stared at her blankly across the width of the bed. "James Lucas's house?"

"Well, yes." June looked at her and hesitated. "It *is* his now, isn't it? Deborah — Judge Knott, I mean — said that if he didn't leave a will, everything would go to Mr. Amos."

"No, it's all Dad's again . . . only . . ."

Despite the years, the graying hair, the fine wrinkles around her mouth and eyes, Betty Hitchcock was still beautiful, but now her normally serene face was troubled.

As if reading her mind, June said, "Don't worry. I'm sure Mr. Amos will do right by Tom. There's always his house. And like he says, nothing's in writing yet. He's sure looking forward to this, though, isn't he? I never saw your dad quite in this frame of mind. You were up at the house. Did you see how he has all those picture albums out?"

She briskly fluffed the pillows, put fresh cases on them, and piled the old ones by the landing to take back to the house and wash.

June had helped Betty and Sandra Kay clear out most of Donny's things shortly after his funeral. Clothes and personal papers had been sorted and disposed of. What remained was a large, sparsely furnished open space. The entertainment center no longer held television or stereo, but furniture still ranged in front of it. The couch, low round table, and a club chair were old yet comfortably inviting. More than once she had missed Jeffy and found him here curled up on the couch, sound asleep.

The tabletop was an abstract mosaic that Donny had pieced from shards of broken pottery and the couch and chair echoed those purple and gray hues. (Not a chip of that famous cardinal red, though, June had noted the first time she saw the table.)

At the far end of the loft a long, ceramic-tiled counter held a cold-water sink, a microwave, a toaster oven, a coffeemaker, and a straight-sided earthenware pot into which cooking and eating utensils had been stuck indiscriminately. There was also a small refrigerator, which Betty had already wiped down with baking soda this morning and plugged in. Above was a shelf full of gray-and-purple Nordan tableware and drinking vessels.

Behind the wall was a homemade bathroom consisting of sink, shower, and toilet, again cold water only.

Betty had moved the bed from its former position. Involuntarily, June looked at the beams overhead and tried to recall which one Donny had dangled from, but even though she'd helped Mr. Amos lower his body, she couldn't now be sure. Her mind went back to that gray November day. Hard to realize that more than two years had passed since then. . . .

It was only her second or third time cleaning for Mr. Amos and she had been washing up their lunch dishes when she missed Jeffy. In the living room, the Muppets had been singing her son's favorite song, but Jeffy wasn't singing along as he usually did.

When she went in to check on him, his plaid wool jacket and red knit cap lay on the arm of the leather couch. The big television screen had been full of colorful furry animals, but the afghan she'd covered him with for his nap earlier lay in a woolen pile on the floor. No Jeffy.

The two-story house held four bedrooms upstairs, but all the rooms were small and it only took a moment to assure herself that he was in none of them. The coverlet on Mr. Nordan's bed was rumpled where he'd taken his usual midday rest and she automatically straightened it. Irritation battled with worry over Jeffy's disobedience. Grabbing up her own jacket, she pushed open the side door of this rustic wooden house and stepped into the yard. No sign of her son.

Tall pines shaded the whole pottery compound and nondeciduous bushes, some of them more than head high, lined the paths and the foundations of every structure. They seemed to be ubiquitous in this part of the country. So different from her native California. Azaleas and rhododendrons, she'd been told, and glorious in the spring. Everyone kept saying that North Carolina would knock her eyes out in the spring. "California may have flowers all year 'round," they said, "but you just wait till you see everything here all pink and white and new green. You won't believe how pretty it'll get around here."

Even in the gray and chill of early November, it was a lovely peaceful setting, but right then, June was too worried to take more than passing notice.

Had Jeffy gone into the showroom? He wouldn't mean to break anything, but he was so clumsy and uncoordinated. He'd gotten her fired from the pottery that first hired her when they came to Seagrove and she certainly didn't want him to upset the people here before she'd had a chance to make herself indispensable to the Nordans.

She mounted the two steps at the rear and unlatched the heavy wooden door. Inside, all was as it should be. Shelves and cabinets held orderly rows of beautifully glazed stoneware in deep purples and grays. A couple of customers were murmuring happily to each other as they lifted the various pieces and marveled at their beauty.

"Mrs. Nordan?"

Amos Nordan's daughter-in-law looked up from her work at the sales counter and shook her finger at June in mock scolding. "Now, what did I tell you about that?"

"Sandra Kay," June said stiffly.

The other woman smiled approvingly. She was easily mid-forties, but fighting every year, with blond rinses, moisturizers, and liquid diet lunches. "You finding everything all right over there?"

"Except that my boy — Jeffy — he's wandered off. He didn't come in here, did he?"

"Haven't seen him," Sandra Kay Nordan said, turning back to the computer, where she was entering receipts. "Did you check the potteries?"

"I've told him not to bother —"

"Oh, he's no bother," the woman assured her. "I'll bet you Donny's got him playing

216

with clay right this minute. You run on down and see if I'm not right. And if that husband of mine is back, tell him I need to ask him something."

"Okay," said June, moving toward the door.

"Oh, and June," she added casually, "if you get a chance, could you just dust off the shelves in here before you go today?"

"Sure," June said, even though they both knew quite well that Mr. Amos was only paying her to clean his house once a week, not the shop. But until she figured out the dynamics of the family, she wasn't about to cross the only other woman at Nordan Pottery.

The pottery belonged to Mr. Amos, and technically, his two sons, Donny and James Lucas, worked for him. Or so she'd heard. Sandra Kay and James Lucas lived in a house on the opposite side of the sales shop from Mr. Amos's house and the younger son Donny had fixed up a bachelor apartment over his workshop, although he still fixed breakfast for his father every day.

The first pottery was shared by Mr. Amos and James Lucas. She wasn't surprised to see one of the wheels standing idle. James Lucas had gone to pick up some supplies over near Charlotte and, from her annoyed tone, Sandra Kay clearly thought he should have been back by now. But Mr. Amos wasn't at his wheel, either. Four newly turned tall vases did stand on the drying rack and the fresh lump of clay that lay on the wheel had a wet cloth draped over it, so he couldn't be gone long.

To her surprise, Bobby Gerard, the pottery's general helper, was at the far end of the shed sanding rough spots off ware that had come out of the kiln yesterday. He hadn't shown up for work this morning and she didn't realize he'd come back this afternoon. A taciturn man in his mid-forties, Bobby Gerard was small and wiry and, from what she gathered from conversation between Mr. Amos and Donny, not entirely reliable, having a capricious thirst that made him disappear from the pottery a couple of days at a time.

"We ought to just go ahead and fire his ass once and for all," she'd heard Donny say this morning.

"Naw, now, Bobby'll do," Mr. Amos had replied. "He may not work steady, but he does work cheap."

"And when he does work, he works hard," James Lucas had added.

"Have you seen my son?" June asked him now.

Bobby shook his head and kept working.

Apprehensively, she moved on to the second structure. It, too, seemed empty when she first opened the door and came out of the cold into the earthy warmth of the workroom. A powdery film of clay dust lay over everything except the dozen or more candlesticks Donny must have turned this morning and the leather-bottomed barstool where he'd half-propped, half-sat as he worked.

Then she heard Mr. Amos's voice raised in anger and a frightened note in her own son's voice.

A surge of protective maternal instinct carried her across the room and up a set of crude wooden steps to an open door on the landing.

The door led immediately to the large loft that Donny Nordan had remodeled for his own use. Despite the gray day, the place was brightly lit from skylights set in the roof.

Jeffy cowered beyond the doorway.

"Just get the hell out!" Amos Nordan snarled. "Git, before I knock the living bejeesus out of you. You hear me, you dumb-ass idiot?"

June's own temper flared at the sight of the enraged man's uplifted hand. "You stop!" she cried, rushing into the room. "Don't you dare hit him. And don't you ever call him an idiot again! He's . . ."

Her voice faltered as she took in the rest of the loft. Jeffy ran to her and her arms opened automatically to comfort her sobbing son, but her eyes were riveted by what lay behind the old man.

It was Donny.

Motionless as a lump of clay, he knelt in the middle of his bed, but his head was suspended by a silky loop of soft white cloth that hung from a hook in one of the low beams. His slender body was nude except for wisps of satin — a white lace bra and lacy white panties.

One hand swung loosely over the side of the bed. The other was caught inside the elastic waistband.

He was clearly dead.

At the sight of her, all the anger had drained from Amos Nordan's body and he had stretched out his clay-stained hands to her.

"Help me," he had whimpered. "Please help me."

"I hope nobody tells Davis how Donny died," Betty said now, abruptly interrupting June's memories. "Not right away anyhow. I've warned the children."

"That's good." June knew she was being warned, too, as if she were a common gossip, when nothing — *nothing* — could be further from the truth. Except for Betty and Sandra Kay, who both had a right to know, and the detectives after they'd figured out that someone had changed Donny's clothes, she had never talked about Donny's death. Lots of Seagrove people had tried to get her to confirm the rumors that swirled around at the time, but she'd just stared them coldly in the eye and kept her mouth shut. If people chose to interpret her silence as confirmation, that was their business. She wasn't responsible for human nature.

They worked in awkward silence for a few minutes, then June said, "I only met your brother a couple of times. Were you close to him?"

"Close?" Betty paused with dustcloth in hand. "I suppose as much as any brother and sister. He was a little younger and Dill and I got married so early. But we were always back and forth, living just up the lane from each other like we were. He was different-natured from James Lucas and me. More the artist. That's what everybody always said: 'Betty and James Lucas are craftsmen, but Donny's the artist.' "

There was an edge of old resentment to her voice.

Well, thought June, it was common knowledge that Mr. Amos had favored him. Even in the few short weeks she'd been in Seagrove before coming to clean here, she'd heard that Donny was Jacob to James Lucas's Esau.

Voicing June's thoughts, Betty said, "I think Dad's expecting Davis to pick up right where Donny left off."

June glanced at her watch, then noticed that Jeffy had abandoned the broom and was no longer on the steps.

"Are you okay to finish up here alone? I'm usually at Ada Finch's by nine o'clock, but I can get there a little late if you want me to stay."

"No, there's not much more to do here," said Betty. "If you'll leave the broom, I'll just sweep down the cobwebs in the bathroom and wipe things off in there."

Jeffy reappeared with a fistful of azaleas. He pointed to a vase standing on the windowsill and said, "I got him some pretty flowers."

As June beamed, Betty said, "What a good idea, Jeffy."

She filled the gray-green vase with water, arranged the pink blossoms, and set it in the center of the coffee table.

She wished she felt as welcoming as the flowers looked.

"Look," Davis said for the tenth time in two days. "It's not like I'm going for good. I'm leaving most of my notebooks and stuff."

He opened his duffel bag wide to show only jeans, sweatshirts, socks, several sets of underwear, and a small black case. "See? I'm only taking my portable CD player."

"I wish I'd never told you." The woman was in her late fifties. While her short straight hair was unabashedly gray, it was stylishly asymmetrical in cut. She had not been conventionally pretty in her youth, but good bones and a level penetrating gaze were proving better assets than dimples and fluttery lashes.

"I'm glad you did," Davis said vehemently. "I'm glad I wasn't that asshole's son."

"Keep a civil tongue. For all you know, Donald Nordan was a bigger asshole." She sat on his unmade bed and patted the various pockets of her blue twill coverall till she found a crumpled pack of unfiltered cigarettes.

"Hey!" Davis protested. "You swore you'd quit."

"I have," his mother said. "But you make

me so crazy I need to hold one once in a while. Smelling it settles me down a little. My nicotine pacifier."

She rolled the cigarette between her strong fingers. Craftsman's fingers. Flecks of dry tobacco spilled from the ends onto her knee and she brushed them carelessly onto the floor.

"Was he?" Davis asked.

"Was who what?"

He added a pair of thick-soled sneakers to the duffel and turned to face her. "My biological father. Was he an asshole, too?"

She sighed and pushed back the hair that had slipped from behind her ear to follow the line of her strong chin. "Don't ask questions you don't want to hear the answers to."

He continued to stare at her relentlessly, one hand on his hip.

Nurture over nature, she thought. He'd picked that trick up from the despicable man who had *not* sired him.

"When you do that, you look just like Jeremy," she said with deliberate malice.

He threw up his hands. "And you say I drive *you* crazy!"

"Okay, okay." She laughed. "The answer is that I really don't know. I'm sorry, baby. I wish I could say that he was the love of my live, that we had an affair that blazed across my skies like the afterburners of an Apollo rocket. Bottom line? I barely remember him. He was an attractive man in a pair of mud-stained jeans and he had magic in his fingers when he touched clay. He came over to do a demonstration class at the museum. There was another, younger woman in the class that could've been a clone of the student that Jeremy was sleeping with at the moment and she was all over Donald. Somehow it got muddled in my mind that if I could whisk him out from under her nose, it would be getting some of my own back from Jeremy and his flavor of the week. I felt I needed to prove something."

She held the dried-up cigarette to her nose, then tossed it into his overflowing wastebasket.

"So I did."

"Where? Here?"

"Yes. It was a rainy spring day. Not unlike today, in fact," she said, glancing toward the splattered window overlooking a quiet street in Raleigh's Cameron Park. "Your sisters were at school and Jeremy had made a point of saying he wouldn't be home for lunch, that he would be meeting with some of his advisees about their term projects. That's when he was still bothering to lie about it. I

225

brought Donald Nordan home for a lunch meeting myself."

"Where?"

A tilt of her head gestured to the big room at the end of the hall. "You were conceived in the master bedroom, in my grand-mother's four-poster. Just like Helen and Claire."

Her son raised an eyebrow at that and she gave a rueful smile. "Okay, maybe not *exactly* like them."

"Was he the first?"

"No. And before you ask, he wasn't the last, either. But the others are none of your business."

She stood abruptly, scattering more flecks of tobacco on the hardwood floor. "I wish you wouldn't do this, Davis. There's nothing for you in Seagrove. You're not a potter. Biology isn't destiny."

"No? Maybe I need to prove something, too, Mom. You said I could have this semester."

"I know, but I thought you'd go to New York. Or Europe. I sure as hell didn't think you'd go to Seagrove."

"Look at all the money you're saving," he said lightly as he tucked a couple of sketchbooks and a handful of drawing pencils in the side pocket of his duffel and zipped it closed. He looked around the room, then slung the bag over his shoulder. "I'm only an hour or so away if I need anything else."

"Promise you'll be careful," she said, following him downstairs. "And don't piss anybody off, okay? Just remember that somebody killed Donald's brother."

Unfortunately, it was reading about the murder in the *News and Observer* last week that had finally led her to tell her son the truth about who he was.

Okay, that and too much wine for dinner, she admitted to herself. Too late now to wish she'd kept her mouth shut.

"Listen to your instincts," she urged. "If things start feeling weird, if you sense danger, get out of there immediately. I don't want you in some lunatic's line of fire. Promise?"

"I promise, I promise," Davis said in that "yeah, yeah" tone he used whenever he felt she was nagging. "And I'll call you as soon as I have a phone number."

He leaned in to kiss her cheek, but she pulled him down to her level and gave him a fierce hug and when he was gone, she went looking for the newspaper article she had clipped exactly a week ago.

"Someone you knew?" Davis had asked casually, not really interested.

If only she'd answered yes, just as casually!

Instead, she'd had to smart-mouth and say no, which of course only whetted his curiosity.

The article was still lying on the dining room table. She picked it up and looked again for the name of the detective in charge of the investigation. There it was: Lieutenant Connor Woodall of the Randolph County Sheriff's Department.

She frowned in concentration. Now, who did she know that might know Lieutenant Connor Woodall?

CHAPTER

17

Pots turned rapidly . . . tend to retain the first imprinting of the shape; the evidence of deft fingers on the malleable clay remains.

> — *Raised in Clay*,
> Nancy Sweezy

I was finishing up the leftovers down at Makely Friday morning in a session as dreary as the rain I'd driven down in. One sad case of assault followed another — "I come in after working all day and she's sitting there watching them trashy talk shows, the house a mess, no supper, the kids yelling, but she's lying if she says I hit her with my fist. It was just a little push when she got in my face."

Or, "She's not a bad daughter, Your Honor, 'cepting when she's drinking, and then she gets mean and my wife and me, we just can't take it no more. We'll keep on looking after the baby, but if you could maybe get her in one of those programs?"

Worthless checks seemed to have been written by everyone from migrant day laborers to prim little middle-class grandmothers, and I dealt with various shoplifters who between them had taken clothes, cigarettes, a pair of work boots, five flats of yellow rooster comb — "Everybody's got red. Red's common" — and three packages of rib-eye steaks that leaked a trail of blood through the grocery store and out the door, where the manager stopped him.

I listened to guilty pleas, not-guilty pleas, and, "Yeah, I done it but if you'll just hear me out, Your Honor, you'll understand why I had to."

At the midmorning recess, a clerk found me in the hallway and told me I'd had a phone call.

"She said it was urgent."

I didn't recognize the Raleigh number she gave me and when I called it, an unfamiliar woman's voice answered. I identified myself and she said, "Thanks for calling back, Deborah. It's Jennifer McAllister. I don't know if you remember me? We sat next to each other at that victory luncheon for

Elaine Marshall last fall?"

Elaine Marshall is the Lillington attorney who whomped up on Richard Petty in the race for Secretary of State to become the first woman ever elected to North Carolina's Council of State. And I certainly did remember Jennifer McAllister, popularly known around the Triangle as Jenny Mack, creator of one-of-a-kind costume jewelry. In fact, I even own a necklace that my brother Will brought home from a craft fair before she'd established a name for herself. Strands of flea-market beads, thin chains, and imitation pearls were suspended above and below an enigmatic female face that had been carved from resin, then subtly hand-painted. Will gave it to me half in jest for passing the bar. He told me it was an "I Am Woman" statement and I think he paid all of twenty-five dollars for it.

These days a Jenny Mack necklace like mine goes for three or four hundred.

"Of course I remember you," I said. "You tried to buy back my necklace. And we had that great conversation about Fred Chappell's books."

(Thinking I needed more culture, I'd just joined my sister-in-law April's book club. One of the selections had been *I Am One of You Forever*, which Jennifer McAllister had

231

recently read, too. I'd been rather pleased with myself for holding my own in an area where I don't usually shine.)

"What *I* remember is that you referred to several friends in law enforcement across the state," she said. "SBI agents, sheriff's deputies, police officers from High Point to Wilmington?"

"Yes?" I said, curious as to where this was going.

"What I was wondering is, do you by any chance know a Lieutenant Connor Woodall over in Randolph County?"

I admitted that I did. "Why do you ask?"

"Look, it's too complicated to talk about over the phone. Could I meet you some-where? Take you to lunch?"

I explained that I was down in Makely and wouldn't be finished till midafternoon. We arranged to meet for an early supper at a cantina just off I-40. It was a little closer to my house in the western part of Colleton County than to hers in Raleigh, but hey, she was the one who sounded in need of a favor.

In the end, I finished court a little earlier than I expected; nevertheless, Jennifer McAllister — "Please! Call me Jenny" — was there before me. Indeed, she already had a frozen margarita in front of her that was half-drunk. It looked refreshing and I ordered one, too.

Liquor-by-the-drink is a relatively recent innovation in Colleton County. When I was a child, everyone had to brown-bag it. If you went out to dinner, you could order setups, but the liquor itself had to come from a bottle you brought yourself and kept under the table. Because the state was rather strict about open containers in a car, diners encouraged each other to finish the bottle so it wouldn't "go to waste," which, of course, only encouraged drunk driving.

(It also built a market for the product my daddy used to make. Shot houses were already illegal, so their proprietors didn't think twice about serving the clientele untaxed white whiskey. Now that liquor-by-the-drink is legal, you'd think there'd be fewer shot houses and, for all I know, there are. All the same, shot house cases do keep turning up in my courtroom.)

Jenny McAllister looked as I'd remembered: a compact body, short once-blond hair that was now almost ash and styled by someone really good with the scissors, clear blue eyes above high cheekbones, and the alert air of someone interested and involved in life. She wore a simple sage green cotton tunic over a matching long skirt. Around her neck was a beaten bronze necklace that I instantly coveted.

"Do people buy things right off your body?" I asked.

She smiled. "They try to."

As we read over the menu and ordered, we made small talk about the weather (rainy/mild/good for azaleas and dogwoods) and about the mushrooming growth in this part of Colleton County (rampant/unchecked/bad for overcrowded schools and roads). When the waitress had gone away with our order, Jenny leaned forward and said, "I don't know if you saw it in last week's paper, but a potter was killed over in Seagrove last week —"

"James Lucas Nordan," I said.

She sat back in surprise. "You knew him?"

"Not very well," I said neutrally. "Was he a friend of yours?"

"No, I never met him." With a wry smile on her lips, she shook her head ruefully. "Sorry. A little moment of déjà vu. This is practically the same conversation I had with my son when I first read about the murder."

"Oh?"

"He was my son's uncle," she said bluntly.

"Oh, I *am* sorry," I told her.

"Don't be. Not on my account anyhow. As I said, I never met him. Didn't even know he existed till I read about it." Again, she leaned forward and the lower rung of her necklace clanged softly against the table. "Look, judges and lawyers — you're both discreet, right? Can I speak to you in confidence?"

I nodded, suddenly realizing that if James Lucas was her son's uncle, then her son must be the illegitimate child Donny Nordan had fathered.

"Twenty years ago, I had what amounted to a one-night stand with Nordan's brother, Donald. I never had any reason to tell Donald or my son, either, until a couple of years ago when my husband finally died. We'd lived separately for years, but never bothered to divorce. He didn't want to be free to remarry and I didn't want to have to give him half of what I was starting to make. Anyhow, my son was nearly grown and I decided maybe they both had a right to know. I drove over to Seagrove one day, found Donald, and told him. If he'd been unreceptive, I'd have dropped it right there."

"But he was happy about it," I said.

"Yes! How did you know?"

"A mutual friend told me about his death and how unlikely it was that he'd killed himself when he was looking forward to meeting his son."

"Suicide?" She looked puzzled. "I heard it was an accident, that he got tangled in a cord or something. I never knew it was supposed to be suicide."

No way was I going to be the one to tell her how her onetime lover had died, especially since it was only a guess on my part, a guess with no more confirmation than Connor Woodall's bright red embarrassment when I tried to get him to talk.

"Only at first," I said quickly. "But they soon got it right."

Her face cleared. "We were waiting for the blood tests to come back before telling Davis. Donald didn't see the need. He said my word was good enough, but I wanted them both to have scientific proof from the beginning. But before I got the results —"

She broke off as our food arrived — taco salad for me, a chicken burrito for her. Much as I hate seeing the building explosion here, the influx of migrant workers has certainly brought in great Mexican food.

"So before you got the results . . . ?" I encouraged when our waitress finally assured herself that we had everything we needed and went away.

"Donald was dead. I called to let him know the tests were back and that they did confirm his paternity. I never got a chance to speak to him, though. Whoever answered the phone said he'd been buried two weeks before."

"Must have been quite a shock for you."

She shrugged. "Well, it's not as if we'd had a real relationship."

"Nevertheless . . . ?"

With a sigh, she nodded. "As you say, nevertheless."

She picked at her burrito, and I added some extra salsa to my salad.

"I'm guessing that you didn't tell your son?"

"There didn't seem to be any point after that and I let it ride till I read about this James Nordan's murder at Nordan Pottery and realized that he must have been Donald's brother."

As we ate, she described how her son had picked up on it while she was clipping the article and how she'd blurted out to him that the dead man was his uncle.

"Unbeknownst to me, he drove over for the funeral this past Tuesday, then went back to the house and met his grandfather and aunt and one of his cousins."

I was curious. "How did they react?"

"With open arms, apparently." She did not sound happy about it. "He left this morning to go stay with them. His grandfather's going to teach him how to throw pots."

"And you want me to keep an eye on him?"

"You?"

She looked bewildered and I realized that in listening to her story, I'd forgotten that she didn't know my connection to the Nordans or that I'd be going back to Seagrove next week.

"You found the body?" she exclaimed when I told her about being there the week before.

She wanted all the details and, under the circumstances, I decided she had a right to know them, so I told her everything I knew about the Nordans and what gossip I'd heard.

"And you're going back this week? I can't believe it!"

I nodded.

"Then would you tell me anything you hear? And would you ask this Lieutenant Woodall to keep an eye on Davis for me? I'm worried about him, Deborah. If there's a killer running around that pottery . . ."

I could understand her concern.

"Sure," I told her.

"You could tell Davis that you and I are old friends, so he won't think I'm checking up on him."

I had to laugh. "If he's half as sharp as my teenaged nephews, that's exactly what he's going to think."

CHAPTER

18

It is most important to realize that the central perception of the traditional potter is that his craft is a trade. This attitude governs the making of shapes in multiples without concern about repetition.

— *Raised in Clay*,
Nancy Sweezy

It wasn't that he'd expected a brass band standing on the front porch to welcome him, Davis Richmond told himself, looking at the CLOSED sign on the shop door, but he'd certainly expected *someone* to be there. He peered through the window. All was dark inside.

He'd already knocked on the front and back doors of his grandfather's house with no results. He'd even walked over to the second house, home of his recently buried uncle, and found no one there, either.

Baffled, Davis folded his lanky frame into his old Toyota and drove back toward town. At least it had quit raining, and from the way the sun was shining, the day was going to be another warm one, a sample of summer to come.

Samples of summer's pests were already around. As he gassed up his car at a service station in Seagrove, two dogflies circled his head. Inside the air-conditioned coolness, he bought a ham-and-cheese sandwich and a bottle of tomato juice, which he ate in his hot car, then drove over to the Pottery Center to kill a little time before going back and trying again.

The modern building was light and airy, all blond oak floors and cases, and completely deserted except for a couple of women at the front desk, who collected his entrance fee and told him they'd be happy to answer any questions. He wandered through the display area, following the sound of recorded fiddle music and voices. At the far end of the hall, a television set was showing a tape about Seagrove's history and some of its more prominent potters. As he sat down to watch, he suddenly heard, ". . . who, along with

Nordan Pottery, began sending their wares all over the country. Amos Nordan, shown here with his young sons . . .".

There on old grainy film was his grandfather, a tall and sturdy young man who turned a large jar on an old-fashioned foot-powered kick wheel as two adolescent boys watched. Impossible to know which was Donald. Davis wanted to stop the tape and run it again in slow motion, but it moved on inexorably to other kilns and other potters. Yet certain of the older potteries kept being mentioned, Nordan and Hitchcock among them, and his patience was rewarded near the end when the camera lingered on old Amos's face, then moved on to "those who will carry on the Nordan tradition in Seagrove: James Lucas Nordan and his wife Sandra Kay Hitchcock Nordan, and his brother Donny Nordan."

As the camera panned across, all three looked up with self-conscious smiles and Davis caught his breath. It was almost like looking in a mirror.

For the first time since his mother had told him, he felt a sense of loss, of missed connections and missed opportunities to know a part of himself he might never know now.

The twenty-minute tape was set on automatic replay and he watched it all the way through again.

When he got back to the Nordan compound, he found a green Chevrolet now parked by the side of the main house, and this time his knock was answered by a tall, plain-faced woman whose hair flared almost straight out from around her face. "Yes?"

"I'm Davis Richmond. I thought Mr. Nordan was expecting me, but —"

"He certainly is." Using both hands, she smoothed her hair back and secured it with a large wooden clasp. "June Gregorich. I keep house for him and he's been waiting for you down at the pottery all morning."

"Oh. I didn't know. I knocked and —" He was talking to her back.

The woman was already leading the way down the slope to a pottery workshop that seemed to have been thrown together from old slab siding. At the crude door, she pulled the string latch, then stepped back to let him cross the threshold first.

Inside, he saw that the rafters were exposed beneath their tin roof and that the floor was dirt, which made sense, Davis thought, immediately noticing how clay dust lay thickly on all the surfaces.

His grandfather half-sat, half-leaned on a

high stool before a motorized turning wheel. A bare light bulb dangled overhead and shone down on the silvery hair, but cast into shadow the short person standing behind him. He looked up from the bowl he was turning and Davis was met with the full force of the old man's glare, a glare that he immediately softened into something like a smile.

"Got lost, did you?"

"Sorry," Davis said, and explained about his earlier attempt to find someone.

"No matter. You eat yet?"

"Yes, sir."

"Well, that's one thing." He looked to the woman. "You show him where he's sleeping?"

"I thought you'd want to see him first," she answered.

Using a thin draw wire, Amos cut the bowl he'd finished off the wheel head and handed it to the . . . boy? short man? . . . who carefully positioned it with a dozen others on a nearby drying rack.

Amos took another ball of clay, centered it on the wheel, and began turning. Mesmerized, Davis drew closer and watched as the clay ball magically opened and the sides curved upward.

"Don't stand there gawking," Amos said

gruffly. "Go put your stuff away and come on back and let's get started."

"I'll show you," June said.

As they stepped back outside into the warm sunshine, she pointed over to the next shed. "You can drive your car right down here if you want. Your room's upstairs."

If possible, this building looked even more dilapidated to him than the first, and after moving his car and retrieving his duffel from the trunk, Davis followed the house-keeper apprehensively into the shadowy depths of the disused workshop. A pile of cardboard shipping boxes were stacked beneath the open steps and made it look more like a storeroom than an active pottery. The large light-filled loft at the top of the stairs came as a happy surprise.

"Cool!"

"More than you know," she said dryly as she pointed out the amenities, or rather the lack of them. "There's no hot water. But you can come over to the house and shower, if you like, and you'll take your meals with us. I work around during the week and Jeffy and I aren't here for lunch some days. That was my son, by the way. Jeffy. You'll meet him when you go back. He's a little shy at times. And Bobby Gerard's around somewhere. He helps around the kiln and mixes clay."

She opened the refrigerator to show him milk and juice. "Your Aunt Betty brought over some butter and jam if you just want toast for breakfast. And if you bring your laundry over to the house, I'll run it through the machines for you. Make sure the worst of the clay's off first, though, or it'll clog the pipes. There's a spigot downstairs where you can hose off."

"Thanks, I'll try to remember that." He took a faded pair of jeans from his duffel and looked all around the loft again. "Was this where Donald — where my father lived?"

"Everybody here called him Donny," she said, "but yes, this was his place."

"What was he like?"

"You'll have to ask someone else about that," she said. "I'd only cleaned for your granddad a time or two before the accident. We probably never said more than twenty words to each other."

"I'm starting to think Nordans don't talk much," he said.

"Listen," she said, "you mustn't take it wrong if Mr. Amos acts a little short with you. He's been through a lot, you know. But he's really glad you came the other night and I think he's been looking forward to today. Now you go ahead and change and get back over there. I'll see you at supper-time. You do like pork chops, don't you?"

"Yes, ma'am!"

"Good."

Ten minutes later, wearing a heavy plastic bibbed apron, Davis stood at the wheel that had belonged to James Lucas. He had been introduced both to Jeffy Gregorich and Bobby Gerard, neither of whom had much to say. Indeed, Gerard soon disappeared out the back door, busy with chores Davis couldn't begin to name.

Amos began by showing him how to start and stop the wheel and how to adjust its speed. Jeffy watched, too, and smiled back shyly when Davis smiled at him.

"Grab that bucket over there and go fill it with water," said Amos. "Jeffy, show him where the hose pipe is."

Obediently, the little man led Davis through a side door and pointed to the hose.

"I can turn it on," he said, eager to help, and when the bucket was full, he carefully turned off the tap.

When Davis was back inside with the water, Amos had him wet the wheel head and his hands, then took a ball of clay about the size of a big orange and plopped it on the wheel as it turned at about half-speed.

"Cup your hands around it and make it into a round. That's right," he encouraged. "Now try to center it. No, just give it a little push with the edge of your hands. Remember that you're the boss. The clay's got to do what you tell it. Here, watch me again."

Davis watched, wet his hands again, and this time succeeded in centering the ball of cool smooth clay. It felt oddly sensuous as it turned beneath his hands.

"Now put your thumbs in like this and open it up."

Davis pressed in with his wet thumbs, but instead of opening up into a bowl shape, the center immediately rose up from a circular channel like a small tube cake pan.

Amos pulled his draw wire across the wheel head to free the misshapen clay and dropped it into another bucket where scrap pieces of clay waited till enough had accumulated to be reworked and wedged again.

"Waste not, want not," Amos grunted. "Clay don't come free for the digging no more."

On his fourth try, Davis managed to open the ball, but the sides collapsed before they were an inch high.

The sides stayed up on his fifth try. Unfortunately, when he drew the wire across the wheel, he discovered his bowl was all sides, no bottom.

Even Jeffy saw the humor of that one.

It took Davis nearly two hours to achieve a passable cereal bowl shape.

"That one'll do," said Amos. "Now all you got to do is practice till it feels natural. Jeffy, run up to the house and tell your ma we need some drinks down here."

Davis straightened up and flexed himself. The muscles in his hands and thumbs were sore and cramped, as were his neck and shoulders from hunching over the wheel with such intense concentration.

Amos had gone back to his own wheel and Davis watched with a new appreciation for the craft that went into such seeming effortlessness. As Amos cut the bowl free, Davis took it and added it to the drying rack. There had to be nearly a hundred bowls sitting there.

"You did all these today?"

"Ain't nothing to making cereal bowls. I used to like doing jars the best, but I just can't manage 'em anymore."

Davis had noticed the inward curve of his gnarled left hand. "Stroke?" he asked sympathetically.

"Yeah. How'd you know?"

"My grandfather — my *other* grandfather

— had a stroke and it left one of his hands like that, too. His right hand."

"Yeah? And what'd he do for a living?"

"He was a painter."

"I wouldn't want to be no painter," Amos said, reaching for another ball of clay. "Up and down ladders all day? No, thank you. If this was my right hand, I could still hold a brush or a roller, but I couldn't do no fancy trimwork."

Davis decided this was probably not the time to explain that his other grandfather had painted portraits, not houses. Instead, noticing that Amos was down to a single ball, he said, "If you'll tell me where it is, I'll get you more clay."

"Too bad we can't send you out with a washtub and a pickax," a light voice mocked from the doorway.

He turned and saw short little Jeffy clutching chilled cans of Pepsi to his chest. Behind him was that tall girl cousin, Libbet Hitchcock, with an open can in her hand.

She took a sip and said, "When Granddaddy was a boy, they used to dig all their clay off the creekbanks."

"On after I was growed, too," Amos said. "We'd take off a couple of weeks, dig out a few tons. Enough to last us all year."

"A few *tons*?"

"Son, even Libbet here can turn two hundred pounds a day if she puts her mind to it." He took the drink cans Jeffy was holding out to him and handed one to Davis.

Davis didn't need their grandfather's dry tone to understand that the subtext was, *And she's just a girl.* He glanced at Libbet, thinking of the eruption such a put-down would have brought from his sisters, but either she was too used to it to notice or she didn't care.

He popped the top on his can and drank deeply. "So where do you get your clay now?"

"Buy it dry in bags from a wholesaler, mix it, wet it, and work it up ourselves." As if reminded, he turned to the girl. "Where's Tom? I thought he was going to come pug us enough for tomorrow."

"He and Dad are out back with Bobby, checking on what's in the drying racks."

A few minutes later, the door opened again and a stocky middle-aged man stepped through, followed by a taller boy.

"Dave, this here's your uncle, Dillard Hitchcock, and your cousin, Tom," said Amos.

"Good to meet you," Davis said, holding out his hand.

Dillard Hitchcock's handshake was strong

and forthright and his eyes met Davis's easily. "Well, now, Davis. Your Aunt Betty was right. You're the spitting image of Donny."

Tom's handshake was equally strong. Almost too strong? "How's it going?"

"Okay."

Tom spotted the bowl at the end of the drying rack and picked it up. "This yours?"

" 'Fraid so. Pretty sad, isn't it?"

"Not for a first try," said Dillard.

"Yeah, he's got the knack, all right," Amos said abruptly. "He's gonna be a real Nordan."

Davis sensed that the old man didn't give praise freely and the scowls that flitted across the faces of both cousins warned him that they were not pleased by that praise.

He wasn't too pleased, either. The bowl was a piece of crap — the sides were too thick, the bottom too thin, the proportions all wrong — and it had taken him hours to get one even that good.

So how come his grandfather was trying to make him sound better than he was?

CHAPTER

19

Whole communities, including potters, are interlocked by kinship, close or distant, direct or by marriage. Wayman Cole says, "They told me they wouldn't let nobody marry into the family [in the old days] unless they promised to make pots."

— *Raised in Clay*,
Nancy Sweezy

Dill Hitchcock went back to the buffet for another helping of the Crock Pot's vegetable lasagna. He wasn't crazy about broccoli, but layered in their homemade sauce like this, he found it real tasty.

"Get anybody anything?" he asked. "Betty?"

His wife shook her head. She'd hardly eaten a bite.

"I believe I'll have some more of those barbecued ribs," Edward said, "but I'll get them, Dad."

"What about you, Dave?" Amos asked.

"Maybe a piece of pie?" Davis said.

Nancy Olson said pie sounded like a good idea and Amos agreed. "Coconut if they got it. If they don't, just bring me some of that lemon meringue."

The waitress was at their table when they returned. "Everything all right here?" she chirped as she refilled their tea glasses all around.

"Everything's just fine," Amos Nordan told her.

Like hell, thought Dill as he sat back down with his plate.

He was acutely aware that Betty was strung tighter than a fiddle string. She had really wanted today to be a family event, a coming together to welcome the addition of a nephew after the loss of her brother, and he thought he'd made it clear to the kids that they were to behave themselves and go along with her plans.

Tom and Libbet hadn't said or done anything yet that he could jump on them about, but they certainly weren't little beams of sunshine, either.

Only Edward was himself, speaking

easily to Davis, who sat on the other side of Nancy, next to Amos. Dill had a feeling that Edward's fiancée was picking up on the tension, too, but she was doing her part to keep it light. Nice girl, he thought approvingly. Of course, she was probably counting on the fact that she and Edward could leave as soon as this midday meal was over. They were keeping the sales shop open at the Rooster Clay Works today while the rest of his family helped old Amos catch up and had only met them here for lunch.

And that was another thing, thought Dill. Usually Amos was tight with his money, but today he'd insisted on taking the whole family out to the Crock Pot and treating them to lunch instead of having June fix sandwiches. He'd even had June call ahead and tell them to save him a table for eight for twelve noon, the busiest part of the day.

"You mean a table for ten," Betty had said. Although it didn't occur to anyone to invite Bobby, she was always thoughtful about including June and Jeffy.

June, however, had shaken her head. "Thanks, Betty, but not this time. I'll stay and keep the shop open. Today's a special family occasion for you folks."

Except that Amos was making it more like a political fund-raiser than a private family party.

As soon as they stepped into the place, he started introducing Davis to everybody. "This is Donny's boy. Don't he look just like Donny? Got Donny's talent, too. A new Nordan for Nordan Pottery's new millennium."

This time of day, especially on a Saturday, most of Seagrove was here at the Crock Pot and every time someone they knew stopped to say hello, Amos made a point of having them meet Davis, like he was running for mayor or something.

And there sat Tom and Libbet, looking grimmer and grimmer with each introduction.

No wonder Betty was getting so wired up. Hell, Davis seemed like a nice enough kid — caught on fast about how to weigh out the clay, help unload the bisque ware from the kiln, grind off the rough spots. He'd carried a full share of the work today without complaint, but damned if Dill could see where that made him the genius Amos was telling everybody.

Besides, fair was fair. For the last two years, Amos had made it clear that Tom was to have Nordan Pottery after James Lucas.

By the time everybody in the Crock Pot went to bed tonight, half of Randolph County would have heard that it looked like ol' Amos had changed his mind and was probably going to give it to his new grandson.

That's why, even though it was tearing Betty apart, Dill couldn't really blame Tom when he stood up and said he reckoned he'd go on back to the pottery and get to work.

"I'll go with you," Libbet said.

Amos leaned back in his chair. "Well, now, just because they're in a big hurry to get to work again, that don't mean the rest of us are." He signaled their waitress. "I believe I'd like a nice hot cup of coffee. How 'bout you, Betty? Dave?"

As Libbet and Tom started out the door, another longtime potter entered.

"Jasper!" Amos called. "Come on over here and meet my new grandson."

"Slow down!" Libbet said as Tom took the curve so fast that her braid slapped the window. "Wrecking another car won't help anything."

"He promised me!" Tom said through clenched teeth. "Dammit, Libbet, he *promised* me!"

"I know."

"I've given him weekends, nights. Whenever Uncle James Lucas needed help stacking the groundhog kilns, wasn't I right there?"

"You were," she answered loyally, bracing herself as he weaved in and out of the slower tourists that crowded these back roads on the weekend.

"God knows what I'm going to tell Brittany tonight."

He crossed the double yellow yet again and a car suddenly appeared over the crest of the hill, hurtling straight toward them.

"Tom, *look out!*"

Car horns blared, brakes screeched. At the last possible instant, he swerved around an SUV and back into his own lane, avoiding a head-on collision by mere inches.

"Sorry," he said, almost as shaken and white as she was. He took his foot off the accelerator.

"You stupid idiot!" she raged. "Nothing's worth getting killed for. *Nothing!*"

"I said I was sorry, okay?"

Libbet took a deep breath. "Okay."

But she didn't really breathe normally till they turned in at the pottery and he brought the car to a standstill beneath the tall pines down by the sheds.

Jeffy Gregorich was there, standing absolutely motionless on the board swing James Lucas had slung between a couple of the pines.

"What's wrong with the idiot now?" Tom muttered.

"Hush! Don't call him that," Libbet scolded. "What if Miss June heard you?"

"Oh, hell, Libbet. You think she don't know he's a dummy? Give it a rest."

"I mean it, Tom. And if Dad or Mom heard you —"

Jeffy spoke a single word, but so low she couldn't make it out.

She got out of the car and went closer. "What did you say, Jeffy?"

He said it again, but when she started to walk over to him, he yelled, "No, no!" and almost danced up and down on the swing, shaking the ropes. "Snake!"

She looked down and there it was on the pine needles between them, no thicker than a pencil and less than a foot long.

Libbet wasn't crazy about snakes, but she did know the difference between harmless and poisonous ones.

"It's okay, Jeffy. It's just a garter snake. It won't hurt you."

Tom had come around his side of the car to peer over her shoulder. He didn't like snakes, either, but now he stepped forward and pinned it to the ground with the toe of his boot.

"Go get me a bucket or something," he told Libbet.

"Why? What are you going to do with it?"

"Just get me the bucket, okay?"

"Okay. But Granddaddy's gonna kill us if Davis tells."

"Over a little old garter snake? Get real."

They carried the snake up to the loft and while Tom prepared his little surprise, Libbet was drawn to a sketch pad that lay open on the coffee table. There were her grandfather's unmistakable gnarled hands, drawn in strong quick lines. The hands were cupped around a lump of clay and something about the way Davis had smudged those lines gave an impression of movement so that the flat, two-dimensional drawing captured the feel of a turning wheel.

For a moment, she was almost conflicted about her hostility to the cousin who could draw like this, then Tom called from the doorway, "Come on, Libbet! I hear a car."

It had been a long day and Davis was exhausted. He hadn't realized how much there was to being a potter. It wasn't just standing at a wheel and shaping a piece of clay into an eating or drinking vessel. The clay first had

259

to be put through a pug mill and de-aired — "Used to have to knead it by hand to get all the air pockets out," his grandfather had said. Then the clay had to be sliced into precise half-pound weights. Kilns had to be unloaded, the bisque ware (he'd thought at first they were saying "biscuit" ware) had to be checked for imperfections, glazes had to be mixed from various chemicals and the bisque were dipped in, then set to dry in front of a large fan before getting a second turn through the kiln in a couple of days.

To Davis's surprise, when the Hitchcocks arrived this morning, his Aunt Betty turned out to be the potter and Uncle Dill was her gofer. She had gone straight to her brother's old wheel, set the jigs so that she could work her way back into the right proportions, and began turning mugs with no fuss or big production. Even though she wasn't quite as tall as James Lucas had been, she'd smiled and said it still felt familiar. "Remember, Dad?"

"Yeah. You used to sneak down here every time his back was turned and try it out till we finally got tired of it and gave you your own wheel when you were, what? Ten? Twelve?"

"Eleven," she'd said.

Tom had planned to work Donny's old

wheel, but Hitchcock pottery was proportioned just enough differently from Nordan that he couldn't seem to get the jigs to work right and Libbet had soon taken over. Freed from the wheel, Tom had gone to pulling handles for the mugs and moved back and forth between the two sheds, keeping them caught up.

With June minding the sales shop, the three younger men had kept hopping with all the support work, since Bobby hadn't come back after lunch.

"When are you going to fire his sorry tail?" Betty had asked. "You can count on Jeffy better than you can count on him."

Davis knew he should call his mother, let her know everything was okay and that nobody had taken any real shots at him. *Although*, he told himself, thinking of Libbet and her brother, *if looks could kill* . . . But he was too tired to go back to the main house.

He stripped off to shower, remembered that there was only cold water, hesitated, and then said to hell with it and stepped in. The night was so warm that it wasn't too bad, but he certainly didn't linger beneath the spray.

He dried off, hung the towel over the curtain rod, then padded barefooted over to the bed, which was looking better and better to him even though it was only nine o'clock. Sliding a CD into his portable player, he pulled back the covers and got under.

Just as he reached over to turn off the light, something moved under his bare leg, and before he could react, he felt it wrap around his ankle.

Davis yelped and jerked back his legs. Player and covers went flying and the lamp and table beside the bed crashed over as involuntary primeval survival instincts kicked in. He fell to the floor in time to see the snake wriggle under the sheet at the foot of the bed, leaving just a tail tip exposed.

"Bastard!" he snarled out loud. "You asshole bastard!"

Almost immediately he was struck by the wry humor in his choice of terms. Whatever else he might be, Tom Hitchcock wasn't exactly the real bastard of the week. Thank God he wasn't here. As Davis righted the table and lamp, he ruefully admitted that his reaction to the snake must have been everything Tom had hoped for.

Which was ironic, considering that he'd had pet garter snakes from the time he was six till he went away to summer camp, where (warned by his sisters) he'd disappointed his cabin mates by making friends with the one they'd put in his bunk.

He hauled the frightened snake out from its hiding place and held it up for closer inspection. It wrapped around his wrist and flicked its small tongue impotently.

"Sorry, little guy," he said softly, "but I've got another job for you."

CHAPTER

20

Each of these labels, in their various ways, conveyed a special meaning or identity to the purchaser and it became important to mark it on every piece of pottery. [One potter] never stamped his wares, though occasionally, on special request, he might incise his name on a jug with a nail or a sharp stick.

— *Turners and Burners,*
Charles G. Zug III

Saturday was breezy and sunny, great for cleaning house, doing laundry, catching up with some yardwork, and just hanging out. In fact, the evening was so fine that a bunch of us — Portland and Avery Brewer included — drove over to Durham to watch the Bulls play the Toledo Mud Hens. Portland had gotten over her early-pregnancy nausea and was now into competitive eating. She downed hot dogs, root beer, peanuts, and pizza slices at the stadium, where the Bulls lost 4–2, and then she wanted to stop for hot Krispy Kreme doughnuts on the way home.

"Anything that doesn't eat her first," Avery sighed.

With nothing planned for Sunday I slept in, and by Sunday afternoon, I found myself lonely and just a little bored. I was too restless to settle into a book, yet I wasn't in the mood to socialize with any of my brothers or their families, so when the phone rang, I let my machine take it. As soon as I heard Jenny McAllister's voice, though, I picked up.

"Oh, Deborah, you're there. Good."

She told me that she'd finally heard from her son. Sounded as if he'd called about three minutes before she was ready to send out a search party. He had described his quarters, the pottery workshops, the kilns, the people, and how he'd spent Friday night looking through old photograph albums of his newfound biological family.

"He *says* everything's fine," she told me. "Says it's a lot like summer camp and he's learning more than he ever wanted to know about throwing pots."

"But?"

"But something," she agreed. "He won't tell me what, though. Just kept saying it wasn't anything he couldn't handle. He's a painter, not a potter, Deborah. He's really talented with a brush or drawing pencil, but he's never had much aptitude for three-dimensional arts or crafts of any kind, yet Donald's father sounds like he's trying to brainwash him into thinking he's a natural. I'll be glad when you get over there."

I wasn't due to hear the Sanderson trial till Tuesday, but I'd already scheduled a day of personal leave on Monday to get my hair cut and have my eyes examined. (Till now, reading glasses from the drugstore have worked just fine. Lately though, I've caught myself holding papers and books further away than usual.) Fortunately, there was nothing urgent about either, and yes, poking my nose into the Seagrove situation sounded like a much more interesting way to spend the day.

"Let me make a couple of phone calls," I told her.

"Impose? Don't be silly," Fliss said when I asked if I could come back earlier than I'd expected. "I have plans for dinner tonight,

266

but I'm sure they'd love to have you, too."

"Don't bother," I told her. "I may have plans, too."

"Oh?"

"I'll tell you when I get there. Has Connor Woodall arrested anybody for the Nordan murder yet?"

"No, but something interesting's happened. Remember I told you that James Lucas's brother had an illegitimate child?"

"Yes."

"Well, the boy's turned up and now everybody's saying he's going to change his name to Nordan and that Amos is going to give the pottery to him."

"Really?" I knew from Jenny McAllister that her son Davis didn't go to Seagrove till day before yesterday. And Fliss had already heard this much about him? "I thought one of his daughter's sons — one of the Hitchcock boys —"

"Tom," she said, supplying the name I'd forgotten.

"I thought he was supposed to get it."

"So did he," she said dryly.

I told her I couldn't wait to hear all the details and that I'd be over in about three hours.

I left cancellation messages on the machines at the Cut 'n' Curl and the optometrist. Next I rooted out the business card that Will Blackstone had given me. I tried both his office and his home but got answering machines both places. Well, it was unrealistic to think that such a good-looking man would be sitting by his phone, waiting for my call, on this beautiful Sunday afternoon. I hung up without leaving a message on either machine, threw some clothes in my overnight bag, stuck a couple of dresses and my robe in a garment bag, then headed west.

As a change from Highway 64, I took two-lane back-country roads and came into Seagrove from the southeast, through Carthage instead Asheboro. I never drive that route without wondering about the lofty aspirations of those earlier citizens who earnestly named their settlements Macedonia, Carthage, Samarcand, or Troy. (When I mentioned it to her once, Fliss reminded me that one can also travel around that area from Jugtown to Whynot to Erect to Climax with less lofty aspirations.)

Since I'd made better time than I expected and Nordan Pottery was right on my way to Fliss's house, I decided to swing past, introduce myself to Davis Richmond. And yes, despite what I'd promised Dwight about minding my own business, I was curious to learn if there was anything new on James Lucas's death. Besides, I was minding my own business. Jenny McAllister had made it mine, hadn't she?

June Gregorich was tending the shop when I walked in. It was busy with customers, but she had time to give me a smile of welcome. "Oh, do you know Davis?"

"His mother and I are old friends," I said. (It sometimes worries me how glibly I can lie about things.) "Haven't seen him in so long, though, that I probably won't recognize him. Jenny says he's grown at least a foot. How's he settling in here?"

"Fine, so far as I know. Of course, I haven't seen much of him yet except at meals. Mr. Amos has kept him pretty busy since he got here Friday."

I watched her wrap a pair of purple candlesticks in newspapers and place them in a brown paper grocery bag. The next customer wanted to buy four place settings of the gray-and-purple ware and was dismayed when June explained that they weren't set up for credit cards.

"But I don't have my checkbook with me," she wailed, and went off to see if her friends had more cash on them than she did.

In the lull, June told me that Davis was

probably down at the main pottery shed, "but if he's not there, try calling up the steps at the one next to it. He's staying in Donny's old loft."

"Oh, is the pottery open today?" asked a man who came up behind me with a cardinal red vase in his hands.

"No, I'm sorry," June told him. "Mr. Nordan doesn't do any turning on Sundays."

I went out the back door, just as I had followed Sandra Kay a week and a half ago. As warm as the weather had been lately, the azaleas and rhododendrons had started to fade a little and dogwood petals lay on the pine straw like random snowflakes. A little ways down the slope, I saw June's son Jeffy poking at something with a long stick. It was a small garter snake. A small dead garter snake.

"See th' snake," he told me in his thick-tongued speech. "Tom an' Libbet, they caught him yesterday. Tom killed it."

Naturalists can preach till they're blue in the face about the vital role snakes play in the ecology. Most of the people I know are still going to grab a hoe as soon as they see one and chop it in half. This harmless little snake seemed to have had its head stomped to a bloody pulp.

Two white Toyotas, both almost equally banged and dented, and a shiny little red Sunfire were parked within a few feet of each other down by the shed. When I pulled the latch and opened the door, I found two teenagers. A tall, unfamiliar youth and a very pretty, very blond girl were working at an electric grinder. They seemed to be taking the rough spots off the bottoms of a table full of purple-and-gray lidded jars.

"Sorry," the boy said, giving me a less-than-welcoming stare. "This building isn't open today."

"Are you Davis?" I asked tentatively.

For some reason that seemed to make him scowl even more. "No, I'm not. I'm Tom. Tom Hitchcock."

So this was the dispossessed grandson. Also the nephew whose whereabouts his Aunt Sandra Kay had questioned the day James Lucas died.

I stepped across the threshold. "I'm Deborah Knott. I was here when your uncle was found."

"You're the lady judge?" the girl exclaimed.

I nodded.

"Cool! I thought you'd be older." She wiped her dusty hand on the back of her jeans and held it out. "I'm Brittany Simmons.

271

What's it like being a judge?"

"I think it's pretty cool, too," I admitted.

"How come you asking about Davis?" Tom asked abruptly.

Again, I ran through my tale that he was the son of an old friend and how I thought I'd look him up while I was here since I hadn't seen him in so long.

"He's gone over to the Rooster Clay with Tom's mother," Brittany said. "She had some pictures she wanted to give him. I'm sure it'd be okay if you went over, too, right, Tom?"

He gave a truculent nod. "And if you see him, tell him I'm going to beat the shit out of him when he comes back."

"Tom!" She looked at me apologetically. "He doesn't mean that."

"The hell I don't!"

"You know good and well he thought you'd be the one to find it. He left before I got here, remember? Even you didn't know I was coming here this afternoon."

"What happened?" I asked.

"Nothing," he snapped.

"Davis," she said, in that patronizing woman-to-woman voice meant to chasten any males within hearing distance. "He put a snake in one of these jars. I guess he thought he'd scare Tom. When I picked up the vase just now and turned it over to start grinding, the snake fell in my lap, nearly gave me a heart attack. It's a wonder I didn't break more than two pieces trying to get it off me."

Tom made a low growling sound, very like a dog about to lunge.

"How do you know it was Davis?" I asked, trying for logic.

Brittany rolled her eyes. "Because Einstein here put it in his bed last night."

I had to smile. So that's what Jeffy meant when he said Tom and Libbet caught it yesterday.

"Sounds like you two are even, then," I told Tom.

From the glare I got as I left, it was clear he didn't agree.

I walked back up the slope to my car. The garter snake still lay beside the path, making Sunday dinner for the flies and ants that had found it. There was no sign of Jeffy until I rounded the shop and saw him swinging on the front porch. As I got in my car, he waved goodbye and cheerfully called out something that sounded like, "Come see us again."

I waved back, thinking how unfair life was for some people. Yet, if June Gregorich had to have a mentally handicapped son, she was lucky that he'd been born with such a sunny, friendly disposition.

The pragmatist who lives inside my head nodded in agreement. *Think if he had Tom Hitchcock's surliness.*

On the other hand, said the preacher who shares headroom with him, *that Brittany seems to have her head on straight and they are spending this beautiful Sunday afternoon working for his grandfather, aren't they?*

Maybe they're just taking care of business, looking after their own interests, said the pragmatist, forever the cynic.

Not being familiar with the lane that was supposed to lead over the rise to the Rooster Clay Works, I took the highway around, turning left onto Felton Creek Road, then looking for the big glazed rooster that marks the entrance to their drive. Unfortunately, tendrils of scarlet honeysuckle had twined themselves around the rooster's neck and I didn't spot it till I'd run past. I pulled in at the next drive to turn around and go back and realized that the woman out picking daffodils was Sandra Kay Nordan.

She recognized me at the same instant and came over to the car with a surprised look on her face. "Well, hey, Judge! I didn't expect to see you again so soon."

"I didn't expect it myself," I said, drinking in the beauty of her yard.

Azaleas, lilacs, and rhododendrons were shaded by mature dogwoods, which in turn were sheltered by a high canopy of tall pines. The house might be a double-wide, but it was dark brown with a peaked roof of brown shingles and it had been customized with screened-in porches and a deck weathered to the same brown shade. It nestled into its setting like the stump of an old oak and one end was covered with scarlet honeysuckle and yellow jasmine. A border of purple tulips and golden buttercups lined the drive and the deck was brightened with large earthenware pots filled with geraniums and ivy.

I switched off the car and got out for a closer look. "How on earth did you get it looking like this in only two years?"

Unlike this color spread out of *Southern Living* that she had achieved, my own yard still looked a lot like the field it had been until last year.

"I wish I could say it was all my doing," she said, "but it was really Uncle Dooley's. Not that he was any kin, we young'uns just called him that. He was sort of like Bobby Gerard, only more reliable. Used to help my daddy burn his pots back when that meant cutting wood and feeding the firebox to keep the kiln at a steady heat. That was right after the war when cash money was so hard to come by around these parts. Daddy put him a little house here and let him live in it free. He dug dogwoods and redbuds out of the woods and planted most of the bushes. After he died, the house sort of went downhill and the roof fell in. This was the part my daddy willed to me." The sweep of her hand took in a couple of acres surrounding the house. "When I left James Lucas, I got the old house cleared away and pulled my trailer right in where it'd been. Only had to cut one pine and two redbuds. Once I got all the vines and brambles cleared out, I found the azaleas and rhododendrons were still living."

Up close, I saw that her eyes were bloodshot and her nose was red as if she'd been crying.

"But we don't need to stand out here in the sun," she said. "Come on in and let me get you something to drink."

"Actually, I was on my way to find a friend at your brother's place," I said.

"Oh, surely you have time for a glass of lemonade?" she insisted. "Besides, I want to show you what I've done with our collection."

"Collection?" Back at Nordan Pottery, I hadn't noticed the disputed collection or even thought to check whether it was still there.

"I sat down and had a good talk with Betty, James Lucas's sister. She's also my brother's wife, I guess you know?"

I nodded.

Sandra Kay opened the screen door, then led me across the porch and into the house. Inside was a little too dark and too consciously rustic for my tastes — the brown leather furniture she and James Lucas had fought over, dark oak chests, iron tools as wall ornaments, and lots of baskets and earth-toned pots as accent pieces. Water was waiting in the one on the coffee table and she filled it with the daffodils she'd picked.

"Betty admitted that Amos didn't care a dogged bit about collecting and she doesn't, either, really," she said, ushering me down a short hallway hung with black-and-white photographs from the twenties and thirties of area potters at their wheels or kilns. "They just didn't want me getting it all. 'Well,' I told her, 'who do you think's going to get my part after I die?' I don't think Betty'd ever really thought about how everything I have will go to her children. So she talked to Amos and they're going to give the Pottery Center the pieces that came from his family and I've signed a paper that when I'm dead, all the rest of it will go there, too. They're going to call it the Hitchcock-Nordan collection. In the meantime . . ."

She opened a door and switched on the lights. "What do you think?"

"Wow!" I said, impressed.

"Well," she said modestly, "it's not like as if I haven't been planning this since the day I moved in."

The second and third bedrooms at this end of the double-wide had been opened into each other with a wide archway. Glass cases with multilevel stands held the collection and baby spots in the ceiling accented colors and shapes. It was like an intimate little corner of the Pottery Center.

"I went over and got the last of it a couple of hours ago when the shop opened up," Sandra Kay said as I marveled over the great job she'd done. "And I've still got to make labels for everything."

Tears glistened in her eyes.

"Is something wrong?" I asked.

She shook her head even as she pulled a tissue from her pocket and blew her nose. "I guess everything's just starting to hit me. Bringing the rest of the pots over and unboxing them made me remember how much fun the two of us used to have when we'd go to auctions and then come home to unpack what we'd bought and enter it on the computer. I still miss that."

"You had a long history together," I said, thinking of my short history with Kidd.

"And not all of it great." She took a deep breath. "Let's get you that lemonade."

As we turned to go, I paused in front of a place setting of cardinal ware and said, "My sister-in-law would give anything for a piece of that for her own collection."

"Oh?"

"When she was over here last year, she tried to buy a bowl or mug out of that display of the old original stuff at the front of the shop. June told her that they occasionally sell an antique piece but that she wasn't authorized to and that Amos and James Lucas were out of town."

"I remember you mentioned something about that the day he got killed." She hesitated. "You like your sister-in-law a lot, don't you?"

When I explained that I'd had about fifteen sisters-in-law over the years and that Karen was one of the best, she said, "How would you like to get her a whole place setting?"

"How much?" I asked warily. I only keep about five hundred in my checking account at a time.

"No charge," she said. "I do you a favor, maybe you'll do one for me?"

"What sort of favor?"

"Nothing to do with you being a judge," she assured me, correctly reading my cautious question. "I heard that you're an old friend of Connor Woodall's?"

"He was in school with my brothers, but I hadn't seen him in years till I met him again over here."

"He was out to see me yesterday," she said, using the edge of her shirt to wipe a finger smudge off one of the cases. "He thinks I killed James Lucas."

"Oh, surely not," I murmured inanely. I mean, what do you say to something like that?

"June told him it was my car that went through the lane after James Lucas went down to the kiln."

"Was it?" I asked bluntly.

Her eyes darted away. "No, of course not."

"Because if it was," I said carefully, "and if you didn't have anything to do with putting him in that kiln, you might be able to say whether you saw anyone else in the lane, or if you noticed anything in your rearview mirror."

She shook her head in exasperation. "But I didn't see a —"

Appalled, she clapped her fingers over her mouth and looked as guilty as an egg-sucking hound caught in the henhouse.

"For Pete's sake, Sandra Kay, why didn't you just tell Connor?"

"Because it puts me right there at the right time. But I didn't do it, Deborah. I swear to Almighty God, I didn't! I think the only thing that's holding him back is that he can't find a reason why I'd want James Lucas dead. The divorce was final. We'd divided everything except the collection. I'm not going to say there weren't times before the divorce when I could have cheerfully strangled him, but that was over two years ago."

"Connor and I saw you two fighting in the Crock Pot just last week," I reminded her.

She sighed. "So did half of Seagrove. He didn't want to talk serious about dividing our pots and he dragged up all that old mess about Donny and me, like those lies would make me change my mind. He wanted all the best pieces, and dogged if I was going to let him get away with that. But once we got to court and you told us how it was going to be, there was nothing left to fight about."

By now we had moved to her spotless kitchen and she poured us each a glass of lemonade, which we took out onto the screened porch.

"So you did drive through the lane at lunchtime?"

"Yes," she admitted. "I didn't mean to, but it's such a habit that the car just turned in before I realized what I'd done. I didn't see a soul, though. Course, I wasn't looking for anybody, either."

"But why lie about it when June asked you? That was before we even knew James Lucas had been killed."

She looked embarrassed and took a sip of her lemonade to cover it. "Because she was there when he yelled at me last month and told me he was going to put a chain up if I kept driving through his yard and I got mad and swore I'd drive my car off Felton Creek bridge before I'd ever use that dogged lane again. And really, that was the first time since then. By the time I realized where I was, I figured that if James Lucas said anything, I'd lie through my teeth and tell him it must've Betty or Tom. Both of them drive white cars, too. Then after we found him, I realized that if I said I'd been anywhere near that kiln, they'd think I was the one that killed him."

Leaning over to clasp my hand in hers, she said, "Please, Deborah. You're a judge. You've known Lieutenant Woodall for years. He'll listen to you if you tell him I couldn't have done it. Please?"

"But surely you must know him better than I do?"

She shook her head. "I knew who he was, of course — his wife's a potter — but the only time I ever talked to him was when Donny died."

"The best way to convince him you're innocent is to tell him the truth yourself," I said.

But she was adamant. "Soon as he knows for sure I was there, he'll quit looking for anybody else. And that's what so dogged bad. There's *not* anybody else."

"Nobody gains anything at all with him gone?"

"Well, Tom, I suppose. He wants to quit school, get married, and set up on his own, but James Lucas would've let him come, long as Tom knew who was boss. They didn't always see eye to eye — too near alike, I always said. Tom can be cocky and James Lucas was as pigheaded as they come. Tom would've had to take orders with James Lucas alive and he still will till Amos dies or deeds it over to him." She gave a rueful shake of her head. "Now, if it was Amos that got himself killed, you could throw a rock and hit a dozen people that he's done dirt to over the years. The only really wrong thing James Lucas ever did was to keep making —"

I almost had to smile. If she couldn't keep herself from blurting out things better left unsaid, it was no wonder she didn't want to face Connor.

"Look," she said, "can you keep a secret?"

"If it's personal and not criminal."

"I don't know about criminal," she said dubiously. "You said your sister-in-law wanted a piece of Amos's old red dinnerware, right?"

"Yes."

"Well, there isn't any."

"You mean except for those few pieces in the shop."

She brushed my words aside. "Not even those. The only authentic pieces left are what's on my shelves inside and three pieces that Betty still has on her mantelpiece. That money-grubbing old man sold off every single one of the real pieces years ago. The government closed the line down about thirty years ago because of the lead content. People knew the dangers before then and most potters had quit using the heavy-metal glazes, but Nordan Pottery was famous for its cardinal red and lead's the only thing that'll give that clear bright color, so he and the boys kept on making coffee cups and soup mugs right up till the end, even though studies had shown that things like juice and soup or tea or coffee can leach the lead out even faster. Ever since the rules changed, the only things he can use his red glaze on have to be purely decorative, and even those have to be labeled that they're not for food."

She gazed out over the bright bushes blooming beyond the screen. "Well, you know how collectors are. Tell them there's going to be no more of something and it drives up the prices. Amos still had a few cartons on hand that he wasn't allowed to ship. When people came around asking, he put the warning labels on the bottom of the pieces and charged them double, then triple, until finally, a cup that was made to sell for fifty cents was going for fifty dollars. Even at those prices, the cartons were empty after a couple of years."

"So I'm guessing he made more?"

"He wasn't the first one in Seagrove and I bet he's not the last. There's some famous potters been dead ten years or more, yet stuff is still being sold with their names or their marks on it. Every two or three years, James Lucas and Donny and Amos would fill up one of the groundhog kilns and burn enough to dole out piece by piece like it was the last of the old. Donny was real good about sizing up a collector. They never sold any of the display. No, Donny would walk you down to his shed, flirting with you if you were a woman or talking about his poor old dad's craftsmanship if you were a man. He'd almost whisper to you about how he'd saved out a few good pieces over the years and how he wouldn't offer them to just anybody, but since you were so interested and knew so much about Nordan Pottery's history, he had a feeling in his heart that you would appreciate the piece and give it a good home."

I had to smile. "Sounds like my brother Will."

"He was good," Sandra Kay conceded. "He once sold a platter for twelve hundred dollars that was so fresh out of the kiln, it was still almost warm."

I glanced at my watch. Her mention of Donny reminded me that I'd been on my way to find Davis Richmond nearly an hour ago.

"Anyhow," Sandra Kay said, "unless you tell your sister-in-law, there's no reason she couldn't be happy with some of the counter-feit pieces."

"There's no way to tell the new from the old?"

Sandra Kay's lips quirked in a wry smile. "Actually, there is. Amos's father had made a metal stamp for stamping the bottom of all their ware. Wait a minute. I'll show you."

She darted inside and soon returned with one of the red plates. There on the back was a small triangle with an NP incised in the middle.

"When the FDA people told Amos he couldn't make any more cardinal ware, he got so mad he stomped on the stamp and said that was the end of Nordan Pottery. After that, they just scratched an np on the bottom. But when they sneaked and started making more of the cardinal ware, they had to have the stamp. Donny and James Lucas straightened it out the best they could, but if you look real close, the left corner of the tri-angle is squeezed a little" — she made a pinching motion with her thumb and index finger over the mark — "and that makes the left side tilt just a hair off center."

So this was the secret she'd threatened James Lucas with at the Crock Pot that first evening? Unethical and dishonest, yes, but "filthy"?

"I think Karen would be suspicious with a whole place setting," I said. "Maybe just a plate or mug."

"Then you'll talk to Connor Woodall for me?"

"I was planning to see him tomorrow anyhow, but I really think he needs to hear the truth."

"Okay," she said finally. "Only, could you do it for me? Make him understand why I lied about it?"

That was something I could agree to and we left it that I'd call her the next day.

CHAPTER

21

[The potter] then wedged the clean clay to beat air out of it. . . . Each half is thrown down hard, one on top the other, onto the board. Cutting and slamming is repeated in a rapid, rhythmical way, a dozen or more times, forcing tiny air pockets to break.

— *Raised in Clay*,
Nancy Sweezy

A fairly new white sedan was parked next to an older white van at the back of Rooster Clay Works, which was closed all day on Sundays. The Hitchcocks were sitting on their deck when I drove up and there were open boxes of photographs on the glass-topped table.

I had met Dillard Hitchcock the day of the murder and now he introduced me to his wife. Both were interested to hear that I knew her newly discovered nephew and said that the boy had left for Nordan Pottery about twenty minutes ago.

"He's probably there by now," said Betty Hitchcock. "I offered to run him back over, but he said he needed the exercise."

She gave me directions on which forks to take through the back lanes and over the low ridge and she warned me to mind the pot-holes through the bottom.

"You really need to dump some more gravel along there, Dill. After all the ice we had this winter?"

"I'll see about ordering it the end of the week," he replied.

If I hadn't already heard that she was the better potter and that he did most of the glazing and firing, I would have guessed the other way around. He seemed to have the quiet, steady patience exuded by most of the potters I'd met, while she came across as edgier. Too, her hand when she shook mine felt limp and soft. His was firm and strong. But the sidelong glance he gave her let me know who held the balance of power here. He was acutely aware of her every movement.

The romantic preacher in my head sighed. *Wonder if you'll ever find such devotion?*

And just as quickly, my cynical pragmatist asked, *Wouldn't it get a little tiring to be adored that obviously for thirty years?*

Not something you're liable to find out for yourself, the preacher said acidly.

"Davis hasn't said much about his mother's side," Betty told me. "Is she in law, too?"

"Oh, no." I smiled pleasantly and edged for my car. Whatever Davis's reasons for reticence, I didn't think it was my place to tell them that his mother was as well known in her field as they were in theirs. "She's a lovely woman, though."

"Well, she seems to have done a fine job with Davis. I just hope he and my children can become friends."

Thinking of Tom's hostility, I figured that would probably happen about the time the devil ordered ice skates, but I just smiled and said, "Well, I've hindered y'all long enough. Better go see if I can find him."

The lane was in even poorer condition than I'd expected and I was forced to creep along slowly. There was no sign of Davis Richmond. Either he'd jogged back or had left longer ago than the Hitchcocks thought. The lane eventually circled around the end of the car kiln shelter. As I passed the bushes, I was startled to see Davis and Tom rolling on the ground in front of the workshop. Fists were flying and bright red blood stained both torn shirts as they pummeled each other.

As I jumped out of my car, I could hear Brittany screaming, "Stop it! Stop it!"

But her screams were almost drowned out by Jeffy's loud sustained squall. He seemed terrified by the violence of the fight and his cries brought June running from the shop. Several customers craned their necks from the doorway to see what all the excitement was and here came Amos, pushing past them and clearing a path with his walking stick.

While Brittany yelled at them to stop fighting, June caught Jeffy in her arms and tried to soothe him and Amos waded in and started whacking with his cane.

Tom Hitchcock came up out of the dirt with a roar and clenched fists and in his anger, he almost hit his grandfather till he saw who it was. One eye was already swelling, his knuckles were skinned, and his ear was bright red.

"You stupid-ass shithead," Amos shouted. "What the hell you doing?"

"Getting the hell out of here," Tom shouted back, equally enraged. He gave Davis's leg such a vicious kick that the other boy fell down again, clutching himself in pain. "You want to give him the pottery? Fine! The hell with it and the hell with you!"

Ignoring Brittany's outstretched hand, he ran over to his car, jumped in, and tore out of the yard.

"Fool, fool, *fool!*" Brittany muttered, and hurried to her Sunfire.

Tom had already cleared the top of the drive and barely touched his brakes as he hurtled onto the highway. There was no way he could have checked for oncoming traffic. A moment later, Brittany followed, driving almost as recklessly in her effort to catch up with him.

Amos watched helplessly till they were out of sight, then looked down at Davis, who was still sitting on the ground, exhausted.

"You okay?" he asked.

"Sure," Davis said gamely.

Right.

Blood still trickled from his nose and a cut on his lip, and from the way he was rubbing his leg where Tom had kicked him, I knew he was going to have a huge bruise there, if not a chipped bone.

"Who started it?" Amos said.

Davis gave a weary shrug. "What difference does it make?"

"He always did have a hot temper. Got it from me, I reckon," the old man said as he turned to June and Jeffy, whose frightened wails had now tapered off into breathy sobs punctuated by hiccups. "Can't you make him quit sniveling?"

He waved his cane testily at the gapers up at the shop. "What are y'all gawking at? Show's over."

Then, leaning heavily on his cane, he hobbled toward his house without even a backward glace at his bleeding grandson.

June wiped Jeffy's face with a handkerchief from the pocket of her denim skirt and shepherded him back toward the shop.

I reached down a hand and helped Davis stand.

"Thanks," he said stiffly, and headed toward the shed next door.

I followed him through the door and up the open steps.

He didn't realize I was there till I said, "Is there any ice in that little refrigerator or should I go find some at your grandfather's house?"

"Huh?" Davis stared at me punchily.

"I'm Deborah Knott," I told him briskly. "An old friend of your mother's. You haven't seen me in ages, but she told me you were over here."

There was a bathroom beyond the far partition and I found washcloths. I wet one and brought it out to him. While he cleaned the blood from his face, I discovered that the single ice tray was empty, so I hurried downstairs and over to Amos Nordan's house. With the back door open and the screen unlatched, I walked right in without knocking and opened the refrigerator and took out an ice tray. I didn't want to go rummaging in Nordan's cabinets, but one of those large counterfeit red mugs sat on the wide window ledge over the sink beside a small ruby-red glass pyramid on a mirrored base. It glowed in the afternoon sun. Strings of crystals hung from the window casing and little rainbows rippled across the ceiling with every small breeze. Outside the screen was a set of bamboo wind chimes that softly clacked in soothing tones — touches of California New Age here on a back road of North Carolina.

I filled the mug with ice cubes and carried it back to the potting shed loft. There, I wrapped some of the ice cubes in a clean dish towel and pounded them with a knife handle until they were crushed enough to serve as a makeshift ice pack.

"That lip needs stitching and for all you know, your nose may be broken or you might have a concussion," I said. "Come on and I'll take you to the emergency room."

"Look, Ms. Knott —"

"Judge Knott," I corrected him. "I'm a judge. And you can come with me or you can wait and go with your mother when she gets here after I call her."

He grimaced as he tried to smile. "Isn't it against the law for judges to blackmail people?"

"Absolutely," I said. "But if you won't tell, I won't, either."

CHAPTER

22

The cemetery seems an unlikely home for the works of the potter, but . . . there remains solid evidence that he produced a variety of grave markers. . . . This was an inexpensive but relatively permanent method of marking a grave.

— *Turners and Burners*,
Charles G. Zug III

The speedometer went from forty-five to fifty, to sixty, seventy, and was edging eighty when Tom skimmed over a low rise and saw that both lanes of this winding road were blocked up ahead.

No room to pass on the left and no time to slow down enough to avoid rear-ending the Crown Victoria in front of him. He floored the accelerator and cut sharply to the right to squeeze by on the shoulder. He was dimly aware of some object shifting on the floor beneath his seat, but adrenaline instantly washed it away as his front right fender clipped a mailbox before he could whip the car back into the now-empty lane.

From behind him now, the Crown Victoria's horn blared in futile protest and Tom raised his fist in reply, his third finger doing all the talking as he zoomed forward.

Still, the incident made him ease off on the gas till the speedometer dropped back to just under seventy, which was still twenty miles over the limit along this stretch of highway.

Rage churned through his body in physical waves that twisted his guts and shortened his breath to ragged gasps for air. His head and eye throbbed from the pounding they'd taken.

Confused thoughts raced through his mind faster than his speeding wheels:

Bastard was asking for it scaring Brittany like that — arrogant prick, who does he think he is, coming in, acting like he already owns the place, and Jesus! but it hurt like hell when that lucky blow landed on my ear, and who'd have thought a wimpy-looking faggot like him could give it back like that?

While Granddad — my own Granddad. . . .

That was it, of course. Beneath his conscious thoughts, over and over, like an endless loop, his anger and pain circled back to its roots: *He promised. Goddammit, he promised!*

The speedometer began to creep up again as he took a curve dangerously fast.

And what is it that keeps shifting down there?

An unmarked highway patrol car met and passed him in the other lane, registered the Toyota's speed, and started looking for a turnaround spot, but Tom never noticed because he'd leaned over to feel around on the floor beneath him. His groping fingers felt something ropelike and flexible and —

Holy shit!

He jerked his hand back, but it was too late.

His prodding had so disturbed the black snake hiding there that it oozed away from his hand and came up between the two seats. Its body was half as thick as Tom's wrist and its blunt head swayed back and forth as it searched for escape.

Fighting panic, Tom jerked away from it in an automatic reflex and the steering wheel followed his motion straight into the path of an eighteen-wheeler.

The truck jackknifed as the driver slammed on his brakes and swerved to avoid the head-on collision.

The Toyota crashed into the truck's right bumper and was flipped end over end into a stand of cedars on the other side of the ditch.

Pulled off balance by the weight of its load, the cab of the rig tottered, swayed, almost fell over, then slammed down four-square on its tires. The driver immediately snapped the release on his seat belt, swung down from the door, then raced for the smashed Toyota just as the patrol car pulled onto the shoulder, siren wailing, blue lights flashing.

"I swear to God he turned right in front of me!" the driver cried hoarsely. "He must've been doing seventy. I couldn't miss him."

"More like eighty," the trooper said, realizing the man was almost in shock. "I was clocking him."

Just as they reached the smashed car, they saw something move inside, then the black snake began to crawl through the broken window. It bled from a ragged gash in its side.

"Goddamn!" the trucker yelped, and jumped back.

Almost automatically, the trooper pulled his pistol and dispatched the creature with one shot.

"I hate snakes," he said, and kicked its carcass into the ditch.

CHAPTER

23

An earthy, canny, and sometimes rollicking perception of human frailties and foibles has served Southerners with grace through hard times.

— Raised in Clay,
Nancy Sweezy

Driving Davis Richmond to Randolph Hospital was like driving one of my nephews someplace they didn't want to go, only he had to be more polite about it since we're not kin. That means he sulked a little; but because he thought I was his mom's good friend, he couldn't tell me to butt out.

We brought along the extra ice cubes and I made him keep the cold pack on his nose and lips. The backs of his knuckles were also skinned, but those were minor abrasions compared to his face. A rather nice-looking face, too, now that the blood was all washed off.

From practice with my nephews, I've become rather good at asking questions that require more than a yes or no answer. (As a rule, my nieces are easier to get talking. The trouble with girls, though, is, if they don't want you to know something, they'll overwhelm you with more verbiage than you can easily process.)

It wasn't long before Davis had told me all about the garter snake, how it first appeared in his bed and how he'd put it in one of the jars he knew Tom would be grinding today.

"I wouldn't have done it if I'd known his girlfriend was going to be the one to find it," he assured me.

"You don't find all this just a little adolescent?" If I was going to be his surrogate aunt, I felt obliged to point out the error of his ways. "You guys are, what? Eighteen? Nineteen?"

"Nineteen," he muttered.

"This is the sort of thing I see in juvenile court all the time. And it just keeps escalating. He disses you, you diss him, and the next thing you know, one of you'll be standing in front of a judge trying to explain how the other deserved to get shot or stabbed."

He glowered. "So it's okay for him to try and scare me but not vice versa?"

"I'm not saying what he did was okay, but you should have been the adult there. Besides," I said with a grin, "if you hadn't said or done a thing, it would have driven him crazy not knowing if he'd got you."

I let him think about that a minute, then asked how the other family members were responding to him.

He allowed as how his aunt and uncle seemed nice. "And Edward and his girl Nancy are okay with me being here, but Tom and Libbet act like I'm doing something wrong just by breathing the same air."

"Well, you can't really blame them. Rumors are going 'round that your grandfather had promised to leave the pottery to Tom, but that now he's thinking of leaving it to you."

"Me? That's crazy! I'm no potter," he said, echoing Jenny McAllister's own assessment.

"That's not what Amos Nordan's telling everybody."

"Yeah? Well, have any of those rumors going 'round said that he might be senile?"

His question was so grumpy that I had to smile.

"No, and he seems pretty sharp to me. I know the stroke left his hand a little messed up, but they say his mind wasn't affected. Why?"

He shrugged. "Maybe it's because I don't know him well enough, but I keep picking up weird vibes. If anyone else is around, even if it's only Jeffy, he acts like you said — like I'm already better at potting than my . . . than Donny. You know about Donald Nordan?"

"That he was Amos's younger son and he died a couple of years ago?"

"No, I meant did you know about Mom and him?"

"It all happened long before I met her." It was a relief to speak with absolute truthfulness. "She only told me about it Friday."

We entered the Asheboro city limits and I drove in silence for a minute while I got my bearings and tried to remember whether the courthouse was north or south of the hospital and whether I'd be better off staying on 220 or getting off to follow Fayetteville Street all the way through town. Since that was the route I was most confident of, I took the Dixie Drive exit.

"How's your ice holding out?" I asked as we stopped for a light.

"It's all melted, but the water's still cold." He dipped the cloth into the soup mug I'd brought back from the Nordan house and held it against his split lip, which was really starting to swell now.

"So how's your grandfather different when you're alone with him?"

"It's like he doesn't care if I'm there or not. When I got over here Friday, he was friendly and all, showed me how to throw a bowl, but it wasn't till Libbet and Tom came in that he started calling me Dave and acting like I was special. Then that night, he was showing me pictures of the family, but as soon as Miss June and Jeffy went upstairs, he shoved the albums in my hands and said I could take them back to the loft with me if I was interested, since they were mostly labeled anyhow."

"Maybe he was just tired and wanted to go to bed," I suggested. "After all, he is past seventy."

"When I left, he was watching a rerun of *Smackdown* wrestling," he said flatly.

The hospital's ER was like most ERs these days, overcrowded and understaffed. I got Davis checked in, then called Fliss and told her why I was going to be delayed.

"Why, you sneaky woman! Why didn't

you tell me you knew Donny's son?"

"At the time the subject first came up, I didn't know they were the same boy. Honest."

"I'll be home by ten," she said, "and I want to hear the whole story, okay? I'm putting a bottle of wine in the refrigerator right now and I'll leave the glasses and corkscrew on the counter in case you get back here first."

She told me where the spare door key was hidden, then she left for her supper date and I went back to Davis, who had found an old issue of the *Smithsonian* magazine and was absorbed in an article on Oscar Nauman, an American artist I'd never heard of.

We waited almost two hours before a doctor could see him. I offered to go in with him, but he said he'd be fine alone.

Forty minutes later, he finally returned. There had been more waiting in the examination room, he said, but eventually it was determined that he did not have a concussion and he did not have a broken nose. His lip required only six stitches. "And the doctor said that everything would've been worse if I hadn't put ice on it right away. So thanks."

On our way out of town, I stopped at a drugstore. Davis bought some over-the-counter painkillers and immediately took two tablets. By now it was well after dark and we also stopped for hamburgers and big cups of iced drinks.

Lights were on all over Amos's house when we got back about nine and a patrol car was parked down by the shed. As we drove up, Connor Woodall got out to meet us.

"Hey, Connor," I said. "What's up?"

"Good to see you, Your Honor," he said formally. "Davis Richmond? Could we go upstairs and talk?"

His manner instantly reminded me of Dwight when Dwight gets official, and that made me apprehensive. "What's up?"

"Tom Hitchcock was killed in a car wreck a few hours ago."

CHAPTER

24

In a cultural sense, those persons were outsiders, foreigners, mediators with the larger world. And not surprisingly, they were greeted with curiosity and suspicion.

— Turners and Burners,
Charles G. Zug III

Judges are not supposed to give legal advice, nattered my internal preacher. *Remember? That's one of the first things they told you at New Judges' School.*

I assured him that I was not going to give advice. But given that Connor must have been told that Davis and Tom Hitchcock had fought, he obviously thought the fight had contributed to the wreck. I didn't plan to act as the boy's attorney, I was just going to be there as a friend while Connor talked to him, and then, depending on where the talk went, I'd probably call Jenny McAllister and let her know what was happening with her son.

And if she asks your advice, you'll tell her she'll have to ask her own attorney. Perfectly ethical, the pragmatist agreed.

"I understand you and Tom had a fight this afternoon," Connor said as we settled ourselves on couch and chairs around a colorful mosaic table at the front of the loft.

Davis nodded. He still seemed shaken by the news that his cousin was dead. Hell, I was shaken, too, although today was the first time I'd ever seen or spoken to Tom Hitchcock and he wasn't even tenuous kin to me. To be that young, that full of youth's fiery passions and exaggerated sense of injustice — and then to be gone in an instant?

Incomprehensible.

"You want to tell me about the fight?" Connor repeated.

"It was pretty stupid," Davis said. The stitches in his lower lip were like a constant annoyance and he kept touching them with his tongue. "He put a snake in my bed last night, so this morning I stuck it where he was supposed to find it. Instead, it was his girlfriend who got scared and that made

Tom so mad that he jumped me when I came back from visiting his parents. He's been on me the whole weekend, so I was ready to give it to him, too."

He looked at Connor and swallowed as if something were in his throat. "He's really dead? Not just hurt bad and in the hospital?"

"He's really dead," Connor said.

"How's my grandfather? And Tom's family?"

"Not real good," he said bluntly.

Davis started to rise. "I ought to go —"

Connor waved him back down. "Not just yet. Tell me about this morning. After Tom came but before you left with his mother."

"I knew he was coming back sometime today to finish grinding that rack of jars that my grandfather took out of the kiln last week, so I slipped over to the shed after breakfast and put the snake in one of them. Okay, I realize now that it was dumb, but he'd been so —" He groped for the right word. "So hostile to me."

I was pleased to hear that my mini-lecture had penetrated. Connor just nodded and said, "Go on."

"Tom got here around eleven."

"Where did he park his car?"

"Out front here, right next to mine. Weird

that we could be that opposite and still drive the same car. Only difference, his is a year older."

"Did he leave the windows down?"

"I didn't notice. I always leave mine cracked so it doesn't get too hot inside. Why?"

"Just answer the question, please."

"Well, when we were comparing cars, he said that his air conditioner was broken, so they probably were down."

"What happened next?"

"I was up here when James Lucas's wife — ex-wife?"

"Sandra Kay," said Connor.

"She came knocking on the door. She'd heard I was here and I think she wanted to see if I looked anything like the rest of the Nordans."

Now, that was something Sandra Kay hadn't mentioned to me when she was being so free and open about everything else. A deliberate omission?

"She was here to get a bunch of pots out of the shop and she'd sent Tom up to the house to get the key, since Miss June doesn't open it till one o'clock on Sundays. Tom and I helped her box them up and carry them out to her car, then we ate lunch at the house." Again his tongue gingerly touched his stitched lip.

"Anything happen at lunch?"

"Not really. Jeffy did most of the talking." He looked Connor squarely in the eye. "I didn't know till Judge Knott told me tonight."

"Told you what?"

"That my grandfather — that Mr. Amos — I know he said for me to call him Granddaddy, but it weirds me out to try to," Davis said plaintively. "Anyhow, she says Tom thought he was going to leave me the pottery. I just wish I'd known about that before all this happened. I would've told him I'd never take it and maybe we could've been friends. I didn't come over here because I suddenly had this huge urge to throw a damn pot. I only came because I wanted to meet my — to meet Donald Nordan's people and get to know them a little."

"I see," Connor said. "Now, what happened after lunch?"

"Miss June opened the shop. Mr. Amos went up to his room to take a nap and I started cleaning up things downstairs where Libbet worked yesterday. I hosed off the wheel head and the shelves and washed out all the buckets. Then Tom's mother came over to see her dad and she invited me to ride home with her to see some pictures and stuff. I was over there about an hour and walked back through the lane. There was another car parked next to Tom's when I got here. Brittany's. As soon as I stuck my head in the door, he just started ragging on me, and the next thing I knew, we were slugging it out. Mr. Amos broke it up, Tom took off, and Brittany went after him and Judge Knott took me to the hospital."

"And you didn't see anyone around Tom's car after he got here?"

Davis shook his head. "I guess we all walked past it at one time or another, and — Hey, wait a minute! Jeffy!"

Connor frowned. "Jeffy was by Tom's car?"

"He was in and out of both sheds after lunch. I don't know if he messed with Tom's car, but he got inside mine. I came out one time and he was sitting in the driver's seat, pretending to drive. Poor guy. I didn't think there was anything he could hurt, so I didn't chase him. Is that why Tom wrecked? Somebody messed with his car?"

Connor didn't answer, just made a note on the legal pad he'd laid on the coffee table. My far vision's good enough to see that it looked like a *J* and a question mark.

"What about Bobby Gerard? Was he here today?"

313

"Not that I saw. He was supposed to work yesterday afternoon, but he never came back after lunch. Betty and Mr. Amos were both pissed about it, but I got the impression that's just the way this guy is."

"Now, son, I want you to think about this real carefully. Did you see anybody put a snake in Tom's car?"

"Jesus! Another snake? That's why he crashed?"

Connor nodded. "A big black rat snake about four feet long. You didn't see anyone do it?"

Davis shook his head emphatically. "No, sir."

"Did *you* put it there?"

"Me?" He jumped to his feet and shook his head even harder. "No! I didn't."

"See, the thing is," said Connor, "if you just did it for another joke —"

"But I didn't!" He was getting more and more agitated.

"It's okay, Davis," I said soothingly. "He has to ask."

"Do the rest of them think I did?" he asked.

Connor didn't answer, but as far as I was concerned, the bright red flush that abruptly covered his face was answer enough.

I was struck by a sudden thought. "Did you check Davis's car for snakes?"

314

Both of them looked at me questioningly.

"Well, think of it, Connor. Two white Toyotas sitting side by side? If someone did deliberately put a snake in Tom's car, maybe they also put one in Davis's. Or, for all we know," I said, warming to my theme, "maybe they thought it was Davis's car they were putting it in, in the first place."

"Tom would certainly know his own car, and who else would want to scare Davis?" Connor asked reasonably.

"Maybe the same person who killed James Lucas," I answered, striving for the same reasonable tone. "Somebody who thought Amos was ready to rewrite his will in favor of this new grandson."

"Except he wasn't," Connor said heavily.

There came such an immediate rush of blood to his fair face that I realized he hadn't meant to let that slip and his look so implored me that I didn't pursue it.

Connor's careless remark had passed right over Davis, who now struggled with the thought that someone might want him dead or seriously hurt. "The same person that killed James Lucas? But nobody else was here. Nobody that I saw. It was just family."

"Anyhow," I said, just full of helpful scenarios, "for all you know, that snake could have been in Tom's car for a week. You can't be sure when it got in."

"Mighty convenient timing, though," Connor said. He asked for Davis's home address and telephone, then stood up. "How long did you plan on staying here?"

"I didn't have any definite plans. Right now, though . . ." He hesitated. "I really ought to go up to the house. See my grandfather. And then go over to the Hitchcocks'."

Connor looked at me awkwardly.

"They *do* think I put that snake in Tom's car, don't they?" Davis demanded.

Connor nodded. "I'm afraid they do."

"Do you?"

"I'm not jumping to any conclusions," he said, "but I'd like for you to keep in touch if you leave Seagrove."

I walked Connor downstairs.

"We need to talk," I said when we were outside under the starry April sky.

"I was afraid you were going to say that." He took a flashlight from his cruiser and examined every cranny of Davis's car. "You going to be in court tomorrow?"

"No, not till Tuesday. But I'll come by your office in the morning, okay?"

He nodded.

Back upstairs, Davis was wandering restlessly around the loft. "I wish I'd never come over to Seagrove. I wish Mom had never told me."

"Really?"

He thought about it a long moment, then sighed. "No, I guess not."

There was only one small window up here and he'd thrown it open and switched on the overhead exhaust fan to freshen the air. He looked so miserable that there was only one thing to do.

"Get your things together," I said. "You're coming with me. My friend's got an extra bedroom and I know she won't mind if you crash there tonight. You can drive back to Raleigh tomorrow."

He gave me a look of pure relief, but then his shoulders slumped and he shook his head. "No, I have to face them, tell them I didn't have anything to do with Tom's wreck."

"You can do that now," I said briskly. "I'll go with you. Just pack your stuff."

I went over to the bed. "These your CDs? What about the travel clock?"

Galvanized, he pulled out a catchall duffel bag and began stuffing clothes into it.

Ten minutes later, we switched off the fan, closed the window, turned off the lights, closed the upstairs door, and latched the workshop door. Davis slung his duffel into the trunk of his car, then we both took a deep breath and walked up the slope to his grandfather's house.

Whatever his problems with Tom and Libbet Hitchcock, Davis had apparently become accustomed to coming and going freely in his grandfather's house over the weekend. He rapped lightly on the side door of the house, then opened it and stepped inside.

June Gregorich turned from the sink where she was emptying the drainboard of its dishes, moving back and forth from sink to cabinets in blue cotton socks that almost matched the faded blue of her denim dress. A Celtic cross strung on a red leather thong hung around her neck. Her thick leather sandals sat neatly beside the door. Her face looked drawn and tired.

"You've heard?" she asked Davis.

He nodded. "How's he taking it?"

"Not good, not good at all. He made Betty and Dillard leave about an hour ago. She's just falling apart and Mr. Amos is almost catatonic — he said he was going to bed, but he just keeps sitting there. Maybe you can get him to go on upstairs."

Despite her solicitous tone, I saw her eyes brighten at the prospect of more drama.

I followed Davis into the den. Amos Nordan's recliner was locked in its upright position and the old man sat just as erectly. It seemed to take him a moment to focus on who Davis was.

"So you come back, did you?"

"I just heard. I'm really sorry, sir."

"You're the one supposed to be dead," Amos said. "I thought I could keep him safe. I didn't know I was inviting another killer to have a go at him."

I didn't know if Davis understood any more than I did what Amos's first words meant, but we both understood the intent of his last.

"I didn't put that snake in his car," he said earnestly.

"Lean down here," Amos said, gesturing him closer.

When Davis did as he asked, the old man spat full force with all the venom of his years.

"I spit on you!" he snarled. "Now get the hell out of my house and get off my property before I put the law on you!"

I was almost as startled as Davis, who stood there looking down at this man who'd sired his father. Then he turned and walked steadily from the room.

As I suspected, June Gregorich had overheard everything and she met him at the kitchen door with a damp dishcloth.

He wiped the spittle from his face and took the first deep breath since entering the house. "Thanks, Miss June. You've been nice to me. I really appreciate all you did."

"You're leaving?"

"You heard what he said."

"But —"

"It's okay," he said. "I was going tonight anyhow."

"Well, maybe it's for the best," she told me as he pushed open the screen door and walked out into the mild night.

I didn't envy her having to stay on here in this bleak and cheerless house. As I said goodnight, I added inanely, "Take care of yourself, June."

She gave me a grim smile and nodded. "Don't worry. I will."

The moon was only two nights from full and when I caught up to Davis down by the sheds, tears glistened in his eyes.

"Let's go to my friend's house," I said softly.

"I feel like a coward," he said, sounding almost as miserable as he looked. "But I don't think I'm up to having anybody else spit in my fa—"

There was a loud gunshot and a bullet ripped a chunk of wood from the shed post beside his head.

We both jumped ten feet.

Another bang. Another bullet. This one a little higher up. Davis grabbed my arm and pulled me down behind his car. Neither of us was reassured by the shooter's poor aim. I carry a gun in the trunk of my car, but there was no way to reach it. Besides, this wasn't the O.K. Corral and I wasn't up to a real shoot-out.

Instead, I yanked the cell phone from my purse and dialed 911 just as a third shot took out two of Davis's windows.

"I'm calling from Nordan Pottery," I screamed when the dispatcher answered. "Someone's shooting at us out back of the shop — hurry!"

A dispatcher's calm voice is meant to steady a person's nerves, but this one wasn't helping much. I answered her questions, but I don't know how much sense I was making. I just wanted a patrol car to magically appear between us and whoever was blasting away at us.

An overhead light at the peak of the shed's roof suddenly came on, dazzling us with its unexpected brightness.

From the house, I heard Amos Nordan

holler, "What's going on down there?"

June called over his shoulder, "Deborah? Davis? You all right?"

Libbet Hitchcock's angry young voice called back, "He's fine."

She stepped into the circle of light dragging a rifle behind her, then let it drop to the ground. "If I'd really wanted to kill him, he'd be dead as Tom right now!"

"Good God Almighty, girl! What the hell you doing?" Amos cried, hobbling down the slope to us.

"What I should've done last week when he sat on the edge of your porch to weasel his way into the pottery. And you!" She was half-crying now with grief and rage as she turned on Amos. "Tom would still be alive now if you hadn't gone back on your word and picked this one over him. How *could* you?"

"You stupid bitch! I didn't!" Amos howled.

Adrenaline pumping, Davis stood up. "Would you both just shut the hell up? Why would you think for one minute that I want this dumb place? I wouldn't have it if you wrapped it up and hung it on a Christmas tree!"

Both of them stopped in their tracks, then Libbet sneered, "Oh, right. You'd say anything now to keep us from thinking you killed Tom."

"Yeah," said Amos. "Putting that snake —"

"I did *not* touch the damn snake!"

Then, mercifully, I heard a siren wailing down the road close by.

At almost the same instant, headlights appeared in the lane. The gunshots had carried on the night air and the place was soon awash in lights from both directions. Dillard Hitchcock got out of the van and ran toward his daughter. "Oh, Lord, Libbet! What've you done? What's your mother going to think of this?"

"Who's the shooter?" asked the sheriff's deputy who strode forward with his hand on his open holster.

Hitchcock picked up the rifle and Libbet collapsed in tears on his shoulder.

Amos Nordan sank down on the bench in front of the shed, while June hovered over him. A wide-eyed Jeffy, barefooted and in pajamas, stared at everything in bewilderment. "Momma?"

"It's okay, son," she kept telling him.

As the deputy tried to sort it all out, Davis walked over to his grandfather. "What did you mean when you said I was supposed to be dead? That you thought you could keep Tom safe by having me here?"

Amos glared back at him. "Somebody's killing my boys and I ain't supposed to try and stop him any way I can?"

I saw shocked realization wash over Dillard Hitchcock's face the same time it hit me.

"You were using Davis for bait?" I was appalled.

"I was going to watch out for him," Amos said belligerently.

"Yeah, like you watched out for him this afternoon?" I was too indignant to sugarcoat my words. "Two white Toyotas sitting side by side. Maybe the killer thought he was putting the snake in Davis's car just like you planned. It could be Davis lying dead at the morgue tonight."

"But it ain't him, is it, lady? It's my real grandson." His words were almost strangled by his rusty sobs. "It's Tom."

CHAPTER

25

Laura Teague . . . believes . . . "If you trim, you leave a lot of thickness at the bottom of a pot while turning it. Then it's hard to get enough of the shape so you know what the whole shape is going to be like. You need to get the shape while it's plastic rather than carving it away. Trimming does something to it. I see shapes not coming out spontaneously, not true, if they have been cut later."

— *Raised in Clay*,
Nancy Sweezy

It was only a few miles from the Hitchcock house to Fliss's place, but I was sorry that Davis was in the car behind instead of on the seat beside me. He'd been hit with a lot of heavy stuff tonight, more than any nineteen-year-old ought to have to handle alone. It probably helped that he was still shaking with anger when we left.

With all the shattered glass in his car, I'd tried to get him to come with me, but he'd stubbornly taken a broom and swept out the worst from around the driver's seat.

"I'm not leaving my car here," he'd said. "Or what's left of it."

"Let me know how much the windows are," Dillard had said stiffly. It wasn't clear whether or not he still thought Davis had anything to do with Tom's death, but at that point, Davis didn't care.

"I certainly will," he'd snapped back.

The deputy, a local man, had placed Libbet in his cruiser. He said it was a shame he had to write all this up for official action, considering how much the Hitchcock family was going through right now, but he got no sympathy from either of us. Far as we'd known at the time, she was shooting to kill when we crouched behind Davis's car.

Even so, I had a feeling that once everything sank in, Davis's anger was going to be battling with deep, deep hurt and maybe even a little guilt for ever coming to Seagrove in the first place.

I used my cell phone to let Fliss know I was finally on my way. She hadn't heard about

Tom Hitchcock's death and was totally shocked. "God! Poor Betty. Both brothers and now her son? Those people are snakebit, aren't they?"

An ironic comment, considering how the wreck occurred.

When I told her that I was bringing Davis Richmond with me and why, she was instantly sympathetic. "I'll go put fresh sheets on Vee's bed right now."

Then, because she's no fool, Fliss said, "Deborah, you're sure he's telling the truth?"

"Oh, Lord, not you, too," I groaned.

She wouldn't back down, though. "We both know that adolescent boys do stupid things that wind up with serious repercussions."

"And then swear on a stack of Bibles they didn't do it. I know, I know. But I've been with this one all evening and if I'm that bad a judge of character, then I'd better hang up my robe."

"Speaking of robes, this probably isn't the time for it, but I ran into Will Blackstone tonight and he was very interested to hear you were back in the area. He wants you to call him."

She was right. Gratifying as that information might be, this wasn't the time. In fact, it seemed almost like another lifetime that I came bopping over to Seagrove hoping for a more interesting afternoon than hanging around my own house.

Be careful what you ask for, said the preacher.

Amen, said the pragmatist.

Fliss met us at the door when we pulled into her yard a little before eleven. As a mother herself, she urged Davis to pick up the phone in Vee's room and call Raleigh.

"I don't want to tell my mom all this on the phone," he protested.

"You don't have to," Fliss said. "Just give her this number and tell her you're coming home tomorrow."

"She'll want to know why," he said glumly.

"Tell her you're having car trouble," I suggested.

That got me a half-smile and we left him to it.

Back in Fliss's study, I was happy to sink down on her comfortable chaise, kick off my shoes, and let myself relax for the first time in hours. She poured us both a glass of wine and I finished sketching in the highlights of my afternoon and evening that I had skipped over during our phone call. She listened raptly and was as appalled as I'd been to hear of Amos Nordan's plan to trip up James Lucas's killer by using Davis as a decoy.

"Decoy?" she snorted. "Staked goat is more like it."

When Davis rejoined us, he still looked sad and shaken. The stitches in his lip weren't helping, either, and he took another pain pill.

"What's going to happen to Libbet?" he asked.

"Juvenile court. Most likely, she'll be charged with misdemeanor assault and damage to personal property," I said. "Depending on the judge, she'll probably get a year's probation and she'll have to do community service to earn the restitution for your car windows."

"And if I know Betty and Dillard," said Fliss, "she'll be grounded till she's twenty."

"Not with them getting ready to bury Tom," Davis said.

Fliss sighed, too. "That's true." Then, more briskly, "Would you like a sandwich or something?"

"I'm not hungry, thank you." He looked at me. "Coming here just now, I was thinking. The night James Lucas was buried, the first time my so-called grandfather ever laid eyes on me, he decided right then that he'd throw me to the wolves to save Tom. He didn't even know me."

"But he did know Tom," I said softly.

"What he did was absolutely cold-blooded and monstrous and there's no excuse for it. All you can do is try to understand his logic. He's an old man, Davis. He's lost both sons and he's scared of losing more members of his family. Rightly scared, as it turns out."

"It's too bad he didn't tell Tom."

"I wonder who he did tell," I mused.

"June?" asked Fliss. "Bobby Gerard? Betty Hitchcock?"

"The elusive Bobby Gerard."

"You haven't seen him around the pottery?" She gestured to my glass with the bottle.

I held out my empty glass for a refill. "I've heard snide remarks about his unreliability, but I'm beginning to think he's a collective figment of the Nordan clan's imagination."

"No, he's real," Davis said. "I don't think he turns, but he seems to do a little of everything else. He was there Friday afternoon and was back the next morning — yesterday morning? Jeez, yesterday seems like a year ago. Guess this is what Einstein meant by relativity."

"What about today?" I asked.

"I don't think so. I didn't see him anyhow."

"This Bobby," I asked Fliss. "Could he have had a grudge against James Lucas?"

"I never heard that he had, but I told you,

Deborah. I don't hear every bit of gossip that goes around the area."

"You didn't annoy him, did you?" I asked Davis, who immediately shook his head.

"What about June Gregorich or Jeffy? Both of them certainly had opportunity."

"Do you really think Jeffy's capable?" Fliss asked sensibly. "And what would be June's motive? She gains nothing from having James Lucas or Tom dead. Besides, if Donny's accident was murder, too, she'd barely met him. Furthermore, if the pottery fails, she'll have to look for another place to stay, and not every place would welcome Jeffy."

"How *did* Donald Nordan die?" Davis asked abruptly. "Nobody's ever come right out and said."

I sat quietly as Fliss said, "So far as I know, he got tangled up in some cords or ropes and accidently hanged himself."

"Ropes? Cords? Sounds like something that could have been rigged, doesn't it? Donny, James Lucas, and now Tom. Has anyone else connected with the pottery died oddly?"

Fliss thought a moment. "Nope, that's it."

We had struck out on motive, but I kept wondering about opportunity. "If the person who killed James Lucas is the same one who put the snake in Tom's car, then when did he do it? Tourists and customers don't roam around the workshops on Sunday, so who could besides the family or someone who works there?"

"Maybe it was sheer coincidence?" Fliss suggested. "If his car window was down, maybe the snake crawled in all by itself. Or if someone did do it, it could have been a couple of days ago. I don't see where that's anything the police could ever be sure about unless that person confesses."

"Sandra Kay was there this morning," I said slowly.

"So was Tom's mother, but Tom and I were with them both the whole time," Davis objected.

"Were you? You said Sandra knocked on your door, so you weren't there when she first drove up. And she'd already sent Tom up to the house for the shop key?"

Davis nodded reluctantly.

"So if she had the snake in a bag in her car, say, she'd have had a couple of minutes to slip it from her car to Tom's."

Fliss's eyes narrowed. "I don't think she was real crazy about Tom, either. It annoyed her that she wouldn't have any say over the pottery if James Lucas died first. And I think there were times that he was too much the heir apparent, if you know what I mean."

"They seemed okay with each other this morning," Davis said. "Besides, the pottery has nothing to do with her anymore once she got her collection out, right? I mean, she'd already divorced James Lucas and now she's decorating for someone else, isn't she? So what would she get out of hurting Tom?"

It occurred to me that Tom might have seen Sandra Kay go through the lane when James Lucas was killed, which opened up the possibility that she really had killed her ex-husband despite all she'd told me. Either way, though, the same question applied to both deaths.

"Cui bono?" I said.

Fliss nodded sagely while Davis looked puzzled. "Excuse me?"

"It's Latin for, 'Who profits?' " she translated.

"Tom would have gained a little sooner by James Lucas's death," I said, "but if Tom's death was deliberately caused by the same person, then I don't see it. What about the potter Sandra Kay decorates for now?"

Fliss shook her head. "They might've warmed each other's bed when she first left James Lucas, but I think it's been strictly business for over a year now."

"Libbet?" Davis asked doubtfully. "Maybe she's the one who'll inherit now."

"Heck," said Fliss. "Maybe it's Amos himself, jealous that anybody's going to outlive him. Or Edward, taking out all the competition to the Nordan-Hitchcock name."

Davis suddenly yawned and picked up the wine bottle. "You know, a glass of this would probably help me get sleep."

"Good try," I said, taking the bottle from his hand. "But with all the painkillers you're taking for that lip, I'm betting you'll be asleep two minutes after you hit the pillow."

He tried to keep from yawning again, then shrugged sheepishly.

His yawns were contagious. The wine had worked its magic on Fliss and me both, and we all decided to call it a night.

CHAPTER

26

Customers seek contact with the potters, watch their work in progress, explore their shops, and absorb the flavor of the past. The potter's lifestyle has at its core a control of product, from the digging of the clay to the firing of the kiln. Such visible wholeness is uncommon today, and its satisfactions extend to the buyer who uses the pottery as well as to the potter who makes it.

— Raised in Clay,
Nancy Sweezy

The next morning, Davis was anxious to get on the road and Fliss had an eight-thirty appointment, so I was alone at her kitchen table, making a dent in the half-full pot of coffee they'd left me while I read the

Asheboro *Courier-Tribune*'s account of Tom Hitchcock's death. It was headlined "Snake Causes Fatal Wreck."

The reporter had asked the right questions, but "Lt. Connor Woodall of the Randolph County Sheriff's Department declined to speculate on whether young Hitchcock's suspicious accident is related to the earlier murder of his uncle, James Lucas Nordan, also of Seagrove."

In a sidebar on the same page, a herpetologist at the nearby state zoo discussed this year's early emergence of snakes from hibernation and gave amusing examples of warm spots he'd known reptiles to seek during spring's chancy weather. And yes, car interiors were certainly one of them.

Happily, nothing seemed chancy about today's mild weather. Although spring showers were predicted by the weekend, only clear blue skies were visible through the open kitchen window. Around the window itself were more of June Gregorich's New Age totems — another small ruby-red pyramid, a string of crystals, and a less complex set of bamboo wind chimes beyond the window screen.

"She appropriates an east-facing window in all the places she works," Fliss had told me the night before. "She says it helps focus her harmonic energies."

A light breeze set the bamboo lengths clacking gently and sunlight made little rainbows across my newspaper. It was so quiet and peaceful that I yawned and stretched and couldn't decide whether to go back to bed for a short catnap or get dressed and see if I could catch Connor at his office. The phone rang at that precise instant and there was Connor Woodall — just like the psychic hotline.

"I have to be down in the Seagrove area this morning," he said. "Why don't you come have lunch at my house? Fern would like to meet you. Eleven-thirty too early?"

He gave me directions and I'd just decided I might as well nap for an hour when the back door opened and in walked June Gregorich and her son Jeffy with a bright purple backpack slung over his shoulder. She was surprised to see me. I'd forgotten that this was the day she cleaned for Fliss, and she'd forgotten that I knew Fliss well enough to stay in her house.

Jeffy said hey with his usual sunny smile, then passed straight on to the den, where he took a cushion from the chaise and lay down on the carpet beside his backpack to watch a children's program.

I offered June a cup of coffee.

"Let me get the sheets and towels started first," she said.

I told her that my sheets didn't need changing and that I'd take care of my room, since I'd probably be here another two nights. "But you might want to check her son's room. Davis spent the night here, too."

She made a *tsk*ing sound. "Poor guy. Yesterday was a nightmare, wasn't it? That fight. Then Tom getting killed and the way Mr. Amos was so mean to him."

"Not to mention his cousin taking pot-shots at us."

"Well, that won't be happening again anytime soon. They confiscated Dill's rifle. There's one judge here that has every gun in a juvenile case destroyed. Doesn't matter if it's an expensive deer rifle or a Saturday night special. If a kid's used it to cause trouble, it's history. I made Mr. Amos lock up his guns and hide the key the second day I cleaned for him." She took a laundry basket from the utility room next to the kitchen.

"I just won't work where there's a chance Jeffy might get hold of a gun," she said as she went off down the hall.

I'd barely finished the sports page before she was back to put the kettle on and load the washer.

"I put fresh towels in the guest bath," she said. "If you need more, the linen closet's at the end of the hall."

I followed her to the doorway of the utility room and watched her measure detergent and fabric softener. "Did the magistrate let Libbet come home last night?"

"Yes, but she has to go back this morning. For some sort of hearing's what Betty told Mr. Amos."

Her thick brown hair wasn't braided or tied back this morning and it fanned out from her head in all directions as she closed the washer lid and started the machine.

"How are they doing?"

I thought of the grief the Hitchcocks must be feeling. They'd probably spend the morning in court with their daughter and the afternoon picking out a casket for their son. And as much as Betty might be hurting, I had a feeling that her husband would be hurting doubly, since he would feel her pain as well as his own.

"They'd probably be doing better if they didn't have to worry about Mr. Amos, too." She shook her head. "He acts like it's all about him. Like Tom and James Lucas and even Donny, too, are all part of a plot to hurt him. He thinks God's got it in for him alone. Never mind that they're the ones dead. The way he's carrying on about nothing left to live for, I think Betty's afraid he'll hurt himself."

"Commit suicide?"

"Not if I can help it," she said firmly. The kettle began to whistle and she made herself a cup of herbal tea from a packet she'd brought along in her pocket. "I know where he keeps the key to the guns. I hid the bullets last night and I gave the key to Betty this morning."

An aroma of oranges and cinnamon wafted up from her cup and filled the kitchen.

"You were working there when Donny died," I said. "Right?"

She looked at me warily and admitted that yes, he'd died soon after she'd started cleaning there.

"Was it murder like Amos thinks?"

She shrugged and stirred her tea, not giving anything away.

I tried to sound as matter-of-fact as possible. "I know that it looked like an auto-erotic accident, but was it really?"

That stopped her in her tracks. "You know about that? How? Amos Nordan would just die if he thought it was all over the Seagrove area. Or did Connor Woodall tell you?"

I didn't deny it and she sat down at the table opposite me and gingerly took a sip of the hot tea. "It makes him feel better now to think it was murder, but when it happened — the way it looked with Donny rigged out like that — it shocked him so bad, it brought on his stroke."

Now that she thought I knew everything, June was not only prepared to dish, she seemed positively eager to. "I used to hear about kinky stuff like that out in California, but I never expected to find it here in the backwoods of North Carolina."

Eyes agleam, she described in salacious detail how Amos Nordan had found his son dressed in frilly white lingerie, slumped over a silken loop that hung from the low rafter above.

"Mr. Amos was beside himself — shocked and embarrassed and mad all at the same time. I helped him get those clothes off Donny and get him dressed in his own clothes and then we got a rope and somehow managed to make it look like he'd hanged himself." She shuddered. "It was awful, but Mr. Amos was in such a state, I couldn't *not* do what he asked me."

"The medical examiner wasn't fooled, though."

"No. Something about the rope marks on his neck. He wasn't stiff yet, but they could still tell whether the marks were made before he died or after." She gave a wry smile. "And I guess it didn't help that we'd put his shorts on backwards. The police found the lacy stuff where we'd stuffed it under the mattress."

"But could it have been murder?"

"I don't know, Deborah. We dressed him after he was dead, so I suppose somebody could've *un*dressed him."

She got up and added a little more hot water to her mug. "Either way, it just about sent Mr. Amos out of his mind. Everybody says he doted on Donny. And just about the time he was finally getting over Donny's death, somebody kills James Lucas. I thought he was going to have another stroke."

"And now with Tom . . . ?"

"It's like he can't take it all in. He keeps saying he might as well be dead himself because it's the end of Nordan Pottery. And I guess it is. Both sons gone. The grandson he counted on gone. And after the way he treated Davis, he'll never come back over here, will he?"

"I seriously doubt it." I could feel the caffeine working in my system, yet I still got up and poured myself a fresh cup.

"So that grandson might as well be dead, too, for all the good it does him," said June.

"What about Libbet?"

"She's only a kid. And a girl. They say she's going to be another Nell Cole Graves, but that doesn't cut it with Mr. Amos. One of the reasons he's so bitter about Sandra Kay is that she and James Lucas never had a son."

"This Bobby Gerard, June. I haven't met him yet. Was he working here when Donny died?"

"If you could call it that. He didn't come in that morning, but when I went looking for Jeffy after lunch, he was back working in one of the sheds."

"What about him, then?"

She shrugged. "He's unreliable when he's drinking, but I never heard of him being violent. The only thing he cares about is where his next drink's coming from."

"Sandra Kay was over at the pottery yesterday," I said.

"To pick up the rest of the collection, yes."

"Who do you think killed them?" I asked bluntly.

"Are you thinking Sandra Kay?" she countered.

"It was her car that went through the lane last week, wasn't it?"

"I thought it was," she said reluctantly, "but really, I don't know much about cars. Just their color and if they run. That's about

343

all. Course, Mr. Amos always thought she had the hots for Donny. . . . I never saw anything, but then I wouldn't, would I?"

I had forgotten that June didn't move into Amos Nordan's house till after his stroke. Sandra Kay had left James Lucas so soon afterward that their overlap time would have been quite short.

"But maybe the way he was left *was* some sort of feminine revenge?"

She let my words hang between us almost as if she were examining them. Examining and then rejecting with a firm "No. I just don't believe Sandra Kay could do something like that. Get mad and fly off the handle, maybe, but nothing like what was done to Donny if he didn't do it to himself."

"So who, then?"

She sighed in frustration. "I've been over it and over it in my mind and there doesn't seem to be any reason to kill all three of them. Maybe Mr. Amos is right. Maybe it *is* about somebody trying to shut down his pottery."

She swallowed the last of her tea, then got up and began unloading the dishwasher.

"Have they set a time for the funeral?" I asked.

"Probably Wednesday morning."

The sink was full of dirty plates and glasses

and as soon as the dishwasher was empty, she started reloading it. "You through with your cup?"

From the den came the sound of Jiminy Cricket's song. I guessed that Jeffy had brought a *Pinocchio* tape in his backpack. I remember some of my sisters-in-law grumbling about endless Disney when their children were little. What would it be like to know that your child would never outgrow Mickey Mouse and Bugs Bunny?

Fernwood Pottery reminded me a little of Cady Clay Works, another relatively new pottery with a modern sales shop attached to the front of the work area.

The showroom at Fernwood was only half as big as Cady's, but it, too, was flooded with natural light and had a much more modern feel than Nordan's. The walls and shelves were painted in a pale green that set off the darker green and cream of her wares.

Capitalizing on her name, Fern Woodall's plates and platters were decorated with fronds and leaves and occasional acorn patterns. Very pretty. She also seemed to model small animals: squirrels, rabbits, and turtles in impressionistic free forms that captured characteristic poses.

"Oh, they're darling, just darling!" cooed

the expensively dressed woman darting around the little shop when I entered. "I want one of all of them."

The blond-haired woman at the sales counter, whom I took to be Connor's wife, gave me a friendly if harried smile and a be-with-you-in-a-moment gesture as she tried to decipher the customer's wants. "One of each animal?"

"Each animal and each pose. They'll make wonderful prizes for my bridge club," the woman said gaily. She was wearing quite a lot of gold on her wrists, neck, and ears and several rings with impressive stones on her fingers. The Lincoln parked outside was probably hers, too. "How many different molds do you have?"

"Molds? These aren't molds," Fern explained. "I model them each individually. No two are exactly alike."

"Really? How perfectly clever you are." She sighed extravagantly. "It must be wonderful to be able to make things with your own two hands. I don't have an ounce of creativity. All I can do is appreciate the work of those who do. Now, let me see . . . three tables times four players . . . If I buy a dozen, will there be a discount?"

I pretended to be absorbed in a set of cream-colored stoneware mugs banded in a narrow border of ivy leaves while she agonized over which twelve she wanted.

As Fern Woodall wrapped each figure in newspaper, the woman wrote out a check, chattering away the whole time. "Your life must be so wonderful. That *is* your sweet little house next door, isn't it? It's so charming. And all you have to do is step out of your door and here you are! No long commutes, no time clocks, no bosses standing over you. You can just spend your days in uncomplicated creativity. I really envy you."

Still burbling about the satisfactions of honest craftsmanship, she eventually carried her package out to the Lincoln and drove off to her terribly complicated but uncreative life in Charlotte or Greensboro.

When she was safely out the door, I turned to Fern and said, "How on earth do you keep from smashing one of your platters over the head of customers like her?"

She looked startled and then smiled. "Deborah Knott?"

I pleaded guilty and she laughed. "It probably helps to remember that I'm married to a sheriff's deputy. Ah! Speak of the devil."

Through the side window I saw a car pull up next door, and Connor got out and waved.

Fern pulled the door closed and we walked across the parking area to join him at their front door.

"I hope you don't mind that it's just soup," she said. "Con didn't give me much notice that you could come today."

"I love soup," I said truthfully. "Anything except borscht."

She grimaced. "Beet soup? Yuck!"

"I see you two met," said Connor as he opened the side door for us to walk in.

The fern motif continued inside, but it wasn't cutesy and it wasn't overwhelming. All the walls were painted white, framed botanical prints were grouped over the green-and-white plaid couch in the den, and baskets of ferns hung in the windows in front of crisp white curtains.

Since Fern would have to leave if more customers came to the shop, we went straight out to the kitchen. The table there was a modern circle of white Formica with green place mats already set with her cream-colored soup bowls, each of which had a fern frond painted in the bottom.

"Well, it's *charming*," I said, mimicking Fern's customer. "Just *charming*. And *so* creative!"

She giggled and Connor laughed, having heard similar over the years. Conversation flowed easily between us as he poured the tea and sliced a loaf of soft brown bread while she reheated a pot of fragrant mushroom and barley soup and set out a simple salad of mixed greens. Delicious.

I gave Connor the regards that Dwight and my brothers had sent, showed him some pictures of them that I had in my wallet, saw pictures of their daughters, who were at school that day, and heard more tales of potting in the modern age.

"The scholars are even worse than the patronizing customers," said Fern. "They worry that too many new potters have come into the area and that the tradition is going to be diluted or polluted. Heck, we *are* tradition. They also think the craft should have stopped dead in its tracks around 1950."

"Tell her about that snob from over in Chapel Hill," Connor encouraged, and she grinned at the prospect of new ears for an old favorite.

"Well, one of them is lecturing a friend of mine for using an electric wheel instead of the old kick wheel," she said. "My friend nods and keeps working, but every once in a while, he cranes his neck, trying to see out the window.

"Then the guy starts ranting about potters who burn in electric kilns instead of wood-fired groundhog kilns. And my friend just nods, but now he leans over to see around the man. The guy starts a tirade about using electric pug mills, but finally he can't stand it any longer. 'What are you looking for out there in the parking lot?' he asks.

"My friend shrugs and says, 'I was just trying to see where you'd tied the horse and buggy you must've rode over on.' "

As we laughed, she said, "These are the same people who disapproved of us when we got together and created a group site on the web. We started posting all the pottery stamps about three years ago so that people across the country would know what they have. The purists think you ought to be able to tell who made a pot just by looking at it."

"I'd be curious to see what the Nordan stamp looks like," I said, wondering if they would have the original on their website or the slightly crimped one that Sandra Kay had described.

Fern jumped up. "Oops! Customer alert. Gotta run. Come by the shop before you leave, and I'll give you the fifty-cent tour and let you go on-line."

Left alone, I told Connor that Davis had gone back to Raleigh and he nodded. "I spoke to the deputy and read his report about last night. You really stepped into it, didn't you?"

He wanted to hear my version of events and I told him everything I'd seen or heard, while he took notes.

"And it was nice of you to try and spare Davis about Amos Nordan's motives for inviting him over to Seagrove, but Amos blew it last night after Libbet shot at us."

Connor turned red from my compliment. "Are you completely convinced that he was telling you the truth? Because he did walk from Rooster Clay back to Nordan's through that lane. He could've found a snake there and decided to up the ante on Tom a little."

"Sandra Kay was through there, too," I reminded him. "And so was Betty."

"I'm trying to keep an open mind about all these people," he said, "but I have a real hard time picturing Betty Hitchcock sticking a snake in her own son's car. Sandra Kay, now . . ."

Even though she'd asked me to, I felt a little like a traitor as I told him about my visit with Sandra Kay and how she'd admitted driving through the lane and past the kiln around the time someone pushed James Lucas into it.

He was not as surprised as I'd expected. "I

sort of thought she might be lying to me about that."

"She's scared you'll think she did it."

"Well, she sure has a habit of being around when things happen. She was there when Donny and James Lucas died —"

"Then you *do* think Donny was murdered?"

"I didn't say that. And neither did the ME. He *had* sustained a blow on the side of his head shortly before he died, but he might have banged into something himself. It was enough to daze him, the ME says, and maybe even enough to knock him out, which could have contributed to hanging himself."

"Or made it easier for someone else to do it," I said. "Sandra Kay?"

"Well, she was certainly there Sunday morning when the snake got in the car."

"I still wonder if that snake might not've been meant for Davis. Amos Nordan was telling anybody who'd listen what a great potter he was and what a happy day it was to have him in the family. Didn't *you* think he was setting Davis up as his heir?"

Connor nodded. "That's what I was hearing all week."

"If the killer was aiming for Davis and accidentally got Tom instead, then it really would be about the pottery, wouldn't it? There's no other reason for anyone over here to kill Davis."

CHAPTER

27

This turning process determines shape possibilities. . . . Fullness of shape on a traditional southern pot comes from curves at the belly and shoulder and, to a lesser degree, at the foot.

— *Raised in Clay*,
Nancy Sweezy

I declined coffee after my talk with Connor and toured Fern's workshop instead. Even though she tried to tell me my money was no good, I bought a lovely little bowl for Karen and a lidded rectangular box about the size of a tissue box for me. I've been wanting a container of some sort for my car keys and loose change when I come home rather than dumping them all over the kitchen counter, and this one was perfect.

She showed me the website she and her friends had put up and I browsed through their index of area pottery stamps, which they'd started posting a few years back. (The Nordan stamp was the crisp-angled original, not the repaired one used on their counterfeit pieces.) Then Fern went back to work and I was left at loose ends for the rest of the day.

I called Sandra Kay and told her that Connor hadn't been overly surprised to hear she'd lied. "He'll probably be out to see you again today, but if you just tell him the truth, you'll be okay," I said, hoping I was right.

"Thanks," she said. "I owe you a cardinal bowl."

"That's okay," I told her. I'd already decided I couldn't give Karen a counterfeit piece. Even if she never suspected, I wouldn't like knowing I'd fooled her.

The afternoon stretched before me as I considered my options. I could check out a few more potteries and maybe find the platters I needed. I could read over what I planned to do about the Sanderson deadlock in court the next day. I could even try to find relatives of the late Ms. Nina Bean and convey my daddy's belated respects.

Instead, I called Judge Neely's office and learned that Will Blackstone was holding court in Carthage that afternoon.

And yes, Carthage is twice as far from Seagrove as Asheboro, but hey, if things worked out, I expected to have twice as much fun.

Mondays are usually pretty busy and the Carthage courtroom to which I was directed was still actively in session. It was a little before four when I got there, having dallied briefly on the way at an irresistible antique store. Judge Blackstone was in a low-voice conference with the DA and defense counsel and I slipped in unobserved and sat down on an empty back bench.

He eventually spotted me, of course, and I was gratified by the sudden widening of his eyes and an involuntary smile that he immediately sequestered. I sat demurely and listened with professional interest, but it seemed to me that he disposed of the remaining cases in record time. When he adjourned promptly at five, he waited for me at the side door that led to chambers.

"This *is* a surprise," he said. "I thought perhaps you didn't get my message."

With a deliberate smile, I said, "Oh, I got your message," then, to keep him confused, added innocently, "Fliss Chadwick is very reliable."

"Are you staying over tonight?"

"With Fliss, you mean?" I teased.

"Naturally." But I saw the spark that glinted in his deep-set brown eyes.

"I have court tomorrow morning, but I was hoping perhaps we might have an early supper?"

We took his car.

The restaurant was a few miles down the road toward Southern Pines, a comfortable old southern inn with antique sideboards in the lobby, starched linen on the tables, and a continental chef in the kitchen. We had a couple of drinks in the lounge while we waited for a table and we talked about the violent deaths stalking the Nordan family. The area grapevine was as efficient here as it was in Colleton County, but I was able to add some details he hadn't heard.

Over smoked salmon and risotto — a pleasant change from the fried shrimp and hushpuppies that Kidd Chapin considered gourmet dining — we discovered mutual friends and acquaintances. Will was easy to talk to and he made me laugh as we compared some of the zanier cases we'd heard lately. It was all still pretty new to him. Indeed, he'd be attending his first conference of district court judges down at the coast in June.

"They're a cool bunch," I assured him. "You'll love it. Lots of really helpful information, too."

"The sessions don't go all night, do they?"

"Only if you want them to," I drawled.

On the drive back to Carthage, he asked if I was still interested in seeing his collection of Nordan pottery he'd acquired while representing Amos Nordan. Not the most original line I've ever heard, but the evening was still young and it would do.

We picked up my car at the courthouse and Will led the way to his townhouse in a newer section of town.

"My ex-wife wanted the house worse than I did," he explained as we went up the short walk to his front door. "I have to say, though, that I don't really miss mowing grass or clipping hedges. The association's maintenance crew takes care of all that here."

Inside was pretty standard affluent bachelor furnishings except for the half-dozen pieces of red cardinal ware that sat on individual ledges over the long low cabinet that housed his sound system.

He tossed his robe over the nearest chair and put his arms around me as if kissing were the most natural thing in the world for us to do. And a very good kiss it was.

Nine-point-six, said my slightly breathless pragmatist, holding up a scorecard.

Here we go again, sighed the preacher.

We kissed again and this time both of us were breathing heavily when we pulled apart.

"Drink?" he asked.

"Just a glass of ice water for now." I hadn't yet decided whether or not I'd be driving later.

Will laughed. "Are you sure you want to cool off so quickly?"

He loaded some smoky piano jazz on his CD player and turned the volume down low. While he fixed our drinks, I took a closer look at the pottery.

"There were times that poor ol' Amos didn't have the cash to pay me," Will said, "so he'd settle his bill with some pieces from his pre-1970 stash before they finally quit making it. I'm afraid I got the better end of the bargain. A bowl like the one you're holding went for almost eight hundred dollars the last time one came up for auction."

"Really?"

He nodded proudly, then picked up his robe and excused himself for a moment.

I turned the bowl in my hands and looked at the bottom. The left corner of the triangular kiln mark was ever so slightly crimped, barely noticeable unless you were actually looking for it.

I checked the soup mug, a plate, a cup and saucer. All had been stamped after it became illegal to use this lead glaze on tableware meant for serving food. It would appear that "poor ol' Amos" had gotten a couple of thousand dollars' worth of legal advice out of Will for less than forty bucks.

"Shall we call this session to order?" Will said from the doorway.

I turned, and to my surprise, he was standing there in his robe.

His judicial robe.

As he walked toward me, I could see that the only thing he wore underneath was a bronze-colored condom.

"What's going on?" I asked as he took me in his arms again and pressed his body to mine.

"I love playing judge," he murmured, nibbling on my ear.

"Really?" I purred. I let him nibble for another moment, then said, "You know something? My robe's in my car. Why don't I go get it?"

"Oh, God! Would you?" He was holding me so tightly, I could feel his need become even more urgent. "Judge to judge would be such an incredible turn-on."

I reached for my purse, where my car keys were, and slipped out of his arms. "Why don't you pour me a gin and tonic while you're waiting?"

He gave a happy smile and headed for his wet bar.

I went out, got in my car, and headed back to Seagrove.

I knew he was too good to be true, said the preacher.

Here we go again, sighed the pragmatist.

Fliss was surprised to see me back so early and she thought the whole account of my abortive evening with Will Blackstone was hilarious. "But I almost wish you hadn't told me. How am I going to keep a straight face next time I have to argue a case before him?" she asked.

"Your problem, not mine," I said heartlessly, and went to bed.

In the darkness of her guest bedroom, though, with only the full moon as my witness, I took a vow of chastity. Worse than being alone, I decided, was making a fool of myself again.

I convened court promptly at ten the next morning. Again, there were only five of us in the courtroom: Nick Sanderson and his ex-wife Kelly, the clerk, the bailiff, and me.

"Have you reached a compromise on the disposition of your office?" I asked.

To my complete lack of surprise, they informed me that they had not.

Once more I tried to establish a reason to award the Lawyers Row property to one over the other, but it just wasn't there. Both were from the Asheboro area, both intended to stay in practice here, both had contributed equally to the purchase of the property.

"I strongly advise you to sell, split the proceeds, and relocate," I told them.

"Your Honor, I was the one who first heard about the property when it came up for sale," said Nick Sanderson. "I was the one who rushed right over and made an offer that she thought was crazy when she heard about it."

"An offer made from our joint account," Mrs. Sanderson responded coolly. "Your Honor, our older daughter is fifteen and she's already expressed an interest in a law career. It's her dream to have her office in this house on Lawyers Row and eventually become a partner there. This is her heritage. Please don't force us to sell it."

I looked at Mr. Sanderson. "It is also your desire that it be awarded to one of you in preference to selling?"

"Yes, Your Honor." He said the words, but somehow he sounded less certain than his ex-wife.

"Very well," I said. "I am going to recess court until twelve-thirty. At that time, I will ask that you each give me a sealed bid for the property. The highest bid, even if it's by only a penny, will get title. In effect, one of you will be buying out the other by making a distributive award. Even though the property will be valued as of the date of separation, the highest bid will become a distributive factor that will effect the ED. This is not going to be an auction. You will have one chance and one chance only to submit a bid. Is that clear?"

"Perfectly, Your Honor," said Mrs. Sanderson.

"Mr. Sanderson?"

"Yes, Your Honor."

"Court's adjourned till twelve-thirty," I said.

The courtroom clerk, Mrs. Cagle, offered to bring me a salad and I spent the break in chambers with my laptop hooked into Lexus-Nexus as I researched case law for a matter I'd have to rule on next week.

Promptly at twelve-thirty, I reconvened.

"Do you each have your bids?" I asked.

"Your Honor —" Mr. Sanderson began.

"Yes, Your Honor," Mrs. Sanderson interrupted smoothly.

He turned in surprise. *"What?"*

She never looked at him, just asked if she could approach the bench to give me her bid. I took it.

"You lying bitch!" he said angrily.

The bailiff stood up, almost as startled as I was.

"Mr. Sanderson, I don't tolerate that sort of language in my courtroom. May I have your bid, please?"

He was white with suppressed rage. "I apologize, Your Honor, but she came to my office during the break and said she'd changed her mind, that we should just go ahead and sell. She said I could draw up the document and she would go along with it. I spent most of the break working on it."

"Is this true?" I asked Mrs. Sanderson.

Unlike her cousin Connor, Kelly Sanderson did not flush hot and red when confronted with pointed questions. "I would suggest that the matter is irrelevant, Your Honor," she answered coolly. "You said you would award the property to the highest bidder. I have submitted my bid in accordance with your ruling. What I did or said to my ex-husband should have no bearing on your decision."

Nick Sanderson looked as if he'd been kneed in the groin, which, figuratively speaking, I suppose he had. I felt sorry for him, but hell! He'd been married to this woman for sixteen years. Surely he must know how her mind worked.

"Mr. Sanderson, I will recess for ten minutes. At that time, I will accept your bid."

Mrs. Sanderson objected to the delay, but I overruled her and she backed down.

I had the bailiff escort Mr. Sanderson to an empty conference room so he could gather his thoughts. It was going to be hard for him. If he lowballed, he'd lose the property. If he bid too high, he might never recoup his investment. I had a feeling Mrs. Sanderson knew to the penny what his bid would be.

In that, I was wrong, though. I opened his bid first and saw that it was well above the appraised valuation. Then I opened hers and saw that she had misjudged his desire to win by eight thousand dollars, bringing her bid to just under twenty thousand over and above the property's worth.

She looked a little green around the mouth as it sank in that she could have won for a lot less, but she'd probably done a cost/benefit analysis and decided it was worth it to her before she ever wrote down her bid.

I could have delivered a lecture about her shabby trick or his gullibility, but nothing I could say would change a thing about either of them.

The figures were incorporated into my final order. The whole process had taken less than three hours and I was free to go home.

"But I thought you were going to stay over another night," Fliss protested when I went by her office to tell her I had finished and would head on back east if I could pick up my things.

She reminded me where her spare key was hidden and we hugged and promised we wouldn't let it be so long before we got together again.

"And call me if Connor Woodall makes an arrest," I said. "I really want to hear how this comes out."

CHAPTER

28

Glaze goes into the kiln as a powder adhering to pots. At the height of the fire it is a thick, viscous melt, which hardens to a glass on cooling. A potter can only see the glaze in this state by looking through a peephole into the white heat of the kiln interior. To see glaze in its melt is so ephemeral and exhilarating an experience that its absence is a loss to potters who burn only unglazed ware.

— *Raised in Clay*,
Nancy Sweezy

At Fliss's house, I stripped the bed and put the sheets on top of her washer, packed up my few belongings, and carried them out to the car. As I set my bag on the floor behind my seat, I saw the bright red soup mug that

I'd coopted for ice on Sunday night when I'd taken Davis to get his lip stitched. I'd totally forgotten about it.

Well, Nordan Pottery was on my way home, so I could easily drop it off.

Almost automatically, I glanced at the triangular stamp on the bottom. To my amazement, all three sides were perfectly straight. I looked again, closer. No crimping of the left angle. It would appear that I had helped myself to one of the original pieces of cardinal ware, an object worth at least a few hundred dollars, if I could believe what Sandra Kay and Will had told me. It was a wonder a warrant hadn't been put out for my arrest. Of course, with all that had happened lately, Amos Nordan probably hadn't had time to miss it.

I wedged the mug very carefully between the two front seats so that there was no danger of it rolling and chipping, although if it had survived my sudden departure from Will's last night, it could probably survive anything.

After locking the house and putting the key back in its hiding place, I pulled onto the highway and headed toward Seagrove. Odd about the mug, though. Only two days ago, Sandra Kay had told me that Amos Nordan was such a money-grubbing old man that he'd sold every single piece of his original cardinal ware. Somehow he seemed to have missed this one.

As I drove, I found myself trying again to make sense of all that had happened. If there was a pattern, I couldn't see it. And if the pottery was the reason for all the attacks, why hadn't Amos been killed? Was it because all his potential heirs had to be killed first, so that the way would be cleared for the killer to inherit?

Unless he'd made a will, that would seem to be Betty. But why would Betty want her father's pottery to go out of business? Or what if James Lucas really hadn't died intestate? A lot of men forget to change their wills when they get divorced.

But no, that wouldn't work because the pottery wasn't James Lucas's to will to his wife.

Ex-wife.

And besides, in North Carolina, divorce automatically revokes all provisions in a will that favor a former wife.

Libbet? Dillard?

I glanced down at the cup beside me, almost wishing I had Maidie here to read the tea leaves for me. Not that I'd ever drink hot tea out of it. The heat and the acid would leach lead right into the tea, which is why

Nordan Pottery no longer sold soup mugs and coffee cups except surreptitiously to collectors who knew better than to use them in daily life.

When I'd toured Fern's place yesterday, she'd told me that she wouldn't use any of the heavy metals. "Yeah, the colors were great," she agreed, "but I couldn't live with myself if I thought anyone could be harmed by what I made."

I tried to remember what I knew about lead poisoning, but all I kept seeing in my mind's eye was a drunken old man that my daddy used to hire to paint the exterior of our house when he was sober enough. Mother accused Daddy of hooking him on moonshine, but Daddy said no, it was a known fact that most painters drank too much because the lead in the old white paints drove them to drink.

"Never knew a single sober house painter," he'd told her.

So thirty years ago, several years after the dangers of lead glazes were known to most potters, Nordan Pottery had been forced to quit making and selling tableware. Yet Amos had stubbornly — arrogantly? — continued to make his cardinal red vases, each with a little warning label on the bottom where he scratched his initials.

Thirty years ago I was just a little kid. Sandra Kay and James Lucas had been courting then but not yet married. Same with Betty and Dillard. And Bobby Gerard had long since taken his first drink.

Okay, bring it closer to the present. Two years ago Donny was killed.

Maybe.

If indeed he hadn't killed himself accidentally, something that sounded increasingly improbable.

So what else happened two years ago?

Well, Amos had a stroke. Then Sandra Kay and James Lucas split, and June Gregorich and her thirty-something retarded son came to live there and take care of Amos.

June?

The soup mug had been in the window with all June's New Age totems.

"She appropriates an east-facing window in all the places she works. She says it helps focus her harmonic energies."

"That money-grubbing old man sold off every single one of the real pieces years ago."

But she'd barely met Donny before he died. Surely she wouldn't have killed a stranger on the off chance of being offered a live-in job? She didn't need a place to live that badly.

"We started posting all the pottery stamps three or four years ago so that people across the country could know what they have."

The stamps are posted on the web and within a year, June Gregorich arrives from California.

Sheer coincidence? Or cause and effect?

I turned onto the road where Nordan Pottery lay and a few minutes later, I was parking my car outside the sales shop. The OPEN sign was in the window, the door was unlocked, but no one was inside. I helped myself to their phone and called over to Fernwood Pottery with muddled thoughts of Portland and Avery and champagne tumbling through my brain.

When Fern answered, I asked her a single question and her reply confirmed my guesses. I told her where I was and what I suspected and asked her to send Connor.

With the mug in my hands, I walked over to the Nordan house and tapped on the kitchen door, but no one answered. The door was open beyond the screen and I stepped inside. June didn't answer even though her car was here. Music came from the den and I looked around the corner. The television was tuned to a children's program and at first glance I thought Jeffy was asleep under the afghan on the couch, but when I went over to him, I saw it was only the way the afghan was bunched up over the cushions and pillow.

Back outside, I started down the slope to the pottery. As I approached the one where Davis had stayed, I smelled wood smoke and the pungent fumes of kerosene. June's voice came shrilly through the open door.

Amos's voice was raised, too. "But I never took the damn mug!" he cried angrily.

As I crept closer, I realized it wasn't anger in his voice, but fear.

Not ordinary fear, either.

June's back was to the door. She held a gun in one hand and the smell of kerosene was even stronger. The smoke came from a pile of cardboard boxes beneath the open steps and I saw flames leap up and around the dry wooden treads.

". . . they'll say you finally snapped," June taunted the old man. "That you set fire to the pottery and then shot yourself."

Amos was facing the door, but he seemed so traumatized by those leaping flames and what she was saying that he never noticed me.

"I was good to y'all two," he howled. "What'd I ever do to you that you'd kill my boys?"

"Why do you think *my* boy's like he is? I

did all the healthy things when I was carrying him. Homemade soups, juice from our own orange trees. No pesticides, no artificial additives. And all served in your pretty red hand-thrown mugs. You knew lead was dangerous. Other potters around here quit using it as soon as the government started telling you people the dangers, but not Amos Nordan. Oh, no! Not Nordan Pottery. Did you know what lead does to unborn babies? Did you care? You and your precious glaze made my son what he is and I swore I'd find you if it took the rest of my life, find you and pay you back for what you did to me. To me, you wicked old man. To *me!*"

The fire was racing up the scaffolding of the stairs and spreading to the walls behind the blazing boxes.

"My only fear was that you'd die or go senile before I could make you suffer a tenth what I've suffered."

As she spoke, I'd been looking around for something to hit her with, but the yard was bare of convenient rocks or sturdy sticks. All I had was the soup mug and I could hardly get close enough to brain her with that.

Amos whimpered in protest as the gun came up.

"No!" I cried.

Startled, she whirled and saw the mug in my hands.

"You?" she cried. "You're the one who took it?"

She fired wildly as black smoke swirled through the shed.

A second shot rang out as I bolted in panic, racing around the corner of the building, anything to get out of her range.

Another bullet zinged past me.

As she swung around the corner and saw me, she fired again and a slug slammed into the wall beside my head. I tried to run, but my foot slipped on the pine straw and I went sprawling.

"Momma! Momma! *Momma!*"

From the open window directly above us came smoke and panicked wails.

"Jeffy?" she screamed. "Oh, God, no!"

Instantly forgetting me, she raced back around the shed.

Jeffy had heard her voice, though, and came to the open window, which was already leaking smoke.

"Push the screen out, Jeffy!" I cried, making pushing motions with my hands. The window was small, but so was he.

"Come on, Jeffy, push the screen away. You can do it. Push!"

Wailing even louder, he pushed, and I had

to dodge as the screen fell to the ground.

"Jump, Jeffy! Don't be afraid. Come on and jump," I yelled. "I'll catch you."

I wasn't sure how much he understood or even heard over his panicky cries and I knew that all I could hope to do was break his fall. But I might as well urge him to fly for all the good it was doing, because he clearly had no intention of jumping out of a high window.

Smoke billowed out around him now so thickly that I could barely see him. But I heard him cough and choke and I was terrified that the flames would reach him any second. I turned to search for something — anything — that would let me help him and almost collided with a small wiry man who reeked of alcohol.

He carried a rickety homemade ladder that he set against the side of the building and immediately started to climb toward the thick black smoke.

"Bobby!" Jeffy sobbed. "I want my momma."

"I know, dearie," the man crooned. "You just come on out with me and we'll go find her."

The ladder wobbled and started to slide sideways and I rushed to steady it.

"Momma!"

"Come on, dearie. Turn around now and

back on out to me. . . . You can do it. . . . That's right. Bobby'll take you to your momma. You just come with old Bobby."

He managed to coax Jeffy halfway out, but then we heard June scream from somewhere behind him and he tried to scramble back in. Bobby gave a tremendous yank, though, and Jeffy came through with such momentum that the older man lost his footing and slid down the ladder. I managed to sidestep him, but Jeffy fell on top of us both.

A moment later, flames shot out of the window and begin licking at the eaves of the roof.

I seemed to have turned my ankle and Bobby was cursing that his arm was broken, while Jeffy just sat on the ground and wailed like a three-year-old with no one to comfort him.

I limped around to the front of the shed and found Amos lying on the ground outside where he had managed to hobble before collapsing.

I couldn't find a pulse.

The interior of the shed was like a raging kiln during the blasting stage and I began to shake as I realized that June's agonized scream only moments ago had come from inside.

★ ★ ★

By the time the fire engines arrived, the
roof had already fallen in on the first shed
and the others weren't far behind. The
firemen managed to disconnect the propane
tank on the car kiln and shift it out of the
fire's reach so it wouldn't explode. After
that, all they could do was wet down the surrounding area and try to keep the flames
from spreading through the pine trees to the
houses and sales shop.

The Hitchcocks arrived, reeling at the
sight of this fresh tragedy. An EMS truck
rushed Amos and Bobby to the hospital, but
despite valiant efforts to resuscitate the old
man, he did not survive this second stroke.

Connor Woodall called someone from
Social Services, who came out and took
charge of June Gregorich's son. Poor bewildered Jeffy was still calling for her as they
drove away.

It was almost dark before we got it all
sorted out.

"Fern told me that you'd asked her what
would happen if a pregnant woman ingested
large doses of lead," Connor said.

I nodded wearily. "Amos's red mugs."

I'd had lots of time to finish putting it all
together while the official work went on.

"Lead crosses the placental barrier and can

cause irreversible developmental damage to a fetus," I said. "I don't know how long she'd been searching for the maker of those mugs, but once she matched the stamp to the one on Fern's website, she came straight here. That's how she knew to kill Donny in a way that would totally shock and humiliate Amos. And she probably sowed the seeds of distrust that helped break up James Lucas's marriage just so she'd be rid of a woman who might have noticed what she was up to. Then she cold-bloodedly waited till Amos was almost over Donny's death before she killed James Lucas."

Remembering how closely she'd questioned me about the likelihood of Davis coming back, I had a feeling that he had been her intended victim with the snake but that she'd muddled the cars.

"If Davis had died, then sooner or later she'd have gone after Tom deliberately. She wanted to strip away every reason Amos had for living."

Connor sighed. "And I missed it all because she'd barely met Donny and she didn't seem to gain anything by the other deaths."

He handed me the mug, which I didn't remember dropping.

"A souvenir," he said.

Miraculously, it was still intact.

"You might as well keep it. There's another one in the window of her bedroom."

"She told Fliss it was to focus her harmonic energies. More like keeping her hatred focused, I'd say."

I looked at the clear cardinal red that shimmered like a summer sunset.

A summer sunset, or a mother's heart burning for retribution?

I hope Karen will appreciate what it cost.

The employees of Thorndike Press hope you have enjoyed this Large Print book. All our Large Print titles are designed for easy reading, and all our books are made to last. Other Thorndike Press Large Print books are available at your library, through selected bookstores, or directly from us.

For information about titles, please call:

(800) 223-1244
(800) 223-6121

To share your comments, please write:

Publisher
Thorndike Press
295 Kennedy Memorial Drive
Waterville, ME 04901